Fairi ♡ Beginnings

A Heartwarming Romantic Comedy

Also By

The Guestbook
One Hundred Proposals
One Hundred Christmas Proposals

Holly writing as Amelia Thorne

Tied Up with Love
Beneath the Moon and the Stars

For young adults

The Sentinel
The Prophecies

Fairytale ♡ Beginnings

A Heartwarming Romantic Comedy

HOLLY MARTIN

Bookouture

Published by Bookouture

An imprint of StoryFire Ltd.
23 Sussex Road, Ickenham, UB10 8PN
United Kingdom

www.bookouture.com

ISBN: 978-1-910751-16-9
eBook ISBN: 978-1-910751-15-2

For my mom and dad,
I couldn't have done this without you, thank you so much for all
your support in helping me realise my dreams.

CHAPTER 1

Milly drove up the steep, curvy, cliff top lanes with the warm sun on her back and the wind in her hair. From up here, she could see the sparkling blue of the sea below her stretching out for miles into the horizon. It was a beautiful day, made even lovelier by the endless yellow fields of rapeseed on the other side of her. It smelt wonderful but she wished it was clover instead as that might be some indication that she was going in the right direction.

She was hopefully heading towards Clover's Rest. The satnav had, of course, stopped working half an hour ago and all she was left with was a flashing question mark on the screen, indicating that the satnav had no idea where she was. Nothing seemed to be known about the village of Clover's Rest or Clover Castle which presided over the tiny dwelling. It didn't appear on any maps, and bizarrely there was no record of it on any kind of historical documentation. That in itself was a mystery and one Milly was keen to solve.

Dick, her beaten up old Triumph, was having trouble with the steep gradient of the inclines and she had spent most of the last fifteen minutes barely coming out of first gear. Her brother, Jamie, had begged her several times to buy a new car but her beloved white Triumph TR2 was her pride and joy.

Up ahead, on the very summit of the hill, she suddenly saw a flash of a blue-topped turret from behind the trees and her heart soared. But no sooner had it appeared, it had gone.

Dick whined as she pushed him round a very steep corner and she leaned forward and gave him a little pat of encouragement. He spluttered and coughed, but thankfully didn't cut out. The handbrake wasn't the best and she wasn't hopeful that Dick could cling to the road surface without sliding back to the foot of the hill again.

Steam started to appear from under Dick's bonnet as she floored the accelerator and crossed her fingers and toes. She glanced down at her multi-coloured star bracelet and absently made a wish that she would make it to the top of the hill.

'Just a little further, Dick, come on.'

Dick was barely moving at all now, Milly could get out and walk quicker. As she begged and pleaded with Dick to just last a little bit longer, a kid on his bike rang his bell and scooted round her, disappearing into the trees up ahead.

How insulting to be overtaken by a kid on a BMX. And Dick obviously thought so too as he suddenly found a last bit of energy and groaned and coughed up the last few metres, where the hill finally levelled out.

They shuffled into a tunnel of trees, which swallowed her up, shutting out all the bright daylight behind her and overhead so she was driving through a canopy of total green. It was very dark, with just a tiny pinprick of light ahead of her that she pushed Dick towards. Movement swirled in her rear view mirror; as she glanced up it almost seemed like the trees were closing the gap behind her, covering the road with their tangle of branches so there was no escape.

Dick finally burst through the trees to the other side. Daylight temporarily blinded her, she briefly saw some houses and a village green and then a thick plume of white smoke burst from the engine and the village vanished from view. Dick let out what sounded like a really big fart and then died, smoke still pouring from underneath the bonnet.

Milly sighed. She had asked too much of him, she knew that. It had seemed like too good an opportunity to pass up; going out in her convertible along the seafront when the weather was so hot, and Clover's Rest was only supposed to be an hour and a half away from where she lived. But Dick was over twice her age and was only really capable of short flat journeys, nothing like the mountainous terrain she had just traversed.

'It's ok Dick, you can have a few days to have a little rest and maybe we can find someone to tinker under your bonnet before we go home. And it's all downhill from here so worst case scenario, we can just roll you home. Plus we're on holiday next week, I promise you can stay at home every day. I intend to sit in the garden and do nothing but read for the entire week.'

Dick let out a sigh of relief and the smoke slowed and then stopped, revealing the most gorgeous, picturesque village she had ever seen.

Milly quickly got out and gazed across the village green, staring at the whitewashed cottages like a kid in a sweet shop. The roofs were topped with yellow thatch that glinted like gold in the sunlight. They were a hodgepodge collection; the nearest ones to her were timber framed and the ones on the far side were made from stone. But all of them came with their unique lumps and bumps, jutting out bits of stone or bent bits of timber indicating that these houses were hundreds of years old.

She quickly grabbed her suitcase, gave Dick an affectionate pat, and abandoned him on the edge of the green as she walked in awe along the cobbled road.

The historian in her picked out key features in the houses straight away. Of course without certain dating tests it would be hard to be specific, but the first house on the green had to be at least four hundred years old, which meant it should be a listed building. But there had been nothing in any historical documents or files that even indicated this place existed, let alone had listed buildings.

Her toes curled with pleasure at the prospect of what this mysterious Clover Castle looked like. Was it possible that she was going to round the corner of the green and see a sixteenth century undiscovered jewel?

She approached the nearest house and ran her hand appreciatively up the oak timber frame. There was something incredible and humbling about touching something that had been around for hundreds of years. What had this building seen and heard, what stories could it tell?

She leaned closer to the wood and sniffed it. The rich smells of smoke, wood and earth engulfed her and she smiled.

She suddenly realised she wasn't alone. Milly looked up from the wood into the bulbous eyes of an old man, dressed in a tatty suit. His skin seemed to have shrunk against his bones, making his eyes seem more bulging and protruding. He was chewing on what looked like a small stone, rolling it around his mouth and back again as if he was trying to work out what it tasted like. His white hair stuck out making him look like he was a crazy scientist but he was looking at her as if *she* was insane, which she supposed she was, standing on someone's front lawn stroking and smelling the side of the house.

He took a drag of his cigarette and then flicked it into the nearby bushes. She winced at the desecration of such a historic place but chose to ignore it as he still had the moral high ground at the moment, being the slightly saner one of the two.

'You can't leave your car there,' said the man, indicating poor Dick, who looked so deflated and exhausted that even his headlights seemed to be drooping. 'It's double yellow lines.'

Sure enough, double yellow lines covered the roads on both sides, as if it was a main road through a busy city rather than a tiny remote village with probably no more than thirty houses. But closer inspection showed the lines to be very wobbly and most likely hand painted. Who would do such a thing? Traffic clearly wasn't a problem up here, there wasn't even another car in sight and Dick wasn't blocking up the road, which was wide enough for two cars to pass easily in both directions.

'Well unfortunately my car broke down, so it will have to stay there until I can get someone to have a look at it.'

The man sucked air through his teeth and shook his head. 'Igor won't like that. It's likely the car will be towed.'

Igor? Wasn't that the name of Dracula's assistant?

'Sorry, what did you say your name was?' Milly asked, deliberately.

'Danny.'

'Danny, I'm sure Igor will understand that a broken down car is not my fault. I'm a guest of Lord Heartstone, so if there's any problem Igor can come and see me at the castle.'

Milly hoped that using Cameron's name and title would be enough to get Danny to leave her and Dick alone, but that wasn't the case. Danny's face suddenly filled with disdain.

'He isn't exactly Mr Popular round here at the moment. He's only been back here a few months and he's sacked all the staff already. Grumpy sod, too, keeps himself to himself.'

'Well it's a big responsibility to suddenly inherit a castle, I'm sure it will take a period of adjustment. I'm here to see if I can help him.'

She spotted a flag flying above the trees and grabbed her suitcase and started walking towards it, hoping that Danny wouldn't follow her, but he did.

'It's the Summer Solstice this weekend, we always have a big celebration and he won't even be a part of it.'

'Well maybe I can talk to him.'

She squinted at the flag, it wasn't like any she had ever seen before. It was hard to see from this distance what was on it, but it looked like a dragon eating a heart.

'Are you staying up there?' Danny yelled after her, finally giving up following her.

'Yes, for a week.'

'You'll never leave. Those that stay there never leave.'

She stared at him. These sinister words sent shivers down her spine.

'And whatever you do, don't go out after midnight. The Oogie will get you.'

'The Oogie?'

'A sea monster who eats unwanted visitors.'

'That's a local myth, surely.'

Danny shook his head. 'The village has lost lots of victims to the Oogie. Just don't go out after midnight and make sure you keep all the doors and windows locked at night.'

He was clearly joking or just insane. Danny wandered off and she stared after him, realising he was only wearing one shoe. Definitely insane. She looked around at this calm, tranquil little village. With the bright sunshine beating down on the little houses, the scent of the roses that twisted round all the doors, she wasn't going to let some crazy nonsense about a sea monster bring her down.

She had a castle to look at and she couldn't wait to see it.

CHAPTER 2

Milly walked round the corner into the trees. Up ahead she could see some large, highly decorative wrought iron gates, with swirls and flowers. The gate was probably Victorian or Edwardian. It was very pretty but her heart sank a little bit. It didn't necessarily mean that the castle was from that era, but she hoped it wasn't. Castle Heritage, who she worked for, would have nothing to do with the castle if it was from the Edwardian era. They were only interested in ancient relics, particularly those from the medieval period.

She wanted to help Cameron, she really did. She had spoken to him a few times on the phone and he'd sounded desperate. He had this deep, rich, voice that sounded velvety and she guessed he was about fifty years old. She had a way of accurately estimating people's ages too, not just the age of houses.

It was the stuff of dreams to wake up one morning and find that not only were you a Lord but one that owned a castle too, yet from speaking to Cameron it seemed it was more like a nightmare than a dream.

He'd spoken to her about burst pipes, broken windows, rotting walls, crumbling masonry and a severe damp problem. It wasn't the inheritance that he had hoped it would be.

If the castle was old enough, Castle Heritage would probably buy it off him or, at the very least, pay to have these things repaired and maintain the upkeep of the place. They might even make it into a tourist attraction if they thought it was a viable option. If *she* thought it was a viable option. That's what she was here to assess. The steep incline of the hill was definitely a negative point. Thousands of people every year visited the big castles in the UK. The road she and Dick had driven up earlier couldn't sustain that many visitors, nor could the tiny village. But if the property was worth it, her company would pay to improve the road too.

She ran her fingers over her multi-coloured star bracelet, as she always did when she wanted something really badly. Most of the time the bracelet let her down but occasionally her wishes came true. Singing the first few lines of the song 'When You Wish Upon A Star' in her head, she closed her eyes and made a wish. 'Let the castle be something truly spectacular,' she whispered.

She opened the gate and it creaked in protest. Clouds skittered across the sun, casting long shadows across the curved drive. As she stepped through the entrance, a cool wind whipped around her, dragging her blonde hair into her face. The wispy summer dress she was wearing hardly seemed appropriate all of a sudden, she should at least have worn a jacket or a cardigan. English weather was always so unpredictable.

She shivered and walked round the corner, pushing the hair out of her eyes so she could get her first glimpse of Clover Castle. And suddenly there it was.

Her heart soared. For someone who had grown up obsessed with all things Disney, and still loved Disney now, years after it was socially acceptable for her to do so, seeing what was quite obviously a real life Cinderella's castle in front of her was something out of her wildest dreams. Turrets jutted out from all parts of the castle, some protruding out of other turrets. There were four towers, all topped with conical blue spires. From her position at the foot of the drive, she could see twenty-three blue spires, some of which topped the turrets, some that were simply large conical topped pinnacles that didn't seem to have any purpose other than for decoration. Each spire had a long, gold flagpole on the top with a scarlet banner, apart from the large flag in the middle that had that weird dragon design. She stared at the flag for a moment, although very different in its design, the theme of the dragon wrapped protectively around the heart was eerily similar to the tattoo she had on her right side.

The castle was beautiful but her heart had already plummeted into her shoes. This couldn't be any more than a hundred years old. It looked Bavarian in its design and was built purely for enjoyment and certainly not to protect.

There was a splendid drawbridge in the middle of the front castle wall but as she walked up the drive she could see there was no moat for the drawbridge to go over.

It seemed as though, at some point over the last hundred years, someone had decided to build a castle, looked at what features other castles had and decided to have one of everything – whether it was needed or not. Or in the case of the spires, twenty-three of them.

Standing on the hilltop with the sea framed dramatically behind it, the castle was an incredible sight. It was magical and arrogant and wonderful all at the same time and … Castle Heritage wouldn't come anywhere near it.

She might as well turn round and head home now. Her birthday was later this week, and she didn't really want to be working on her birthday. If she left now she might even be able to start her holiday a few days early. But she had promised Cameron she would stay for a week to do all the tests and surveys. He had already paid Castle Heritage quite a significant sum for her time and services and although she could refund the money there must be something she could do to help him. At the very least she could stay for a couple of days in order to get a feel for the place.

She couldn't feel too disappointed at her wasted trip, the place was spectacular and she got to sleep here, hopefully in a room fit for a princess in one of the tallest towers.

As she stared up in wonder at this thing of beauty, she heard two deep barks. She turned in time to see a heap of black, shaggy fur before she was knocked to the ground.

'Gregory, NO!' a deep voice yelled out.

But Gregory, if that was indeed the beast's name, was not to be dissuaded. Standing over her, Gregory started bathing her face in pungent wet licks, his coarse tongue tickling her face and making her giggle.

Suddenly the dog was snatched from over her and she was yanked to her feet. She slammed into a hard wall of muscle and looked up into a pair of eyes that were so dark they were almost black. Dark, curly hair topped his head, but she was too close to see any other features. He smelt amazing though, all woody and earthy and wonderful.

'Oh God, I'm so sorry, I didn't realise I pulled you so hard.' He took a step back and Milly stared up at him, aware that her throat was completely dry. This guy was frigging hot. Dark stubble lined his jaw bone. He was huge too, muscles screaming from every single part of him. He was wearing a suit that was very tight around his broad, muscular shoulders. She felt very under-dressed all of a sudden in her beach dress and sparkly pink Converse trainers.

'Oh God, your dress, I'm so sorry.' He stepped forward and brushed her breasts, trying to wipe off the two muddy paw prints that had been imprinted onto the material. His face immediately turned pale as he realised what he had done. He leapt back, looking horrified. 'I'm so sorry. I … God, I'm so sorry.'

Milly couldn't help but take pity on him.

'It's not the usual greeting I get, normally a handshake would suffice.'

He stared at her for a moment, then laughed, a deep, booming laugh. He offered out his large bear paw of a hand, and she shook it. 'I'm Cameron Heartstone.'

This gorgeous man was Cameron Heartstone? She had expected someone so much older, probably smoking a pipe and wearing tartan slippers.

'Milly Rose. We spoke on the phone. It's good to finally meet you.'

'Yes of course, come in.' He bent down to pick up her discarded suitcase. 'Gregory, Sit! Stay!' He commanded the black, hairy beast by his side. Gregory was so big Milly thought she might be able to ride him. His eyes were lost under a mass of fur, his pink tongue lolling out the side of his face. He gave a wag of his tail before running off and disappearing round the side of the castle. Clearly very obedient. Cameron sighed and ushered her through a small side door, with his hand in the small of her back. 'He's not my dog, he sort of came with the castle. The first day I arrived he turned up and hasn't left since. He doesn't belong to anyone in the village, so I guess I'm stuck with him.'

He was clearly nervous, though she wasn't sure why. He pulled at his collar, obviously not comfortable wearing a shirt and tie. Had he dressed up for her?

She stepped through into a warm kitchen, with a large wooden table standing in the middle and wooden benches either side. The walls were painted a cosy terracotta. Delicious, tangy smells reached her and her stomach gurgled appreciatively. An Aga stood at one end of the room and something was bubbling away in a huge pot on top.

'I'll make us some lunch. Will your boss be joining us soon?'

'My boss? I don't really have one. Well, the board of directors at Castle Heritage are sort of my bosses, but I mainly work for myself.'

Her heart sank a bit. He had been expecting someone older, too.

'Oh, well, the science people, the historians, the ones who will do all the tests?'

'That would be me.'

He stared at her, disappointment registering on his face. He looked her up and down disdainfully. 'They've sent me a child, is this someone's idea of a joke? Your idea of history is probably what happened in *EastEnders* last week.'

Milly felt her mouth fall open. She was used to getting some prejudice when she turned up at these historic places. With her long blonde hair, large blue eyes and Mary Poppins style rosy cheeks, no one thought she was capable of having any knowledge of history at all. She knew she didn't help these first impressions by having pink tipped hair and sparkly clothes and shoes, but generally the comments she got were little jokes. That remark about her historical knowledge hurt. And she had never been called a child before. This man couldn't be any more than five years older than she was, although, being so short, she knew she looked a lot younger than her actual age.

She drew herself up to her full height, which did nothing to diminish the height difference between them.

'I am not a child. I'm twenty-eight years old. You judgemental ass. You see the blonde hair and the pretty dress and automatically assume that I'm some kind of bimbo. I have a Doctorate in Archaeology and Historic Architecture. I have a

Master of Science degree in Heritage Conservation and a Bachelor of Science degree in Medieval History. I have extensive experience in dendrochronological and geophysical surveying and my PhD studies required detailed research into archaeological remains, excavation and historic building construction. I guarantee I know more about this castle than you could possibly ever know but if that isn't good enough for you, I will quite happily leave right now and take every chance of you ever working with Castle Heritage with me.'

She stormed to the door but he beat her to it, slamming it closed before she'd only opened it an inch.

'You can't leave.'

'Just watch me.' She tugged at the door but he leaned against it, so it didn't budge. She tried again.

'I'm sorry.'

She stopped tugging, but didn't let go of the handle.

'I really am.'

She looked up at him and his eyes were honest and concerned.

'I've hurt you and it really wasn't my intention to do that. It's been a really bad couple of weeks, well, a bad couple of months if I'm honest. Since my dad died and I inherited this place, it's been one problem after another. He was in so much debt and that debt doesn't appear to have died with him. There is no money in this estate, none at all, and he was still paying all the staff here right up till he died but I can't see how or where the money came from. I've had to let them all go, which means everyone in the village hates me and I've been going through all his paperwork and keep uncovering more and more problems. Without the staff the place will fall into ruin. I have no money for any of the repairs or to pay any of his debts and quite frankly the idea of selling the place to Palace Hotels and making it into

a five star resort is looking very appealing right now. You are my
last hope. I looked at you and thought ...'

'You thought wrong.'

'I know, I'm sorry, I had no right to judge you by your appearance. I'm a terrible judge of character, I really am. I should
have learned my lesson by now, not to judge a book by its cover.
The people I've trusted have sold me out and betrayed me. I've
had my share of model girlfriends, the types that look good on
your arm but with not a lot else going for them and ... I ...
Well, I'm really sorry. Please stay, at least have some lunch whilst
I beg your forgiveness some more.'

Milly felt all the fight go out of her. She couldn't hold a
grudge for long. Besides, she was starving and the soup that was
bubbling on top of the stove smelt amazing.

'Ok. I'll stay for lunch, but it depends how good the soup is
whether I stay longer.'

His mouth lifted up into small, cautious smile and he gestured for her to sit down.

'There's a hell of a lot riding on this soup then. If I'd known
that perhaps I would have thought about the recipe a little more
carefully instead of just throwing everything into the pot with a
bit of seasoning.'

She sat down on the bench and watched him fill two big
bowls. There was nothing graceful about him. The soup splat-
ted into the bowl and over the sides and he didn't seem to care.
There were big chunks of meat, large slices of potato, whole
florets of cauliflower, all of which should have been blended or
at least chopped smaller. He grabbed a large round loaf and tore
it into chunks. He plonked the bowl down in front of her and
left her half of the loaf on the table next to her bowl, not even
on a plate. The man really had no finesse. He sat down opposite

her and took a big bite of the bread. He was like a caveman and strangely she found his raw masculinity a bit of a turn on.

'Do you normally have such gay abandon with your food?'

He paused with the spoon halfway to his mouth. 'It seems to work.'

He gestured for her to try it and she took a small sip from her spoon. It was incredible, so thick and full of flavour. 'It's really good. Did you make the bread too?'

He nodded, before biting off another huge chunk from his loaf. 'It's potato bread.'

She took a small piece and bit into it. It tasted delicious. 'You're actually really good at this "throw it all into the pot and see if it works" method.'

He shrugged shyly. 'It's kind of how I write my books, too.'

'What kind of books do you write?'

'Children's books, with magical forests and super powers and fantasy adventures. But I never plan anything or follow any set rules. A lot of my author friends will have post it notes and charts and character interviews or CVs but I never do any of that, I just sit down and write. People seem to like it. I mean, I have enough to live off and pay the bills but I'm not going to be buying an island in the Caribbean any time soon.'

'Well if you have enough money to write full time, you must be doing something right.'

He shrugged again, obviously not keen to admit that he was any good.

'I'd like to read them.'

He shook his head. 'They're just kids' stuff, not your thing at all, I'm sure.'

'As we've already established, my thing is very different to what you think my thing is.'

'Right, of course.' He swallowed a big lump of bread and didn't look up at all after that.

She sighed. She didn't want him to feel uncomfortable around her. She already regretted her little outburst earlier, she was normally much more professional than that.

'Thank you for letting me stay, there was nowhere else anywhere near here apart from the tiny B&B I booked and when their pipes burst and flooded the house, I was at a bit of a loss for what to do.'

'It's fine,' Cameron said, in a way that said it really wasn't fine.

'Don't feel that you have to cook for me or anything. This is lovely,' she gestured to the soup. 'But I can look after myself. I presume the village has a shop. I can buy some food and make my own meals. You don't have to worry about that.'

'I have food here, it's silly for both of us to be cooking separate meals, unless you're on some weird diet,' he glanced briefly at her slender frame. People always assumed she ate really healthily when the truth was miles apart.

'I eat anything.'

'Then we might as well eat together.'

'I don't want to be in your way.'

'You won't. I have work to do and you'll have tests and measurements to do so I hope … I mean I guess we won't be getting in each other's hair too much.'

He didn't want her there and her heart sank even more at this. Well, if he didn't want her to stay and she probably couldn't help him anyway, maybe she would only stay one night after all.

'Tell me about the castle.'

He looked across the table at her. 'I don't know a lot. I used to live here when I was very young, but my mum took me away when I was about six. I never saw my dad after that and I never came back here either. They were always arguing, mainly about the lack of money, even back then. Mum wanted to sell the place and move, my dad refused, so she left. I know it's been in the family for hundreds of years, hence the rather obnoxious title of Lord that I've been bequeathed.'

Milly sat up straighter. The castle she had seen from the outside was not hundreds of years old, but that didn't mean there hadn't been some recent modifications to the original structure. Perhaps the *Cinderella* façade was hiding something far more exciting and mysterious.

CHAPTER 3

'So, do I get the grand tour?' Milly asked as she finished off the last of the soup.

Cameron nodded and stood up.

'Oh, let me wash these things up first, it's only fair as you did all the cooking,' Milly said, reaching for his bowl.

He moved it out of her reach. 'Oh don't worry, I'll just stick it all in the dishwasher later. Well, these are the servants' quarters, which have been heavily adapted and modernised since they were originally built. Through here is my lounge.' He opened the door on a cosy looking room with squishy red sofas round an open fireplace and a TV. 'And my bedroom is just off there.'

'Is my bedroom down here too?'

He stared down at her in an intense way, as if he was trying to fathom her out. It made her gut clench with desire and she hated that he had this effect on her. She had a good reputation amongst her colleagues and the people she worked with. She was efficient, highly organised and worked damned hard at her job, yet the mere mention of his bedroom and the sleeping arrangements had her insides quivering like jelly like some silly girl. Rather bizarrely, she could already imagine herself living here, swanning around in beautiful medieval style gowns as she linked arms with her husband, the Lord. The image made her grind her teeth in annoyance. Fairy tales didn't happen in real life, she knew that better than anyone. That was why she loved her Disney films so much, it was the closest thing to a happy ending she was ever going to get.

'Your bedroom is up in one of the towers, I thought …' He hastily backtracked. 'No, of course not. You can sleep in my guest room if you like.' He indicated the door opposite his own bedroom.

'You thought what?' she said, staring up at him.

'That you might appreciate staying in one of the original rooms of the castle, rather than a normal modern bedroom. The tower room has a four poster bed with a curtained canopy. I believe the bed was part of the original castle too, although of course the mattress has been changed. The views are quite spectacular and it has an open fireplace, so I can build you a fire if you are cold. It's erm … quite beautiful.' He cleared his throat. 'But to be honest, since I didn't know how many of you were coming, I made five bedrooms up, most of them along the ground floor, so you can take your pick where you sleep, you don't have to sleep in the tower.'

'I'd like to.'

He smiled down at her, his eyes were like pools of melted chocolate when he wasn't guarded or angry. 'You would? It's not too cliché? I wouldn't want to assume anything.'

He was playing with her and she liked it.

'Some clichés never get old. What woman wouldn't want to sleep in a four poster bed in a tower overlooking the sea? It sounds very romantic.'

He stared at her again and then he frowned, the shutters came down and he took a deliberate step away from her. 'Well, there's lots to see. Let's start with the banquet hall.'

He strode ahead through a large door, leaving her behind. She stared after him in confusion.

It seemed that it wasn't just the castle that might hold secrets, Lord Heartstone had some secrets of his own.

—

Cameron walked quickly away from her, determined to just have a few moments to clear his head. This was turning into a disaster.

He'd grabbed her breasts. That was probably the worst crime he'd committed today. What on earth was he thinking? He had never particularly been a gentleman around women, but he'd never been such a Neanderthal either. He had been so nervous about this meeting and so desperate for it to go well. He'd prepared a speech which had completely disappeared from his brain when he had this beautiful blonde woman pressed against his chest. And then he'd become a bumbling idiot and accidentally groped her. What would she think of him? His stupid dog had knocked her over, ruining her dress. He'd accused her of being a child, immediately judging her on her pink tipped hair and pink sparkly Converse. And to top it all, with the whole discussion about bedrooms, there had been only one place he had wanted her to sleep and that was in his bed with him.

What was wrong with him? He'd been swayed by a pretty face before, hell, who hadn't? But he'd sworn he wasn't going to go down that road again. She'd recognised him too, that much was very clear. When she'd first looked at him, she'd stared at him in shock. He didn't need another gold digger fawning all over him. He would not be led by lust anymore and he certainly wasn't going to have a fling with the one woman that could save his ass and save the castle. He had to keep this on a professional level and he absolutely had to stop thinking about what it felt like to have her pressed against him.

He'd show her the castle and then keep out of her way over the next few days while she conducted any tests or surveys she needed to do.

He just had to hope that she was ok with ghosts.

—

'So that's the grand tour,' Cameron said, as he showed her the bedroom she would be sleeping in for the next few nights.

He had kept his distance as he had taken her round the castle, answering all her questions professionally but she never saw him smile again. Any warmth that had started to materialize over lunch had completely vanished, making Milly wonder if she had imagined it in the first place.

The castle was causing him a lot of worries, she knew that. She was determined to do something to help him.

As she'd wandered around, she had seen furniture and parts of the castle that were definitely a lot older than she had first thought. Some of the rooms had been built hundreds of years before, maybe mid to late sixteenth century, judging by the material used and the way they had been built. The room she was in now was quite a bit younger, probably early nineteenth century, despite Cameron's claims that the towers were part of the original structure, it seemed that the towers were added about two hundred and fifty years later, suggesting that the building probably hadn't started life as a castle at all. Another reason Castle Heritage probably wouldn't touch it.

It was a hodgepodge of historic periods, the banqueting hall especially seemed to be a right mixture, with the intricate patterned plastered ceilings of the late eighteenth century and the square oak panelled walls of the sixteenth century. It had clearly seen lots of renovations over the years. The bottom of the main staircase was definitely Jacobean with its carved and painted bannister, balusters and newel posts which set it in the early seventeenth century, while the carved staircases further up the towers were definitely more Georgian, as were the bedrooms on the first floor. The furniture dated from a range of periods, with some beautiful unique pieces that the museums of the world would be desperate to get their hands on.

She moved to the window. Out on the slopes behind the castle was a huge maze that looked very wild and overgrown at the moment. The castle seemed so much bigger on the outside than it was on the inside. Although she had seen lots of beautiful, dusty rooms on her tour, it felt like there were parts she hadn't seen at all.

She stared at the external wall that dropped below her and tried to map out everything she had seen and where it was in relation to where she was now.

'Have I seen everything?'

She felt Cameron standing behind her; the heat of him seemed to sizzle against her skin. Her body erupted in goosebumps at his proximity and she tried to quietly breathe through her mouth instead of her nose so she wouldn't smell his amazing scent. It didn't work. She hated that he made her feel this way. She had long ago accepted that she was never going to get a happy ending and decided that relationships simply weren't for her. For over four years she had barely even glanced at a man and that had worked out great for her as being single meant there was never a risk of getting hurt, but now Cameron was pushing at the barriers she had built without even trying and she didn't like it one bit.

He leaned round her and pointed to the external wall and the battlements below that stretched towards the other tower. 'The banqueting hall is down at the bottom and the portrait gallery that overlooks it is where those windows are, on the second floor. The library and study are on the floor above that.' He pointed to the smaller windows. 'The eight bedrooms, including this one, are on the two top floors in the four towers, two in each tower. The only other rooms are the servants' quarters which are all the modern rooms at the back of the banquet hall, near my kitchen and bedroom.'

'It's not a conventional castle,' Milly said, tentatively.

Cameron sighed, and his warm breath on the back of her neck made her heart gallop. 'No, it isn't.'

'What about all these turrets, are there not rooms in there?'

Cameron shook his head. 'I think these were the four original towers, everything else was just added for show about a hundred and fifty years ago. My great, great Uncle Boris Heartstone was outrageously rich and held banquets and parties that were legendary. He wanted a castle that would be seen for miles around, one that everyone would talk about, so he had all these turrets put on. I believe the entire family fortune was spent on this renovation, leaving his descendants struggling to make ends meet over the last hundred years. I'm sure it looks quite ridiculous to someone like you.'

She turned to look at him. He was standing very close but he didn't move back. Sparks crackled between them. There was an air of tension; of waiting for an explosion to happen.

'It's wonderful,' Milly said.

His eyes crinkled with confusion. 'Really? But it's not historical at all?'

'It's fanciful and silly and it makes me smile.'

'It's arrogant.'

'I think it's the most beautiful castle I've ever seen.'

He smiled down at her. 'You're full of surprises, Milly Rose.' He stared out the window over her head, trying to see it through her eyes. 'I think it looks a bit Disneyish.'

'Exactly, that's probably why I love it.'

'Miss "I've got a Doctorate and Master of Science" doesn't strike me as the Disney princess type.'

'I do love a fairy tale happy ending. They never happen in real life, at least not for me. Other people seem to get theirs. I think this – sleeping in a four poster bed, in a tower in a real Disney castle, is the closest I'm ever going to get.'

He stared down at her and for a moment his eyes drifted to her mouth before he quickly stepped away.

She blinked and cleared her throat, silently cursing herself for having opened up to him. Her professional façade had slipped again. She quickly straightened her shoulders.

'Any dungeons?'

His face fell. 'They're very dirty, I'm sure you don't want to see them.'

'I don't mind a bit of dirt.'

'It's muddy and wet. I could take some photos for you if you like, save you the trouble of going down there.'

What was he hiding down there?

'I'd really like to see them. The foundations of the building will give me a good clue as to how the building was made and I should be able to see the square footing of the original structure too.'

He sighed. 'I'll show you the way.'

CHAPTER 4

Should he tell her? She might not notice anything amiss, in which case if he'd already spoken about it, he would look a complete idiot. Some days were very quiet. Maybe today would be a quiet day. But maybe he should prepare her. He didn't want to do anything that might scare or upset her. In fact, he would rather she didn't go down to the dungeons at all. What if it put her off working with him altogether?

She walked by his side, a determined look on her face. He had intrigued her with his evasiveness. He should have told her he didn't have a key for it.

He approached the door, slid back the giant bolt and unlocked it with a large black key that was hanging on the wall. He wondered if she thought it odd that he kept the door locked even though there were no prisoners down there. It was quite obvious that the idea wasn't to keep people out, but to keep something in.

He had been curious about the protection on the door when he had arrived. And although it was silly to keep up these measures, bearing in mind what was on the other side, he knew he slept better at night knowing the lock was firmly in place.

He flicked the light on, thankful at least that someone had seen fit to install electricity in the dungeons, even if the light was sporadic and dim. He knew he would have to replace some of the bulbs at some point but prolonged time in the dungeon wasn't fun so he had been putting off the job.

He turned back to Milly, wondering which words he could use to explain, to warn her, but he had nothing. Instead, he took her hand and pulled her close to his side. He didn't relinquish his hold on her as he walked down the cold dark stairs and he found her inching closer with every step he took.

It stank down here, the smell of stagnant water somehow prevalent. A cold draught seemed to come from somewhere but he didn't know where.

As they reached the bottom step, she stepped in closer to him, the heat from her searing up his right side. A long tunnel stretched away from them into the darkness, the dim light glistening off the muddy puddles on the ground. There were cells either side, some with barred doors, some without.

He would just make it quick. He'd go to the end of the tunnel that stretched underneath the castle into the large chamber that was directly under the banqueting hall and come back out. Hopefully no one would notice they were there.

An ice cold blast blew past them and he sighed. Today was not going to be a quiet day.

'Is it haunted?' Milly whispered, her large eyes looking up at him in the semi darkness.

He stared at her, wondering what to say, and eventually nodded.

Her eyes widened in shock at this confirmation. 'Are you serious?'

He nodded again. 'It seems they like to congregate down here.'

'They?'

'There's one that I've seen. I think there may be more that don't show themselves…' he trailed off. She looked absolutely terrified. He put his arm around her. 'We can go back up to the main castle. There really isn't a lot to see down here. I can take any photos or samples you need for your survey.'

She shook her head. 'No. I want to see them.'

He felt his eyebrows shoot up. She was going to continue to surprise him, he knew that.

He stepped forward and he could feel her heart battering against her chest.

'Had much experience with ghosts?' he asked as they stepped past the first cell, which was open but empty.

'A bit, a few shadowy figures, a few bumps and bangs in old castles or houses, sometimes just a feeling that someone is there. What have you seen?'

'A woman, the Grey Lady, dressed in what I assume is a Victorian dress. I thought once that I saw a little boy up in the study, but I'm not sure. I've heard a child's laughter down here though.'

She stared up at him, wondering if he was serious. He wished he was joking. He had never believed in ghosts before, always thought the idea was ridiculous, until the moment he had walked down into the dungeon for the first time and seen the Grey Lady, almost as clearly as he could see Milly now. He wasn't ashamed to admit that he'd run out screaming the first time he'd seen her, but he had made himself come back several times since, mainly to convince himself he wasn't going mad.

'Are they friendly?' she whispered.

He shrugged. 'Mostly indifferent. They don't seem to be too aware of me. I've spoken to the woman a few times. I know she hears me, but she never answers.'

A cell door clanged behind them and Milly jumped.

'Yeah, they do that a lot.'

'It could be the wind,' Milly suggested.

'It could be. There does seem to be some kind of draught down here.'

A low moan sounded in the darkness and they both strained their eyes to see if there was anyone there. If so, they stayed veiled in the darkness.

A few bangs sounded in quick succession in the large chamber up ahead. Another draught of wind rushed towards them that held whispers and a sweet scent of flowers and then the Grey Lady appeared, gliding straight out of the cell in front of them and along the tunnel towards the main chamber.

'Holy shit!' Milly croaked.

She took a tentative step to follow the lady. He had to hand it to Milly, although she was terrified, she had big balls.

'Hello,' she called out and the Grey Lady stopped, facing away from them. Milly took another step towards her. 'I'm Milly, do you have a name?'

The Grey Lady carried on walking but as she turned the corner and disappeared into the large chamber she turned her head and looked directly at them, her eyes were cold but curious. There was an air of anger about her, as if she was insulted by the intrusion. Cameron had never seen her engage with him before. She mainly ignored his presence but Milly had somehow piqued her curiosity. He had heard rumours from the villagers of the terrible moods of the ghost against those that had angered her. The last thing he wanted was for that anger to be turned on Milly.

'Come on,' Milly whispered, pulling him along in the Grey Lady's wake. They stepped into the chamber but the room was in total darkness. 'Are there lights down here?'

He fumbled around on the wall and flicked the switch. One lone bulb lit up the far side of the room but it was enough that the light dimly filled the whole room. It was empty. The Grey Lady had gone.

Cameron was trying to make a cup of tea with one hand. The other was wrapped tightly in Milly's, she hadn't managed to let go of him yet since they had left the dungeon. She was standing next to him, very quietly. Too quiet. Despite her bravado at the time, she'd been spooked by seeing the ghost. He wasn't surprised, the first time he'd seen the Grey Lady, he'd been terrified himself.

'You ok?' he asked softly.

She blinked and looked up at him and suddenly realised where she was, that she was still holding his hand.

'God, sorry, I was miles away.' She relinquished her hold and his hand felt cold without her.

'Sit down a moment, it's quite a shock. I couldn't go down there for a week after I first saw her. Scared the crap out of me.'

She smiled. 'You're just saying that to make me feel better. I'm sure a big, burly man like you never gets scared of anything.'

'Oh I get scared all the time,' he pushed her gently down onto the bench. 'Don't like snakes, creepy little buggers.'

She half smiled. 'That wasn't a trick, was it? Something that you set up to … I don't know … make the castle more appealing?'

'No, I swear. I wouldn't even know where to begin creating something that realistic. And I'm not sure ghosts would make the castle more appealing. It could mean that people would be too scared to come here.'

'Good God no, people would flock here in their droves to see a real ghost. We could sell ghost tours, every weekend. We offer them rooms in the tower – the real, authentic rooms rather than rooms down here – people would love it. We could give them bed and breakfast too. We make up a few ghost stories associated with the place, like the history of the Grey Lady and how she died. People would lap it up.'

He passed her a mug of tea and sat down opposite her. 'We?'

Her eyes widened slightly, a pink blush colouring her pale cheeks. 'I meant you.'

He pulled a face. 'I'm not really a people person. I like solitude.'

'People need company, Cameron, we can't be anti-social all of the time. You can be a hermit during the week and grit your teeth and smile at the tourists at the weekend. Besides, if Castle Heritage take it on, there'll be tourists teeming over this place.'

'But I won't actually be living here if that happens, I can go back to my house in London and write books all day and not have to speak to anyone ever.'

'Really? If I lived here, I don't think I'd ever leave. I'd swish around in big gowns all day, just because I could …'

He smiled at this.

'… That view is spectacular. I can imagine walking Gregory over the cliffs and on the beaches. I could chat to all the villagers every day.'

'In your big gowns?'

She laughed. 'Yes, why not? No one speaks to anyone where I live and I bet it's the same for you too.'

'That's the way I like it.'

'Wow, you really are a grumpy sod. You really wouldn't want to live here?'

He looked around. The castle needed so much work and he'd inherited so much debt because of the place it was hard to find any appreciation for it at the moment. But Milly was right. Most people would give their left arm to live in a place like this. It was impressive and in many ways beautiful. Could he really stay?

'Can you imagine writing your stories here? What better place to inspire you than a fantastic castle that has real ghosts? There's something incredible about this place, something magnetic, it draws you in,' Milly said.

He smiled at her as she looked around with such enthusiasm. He had never met anyone like her before, she lived in a permanently rose-tinted world.

'As lovely as that picture postcard life sounds, I won't even be able to keep the castle unless Castle Heritage can help me. Do you think they will?'

A tiny spark faded from her eyes. 'What about your house in London? If you really do want to live here, you could sell that. How much would you get for it?'

He hated talking about money with anyone, but somehow Milly was different.

'Maybe half a million.'

'And do you owe any mortgage on that or do you own it outright?'

'It's mine, I paid for it with the proceeds from my books. Maybe I could sell my car too.'

She pulled a face. 'You might get a few thousand for that.'

'It's a Vanquish.' He waited for her eyes to light up, like girls' eyes normally did when they heard what car he drove but she stared at him blankly.

'Aston Martin,' he clarified, but still she showed no sign of recognition.

'Second hand I could probably get two hundred thousand for it.'

'Wow, you are doing well if you can afford to buy your own house and a car like that.'

He stiffened, suddenly regretting telling her anything. He'd had these sorts of conversations before.

'That money wouldn't last long, it'd just about cover the rest of the debts and do a tiny bit of maintenance. I'm not sure what I would do then.'

'At least it would take a lot of your worries away. There's no point having two properties if you only intend to live in one.'

He sighed. 'I'm not sure what I'm going to do. Castle Heritage is my last hope. I hadn't really thought beyond what I would do if you don't help me. Do you think it's a project that you could take on?'

She stared down at her tea and cleared her throat. 'I'd need to do all my tests and surveys first. There's a lot of work to do, it will take me a while to cover all the rooms. I'll let you know in a few days.'

'Of course,' he nodded, disappointed. Although Milly had originally said it might take her one or two weeks to complete her tests, he had hoped she might give him some indication once she'd seen it.

'I'm going to go for a walk around the grounds, get an idea of the size and footings, see if there are any original features. You can come with me if you like, tell me more about these books you write.'

He found his jaw clenching. 'Why do you want to know about my books? You're here for the castle. We're not about to become best friends. And I've got some work to do actually, so …' he indicated the door and tried to ignore the flash of hurt that crossed her face.

'Right.' She got up and he watched her go as she closed the door softly behind her.

That's how all the conversations with women seemed to start. *Tell me about your books. How much money do you earn?* Then, later, *Can you buy me this?* He wasn't going to go down that road again. And annoyingly, Milly, with her sweet, honest face and childlike enthusiasm, had managed to get more from him in the first few hours they'd known each other than most women got out of him in weeks. It was much easier not to trust someone than to trust them and then be betrayed. And he had to keep things professional between them, he had no choice about that.

———

Milly stared out over the cliffs, at the water crashing theatrically onto the rocks below. The wind tugged at her hair and her clothes and intermittently she could feel the salt spray from the sea. The sun was beating down on top of her head and creating slashes of gold on the crests of the waves.

Cameron was an ass and he certainly didn't deserve her help. She should just march straight back to the castle now and tell him that Castle Heritage wouldn't help him. But there was a vulnerability about him, he had been hurt before and he was clearly trying to protect himself from it happening again. She couldn't hate him for that. She'd been hurt before too.

There was something about this place too that seemed to have some sort of hold on her. There was so much more that she needed to find out.

She turned back to look at the castle. It annoyed her that Castle Heritage probably wouldn't take it on. They had so many rules about which properties would qualify for their help and they had turned down so many beautiful places over the years.

She started walking back up the slope towards the castle. From the outside, she could see that it was indeed a lot bigger than it had seemed from the inside. Even allowing for the fact that the turrets created the impression of extra size.

The castle was roughly rectangular, which could mean that it was possibly some kind of lookout house, with an added extension part with extra rooms on the ground floor which was now the converted servants' quarters.

All the windows in the banqueting hall were stained glass but there were four on this side of the building that weren't. Were there rooms that Cameron hadn't shown her? And if so, what were they and why was she not privy to them?

She squinted her eyes against the sudden sunlight that burst out from behind one of the towers as she walked up the hill. She stepped forward, shielding her eyes and suddenly the ground disappeared from beneath her feet. She reached out blindly to stop herself from falling, grabbing at nothing as she tumbled through the air and landed face down in the dirt in a dark hole.

With a groan, she rolled onto her back to look around and could see the opening some eight feet above her head. There didn't appear to be any way out.

—

Where was Milly? It had been hours since she'd walked out the kitchen and the pie he had made to apologise for being such an arse had long since gone cold on the table. It had got dark outside and had started to rain.

Maybe she was avoiding him.

It was possible that she had gone back to the village and sought refuge from him in the local pub, though they wouldn't make her any more welcome than he had.

In fact, the thought of the villagers getting their weird hands on her suddenly filled him with dread. He grabbed his torch and his jacket and headed out.

Wind roared over the cliff tops as he strode down the drive towards the village. The warmth of the day had well and truly disappeared now, leaving behind an icy chill.

He walked into the village. The cute little houses were seemingly sleeping in the darkness, though the lights of the pub were ablaze.

He pushed open the door and every face inside turned to look at him, as the pub fell deadly silent.

'Is Milly here?' He looked around. She wasn't there, her beautiful blonde hair would light the room like a beacon.

'Maybe the Oogie has taken her,' shrugged Igor, one of his eyes roving over Cameron as if he had no control over its movements.

'There is no Oogie,' Cameron snapped. Bloody stupid myth.

'Oogie, Oogie, Oogie,' Igor chanted as slowly the others all joined in too. 'Oogie, Oogie, Oogie, Oogie.'

Cameron quickly left and as soon as he closed the door behind him, he heard the pub erupt into laughter. Bunch of weirdos.

He looked around the village, every other house was in darkness. Where the hell was she?

He strode back towards the castle. What if she had slipped over the cliff tops and fallen to her death? His stomach rolled with a sudden fear.

He ran through the gates and started calling her name, his torch beam zipping over everything it touched. There was no answer.

He ran towards the cliffs, still yelling for her, but the wind snatched the words from his mouth as soon as they left. If she was out here she wouldn't be able to hear him.

He stood on the cliff top and shone his beam on the rocks below. If she had fallen, she was no longer there now.

The wind suddenly changed direction and he heard his name faintly from behind him.

He turned round and walked forward towards the castle. He heard it again, this time it was louder.

'Milly!' he yelled.

'Cameron! Down here!'

He shone his torch along the ground and saw a hole straight in front of him. Jesus, had she fallen down a rabbit hole, just like Alice?

He hurried to the edge and peered over and there was Milly standing at the bottom of the hole, covered with mud and soaking wet. She smiled, bravely, though he could see she was freezing cold. God knows how long she had been down there and yet she was still smiling. He felt relief rush over him that she was ok.

'I fell down here like a complete idiot.'

Cameron felt his mouth go dry as his torch scanned over her. Her white dress had gone completely see-through in the rain and it was very evident that she wasn't wearing a bra. Two dark nipples stood proudly to attention under her strapless dress and she had no idea how exposed she was. He quickly looked away. Shit. He would have to try to rescue her without looking at her. Surely he could do that.

He lay down on the edge of the hole and thrust his arm inside, reaching down to her. She jumped up and down trying to grab his hand, but it was futile. She was a good few inches away from the ends of his fingers and her breasts were bouncing up and down with her exertions. Bloody woman and her breasts.

'Hang on, I need to get something for you to hold on to.' He stood up.

'It's ok, I'm not going anywhere.'

He smiled briefly and ran back towards the castle. She hadn't seen the hole because the grass was overgrown and the grass was overgrown because he'd fired the groundsman the month before. If she had hurt herself, it would be all his fault.

He ran round the back towards the garage, he was pretty sure there was a rope in there amongst a load of other junk. He burst into the garage and searched though the shelves until he found one lurking at the back. He grabbed it and ran back, untangling it as he ran. The torch he'd abandoned at the edge of the hole showed the way.

'Stand back,' he called, before tossing one end of the rope down the hole. 'Tie it round your waist.'

He felt the rope tug for a few moments.

'Ok,' Milly called.

He braced his legs and started pulling the rope through his hands. He felt the rope take the strain but she weighed next to nothing, he had bench pressed heavier than she was. After a few more swift yanks, she appeared out the hole and he felt bad as he dragged her across the grass.

She stood up, smiling weakly, even though she looked exhausted. The light from the torch illuminated her whole body. Cameron could quite clearly see a large, black dragon tattoo on her right side, whose tail dipped below the waist of her knickers and ended up Lord knows where.

Cameron quickly tossed the rope to one side and ripped his jacket off, wrapping it around her, partly so he wouldn't have to see her incredible figure anymore. If he didn't know better, he would think she was doing this deliberately.

'Are you hurt?'

'No, well my ankle is very sore but it's my pride more than anything, I should have been looking where I was going.'

Her hair was matted against her head, any make-up she had been wearing was long gone and yet he had never seen anything quite so adorable in his life as Milly, bedraggled and staring up at him with those wide, sea blue eyes.

She shivered against him and he suddenly found himself scooping her up in his arms and carrying her back to the castle.

She giggled against him. 'Cameron, I'm perfectly capable of walking.'

'And falling down another hole? I don't trust you.'

She sighed and linked her arms round his neck to stop herself from bouncing around as he walked. The warmth of her breath on his skin did nothing to stop the inappropriate thoughts from running through his head.

He burst through the back door and sat her down on the table.

'Are you sure you're not hurt?' He scanned her, thankful that the only part of her body he could now see was her lower legs.

'I'm fine, freezing but fine. Please stop worrying. I promise I'm not going to sue you or anything.'

That hadn't even crossed his mind.

'I'll run you a bath and then I'll make you some dinner.'

'Cameron …'

He strode off towards the bathroom before she could protest and started filling the oversized tub with hot water.

He came back out and gestured for her to go in, hopefully giving her a look that was not to be argued with.

She sighed and slid off the table, causing his jacket and her dress to ride up her thighs. What was she trying to do to him?

She kicked her shoes off and shuffled past him into the bathroom and closed the door. He leaned his forehead against it and closed his eyes.

Having her here was going to be trouble.

'Cameron Heartstone, I can still see your feet under the door. If you're spying on me, there's going to be trouble.'

She was playing with him but he stepped away from the door regardless, little did she know that he had already seen her nearly naked body in its full, spectacular glory.

He tried to occupy himself so he wouldn't think about her lying in his bath mere metres away from where he stood. He tidied her shoes to one side of the room, since she had left them in the middle of the floor. He put the pie back in the oven with a tray of chips and made a fire in his lounge. He went to retrieve the rope and torch and as he was trying to distract himself with reading the paper, he heard the bathroom door open and a few moments later she appeared in his lounge, wearing just his robe, her hair wrapped up in a towel.

She was naked underneath his robe. He swallowed, trying to take his eyes off her. She smelt like him, having evidently used his shower gel and his shampoo. The fact that she had inadvertently marked herself with his scent somehow appealed to his inner caveman. How could something so simple turn him on so much?

He stood up. 'Sit down, I'll just finish off the dinner.'

She did as she was told and he walked out into the kitchen just to be away from her. He dished up the pie and chips and carried them back through to his lounge. She was curled up in one corner, drying her hair.

'It smells delicious, you didn't have to do this,' she said, taking the plate and tucking into the pie, before he had even sat down.

He sat down next to her and started eating his own, deliberately not looking at her in his robe.

He wanted to say something to clear the air after he had been so grumpy with her earlier, but apologies never seemed to come easily to him and he'd already used up his quota today.

She finished eating and put the empty plate on the coffee table, leaning back into the sofa.

He stared down at his food, which seemed to be sticking in his throat along with the apology.

He finished his dinner slowly and then, when there was nothing else to distract him, he took a deep breath to deliver the apology. 'I wanted to say sorry for my attitude earlier, when you asked me about my books.'

He turned to look at her to gauge her reaction and saw that she was fast asleep. He put his plate down on the coffee table, scooped her up and carried her through to his bedroom. He put her in his bed and covered her up, going back into the lounge.

There were lots of beds along the ground floor he could have put her in which would have saved him the trek up to the tower, but his bed was closest.

He rolled his eyes as he lay back on the sofa and flicked the TV on quietly. That was a pathetic reason and he knew it, but that was his excuse and he was sticking to it.

CHAPTER 5

Milly woke the next morning and looked around her in confusion. She was in a bed but certainly not the bedroom in the tower. She'd obviously fallen asleep on Cameron's sofa after dinner and he'd brought her to one of the rooms in the servants' quarters.

She was still wrapped in his robe and it smelt divine; wonderfully clean and woody. She buried her nose in it and inhaled deeply. It was an intoxicating scent and it made her gut clench with need. What was wrong with her? She had never, ever had feelings about a client before and had always declined those who asked her out, for professional reasons.

But there was something about Cameron that she couldn't seem to shake.

She got out of bed, determined to find the toilet but when she opened the bedroom door she had two shocks. The first was that she was standing in Cameron's lounge, having clearly spent the night in his bed. The second shock, which had her welded to the floor, was Cameron, soaking wet and stark naked standing in the corner of the lounge, rooting around in his towel cupboard.

She couldn't move, couldn't even breathe. Holy crap, this guy was huge. Hulking muscular arms, massive thighs, even a broad, muscular back. His bum was toned and tanned just like the rest of him and she had a sudden urge to sink her teeth into it.

Suddenly he turned around with a towel in his hand and she gave a little yelp at being caught staring at him so openly. She quickly ran back in to the safety of his bedroom and closed the door. But not before she'd seen that his huge size was prevalent ALL over his body. Holy frigging crap indeed.

'Milly, I'm sorry, I didn't mean to scare or embarrass you.' Cameron called through the door. 'I took a shower and forgot that you had my robe and my towel.'

'I can't believe I saw you naked.' Although it wasn't the fact that she had seen him that was causing the burning blush over her cheeks, it was that he had caught her staring with wide, hungry eyes and an open mouth. What on earth must he think of her? Her professional façade was slowly crumbling.

'If it helps, I saw you naked yesterday,' Cameron called.

Her eyes snapped open and she yanked open the door. Thankfully Cameron had had the foresight to wrap a towel round his hips by this point, though it did nothing to detract from the magnificent wet chest right in front of her eyes. 'You saw me naked?'

Cameron blushed. 'That probably doesn't really help things, does it? And not properly naked, just …' he trailed off.

She put her hands on her hips. 'Just what?'

He looked down, staring at his massive feet. 'Your dress was wet and very see-through yesterday, when I pulled you out of the hole. I could see that you weren't wearing a bra,' he mumbled.

She felt her mouth fall open. 'I was absolutely wearing a bra. Do you think I turn up for business meetings not wearing a bra? What made you think I wasn't wearing one?'

'I could see your nipples.'

'My nipples,' Milly squeaked. They hadn't known each other for twenty-four hours and she had seen his willy and here they were talking about her nipples.

He nodded 'And your dragon tattoo.'

'And you never thought to tell me?'

'I didn't want to embarrass you.'

'Like you are now.'

'Well, I wasn't planning on ever telling you.'

'Just keep it to yourself, you dirty pervert.'

His head snapped up, flashing her a smouldering look. 'I wasn't the one that was standing ogling for a good five minutes, at least I had the good grace to cover you up when you were exposing yourself to me. You could have looked away.'

Holy shit, the atmosphere was so electric between them. The way he was staring at her so angrily yet so hungrily was such a turn on. She wanted to grab him, kiss him hard and drag him back into the bedroom. She had never had such unprofessional thoughts before. In fact, she had never wanted any man as much as she wanted him.

A bubble of laughter suddenly burst from her throat at the ridiculousness of the situation.

The look of hunger completely vanished from his eyes and was quickly replaced with the cautious look of someone dealing with an insane person. It made her laugh even more. Any professionalism she was desperately clinging onto was slipping through her fingers like sand.

'For God's sake, put some bloody clothes on and I'll make us some breakfast,' she said, stepping out of his way.

He stared at her in complete confusion then shuffled into the bedroom and closed the door.

Gregory was waiting for her in the kitchen wagging his tail, his tongue lolling out of his mouth as if he found the whole thing hilarious too. He was a big, tatty, muddy beast who clearly hadn't had a bath for weeks or even months.

She gave him a little curtsey. 'Will Sir Gregory be wanting his breakfast too?'

Gregory licked his lips as if in answer and she laughed. She moved to the fridge and pulled out some bacon and eggs, determined to move things on to more friendly grounds with Cameron when he came out.

—

Cameron walked into the kitchen and sighed with annoyance. She was still in his robe and he didn't think anything could be sexier than Milly wearing it, with her tangle of blonde and pink hair tumbling down her back. She was barefoot as she padded round the kitchen, singing to herself and it was almost impossible not to remember that underneath she was completely naked. He didn't want to be attracted to her. After the last three women he dated had sold their stories to the papers, he had sworn off having any kind of relationship ever again. Yet the feelings he had for her were beyond inappropriate and he was a little bit angry with her for making him feel that way.

She turned round and caught him looking at her. Whatever she saw in his face made the smile fall from hers.

'What is it now?' she said.

'I would have thought you'd have put some clothes on by now. Walking round my home, half naked, it's not the professionalism I expected from Castle Heritage.'

'I was making breakfast.'

'I don't need you to make breakfast for me. You are a business associate, not my girlfriend. I'm quite capable of making my own breakfast.'

'You said we might as well eat together.'

'I didn't mean for you to cook for me.'

She stared at him for a moment in shock and he regretted saying it immediately. It wasn't her fault he was attracted to her and didn't want to take it any further.

She turned back to the stove, grabbed a plate filled with all manner of breakfast delights and slammed it down on the table next to him so hard that the sausage rolled off the plate onto the floor, where Gregory immediately gobbled it up.

'If you don't want it, give it to Gregory, I'm sure he'd be much more appreciative.'

She took her plate and sat down opposite him. With no words in his head, he sat down too.

He speared a mushroom on his fork and tried to swallow it, eventually forcing it down his throat. 'I'm sorry.'

She nodded, curtly.

'This is lovely, thank you,' he said, quietly.

She continued eating her breakfast in silence, refusing to look at him. He tore his eyes away and stared at his food.

Milly finished her meal first and looked across the table towards him. 'Oh I forgot to tell you,' she said, lightly, as if the conversation minutes before hadn't even happened. 'The hole I fell down yesterday. It wasn't a hole.'

He took a big slurp of tea. If she wanted to play it like this then he could pretend to be civil too. 'It wasn't? What was it?'

'A passageway, from the castle.'

His eyes widened in surprise, his forced pretence completely forgotten. 'A secret tunnel?'

'Yes. It had collapsed, so there was no way for me to get back, but it might be worth at least seeing where the secret passageway started. I wonder if it was originally a priests' bolt hole.'

'Well that's interesting.'

'Very,' Milly agreed. 'Why don't I get dressed and we can do a bit of investigating?'

He nodded and watched her go.

—

Milly joined Cameron back in the kitchen and he stood up, his eyes scanning over her for a brief moment. She doubted it was an appreciative gesture. She was wearing long denim shorts, a red and white polka dot shirt and purple sequined Converse trainers. It was a defiant gesture, sticking two fingers up at the professionalism he so desperately wanted. Besides, she doubted whether anything she wore would gain his approval. He really didn't seem to like her much. The chemistry she had felt between them was very clearly one sided.

He was right though, making breakfast for him was a bit too domesticated. Despite his hostile attitude to her staying with him, somehow she felt at home here, she felt completely at ease pottering about his kitchen making tea and food and it made no sense to feel like that. But he didn't like the cosy arrangement and she could understand why, so maybe it would be best to eat separately from now on.

'I think we should go back out to the hole first, get an idea of which direction the tunnel was going in. The parts of the passage that I could see through the rubble seemed straight, so once we have an idea of which area of the castle the tunnel was pointing towards, that will tell us where to start looking.'

'Good idea.' Cameron nodded.

Well, he was clearly going to try to be pleasant and polite even if he didn't want her here. At least for now.

He opened the door for her like the perfect gentleman.

'By the way, for your information, I am wearing a bra.'

His face split into a huge genuine smile. 'That's good to know.'

She strode ahead of him. Despite the earliness of the morning the heat hit her almost as soon as she stepped out. There was no shelter from it here on the cliff tops and she liked the way the castle seemed to bask in the sunlight. With its blue roofs and pale sandstone walls, it had a slightly Mediterranean feel.

years. This kitchen, which wouldn't have been privy to the modernisations over the centuries because it was beyond the realm of the lords and ladies that lived here, seemed to be pretty much as it had been when it was first built. Milly stared around her. She thought it might date back to the fourteenth century. She swallowed down the shock of this sudden unexpected discovery.

It was possible that Castle Heritage or their sister company, National Heritage, might take this place on after all. She'd seen it done before where they had helped to restore an old building to its former glory, but the recent modifications of this castle would probably be too much to remove. And how much would be left? Would it just be the kitchen and maybe a few other smaller rooms around it? She needed to ascertain how big the original building was. Maybe Cameron had some books or documents somewhere that might give her some clue. But finding this little undiscovered gem was even better than finding a secret passageway.

'You ok?' Cameron asked, obviously concerned by the way she was frozen in the middle of the room.

'I can't believe you didn't show me this yesterday. This room is years older than some of the other parts of the castle. It's something like this that could be the difference between Castle Heritage helping you or not.'

'I'm sorry, I just assumed …'

'It's ok, but if I'm going to help you I need to know everything, even if you think it's trivial, it's probably not.'

He nodded, suitably chastised.

'Um … here's the larder.'

He pushed open the little door in the corner and they stepped out onto the top of the stairs that led down below the surface of the ground into a very small, cool, dark room with no windows. There was a large, wide wooden shelf running up one end of the room, fitted over a jutting out stone wall, a few hooks and a couple of smaller, thinner shelves, but nothing else at all. The room was notably cooler than the other rooms in the castle, which served its purpose of preserving the food.

'I can't see a secret passageway coming from the larder, there's nothing in here.' Cameron said.

'But that's the point of secret passageways, they're not supposed to be obvious.'

She walked down the short flight of stairs and looked around, though she had to agree with Cameron that there didn't appear to be anything that could turn out to be an entrance to a tunnel. She ran her hands along the walls, hoping one might be loose and be the much needed switch that she was looking for. Nothing happened. She pulled on the hooks hoping they might be switches too. Nothing.

'Maybe it's in the kitchen,' Cameron offered, moving back out to the other room.

She slid her hand underneath the wooden shelf but just as she was ready to give up, her hand bumped across what felt like a bolt. She pulled the handle back towards her and something clicked, although what it was, she wasn't exactly clear.

She tried to lift the wooden shelf up and to her surprise it came clean away from the wall underneath, revealing a set of stairs leading downwards and round a corner out of sight.

She squealed with delight and gave a tiny little dance before she regained her professional face.

'Cameron, I've found it.'

She heard his footsteps come running and his eyes lit up when he appeared in the door of the room and saw the secret steps leading below the castle. Any sign of the grumpy man she'd come to know had suddenly vanished and in his place was a big kid who had just learned that Christmas had come early.

'Are you kidding me?' he said, running down the stairs from the kitchen.

She shook her head and quickly clambered over the wall. Cameron was already throwing his leg over to join her. She tentatively crept down the stone stairs and he followed.

They reached the bottom and as they rounded the corner, they could clearly see the caved in area of the tunnel ahead of them and the light from the hole that Milly had fallen down beyond that.

'Careful,' Cameron warned as she took a step down the passage. 'If it's caved in already, I doubt the rest of it is that secure.'

She hesitated. He had a point and there was nothing else down this tunnel worth investigating, no other routes or rooms led off it. But what an exciting find.

She turned back to him and smiled at the wondrous grin on his face. Sharing this little secret together, she felt an overwhelming urge to hug him. She liked Cameron like this, smiling and worry free, even if it was only for a few minutes. She wanted to do anything possible to keep that smile on his face.

'You do know what this means, don't you?'

He frowned and shook his head.

'If there is one secret passageway from the castle, there are likely to be several more.'

His eyes widened. 'Seriously?'

He went back up the steps and she followed him. When he reached the wall, he climbed over easily then turned and lifted her out as if it was the most natural thing in the world to have his hands round her waist.

She tried to ignore the feeling of his hot hands on her body. 'Well, your castle is very unconventional, but there's never normally just one. I wouldn't be surprised if we find a tunnel that leads to the maze too, as that was quite popular in old houses with mazes.'

'How will we find them, what do we look for?'

'Bookshelves are a great place to start.'

'You mean, like in those films with books that you pull out that act as a switch for a secret doorway, those things are real?'

She nodded. 'I've seen several passageways like that, or fake book spines which cover a door handle.'

'And should we be looking for light fittings that are handles and secret buttons inside the heads of statues?'

His eyes twinkled as he spoke, she loved the way he teased her.

'Don't rule anything out. I think we should split up, see what we can find.'

'Ok, but no exploring any rooms or tunnels without the other person, we'll let each other know if we find anything.'

She nodded and he ran off, obviously keen to find his own secret passageway. She smiled at his enthusiasm.

She walked out of the kitchen and into the hall that led to the banqueting room. She could see Cameron moving around in there, running his hands over the walls, so she decided to try the study and the library first, since both rooms had bookcases.

She headed upstairs and into the study. There was a large desk and several chairs around the room and a whole wall of bookcases along one side.

She carefully examined the books on the shelves for any that looked out of place or fake. It would take a while to try every single book in here, but she should be able to spot something that looked a little odd.

It was the third bookcase that caught her eye. It was set back from the others by about two centimetres. It wasn't something that anyone would notice unless they were specifically looking for it. It didn't mean that it was necessarily a secret doorway, but the faint scratches on the floor suggested that something was amiss.

She scanned her eyes over the books, trying to spot any that looked suspicious.

Many were various shades of red, green and brown but one at the top was a pale blue.

She couldn't even reach it. Loath as she was to climb up onto this bookcase that was clearly hundreds of years old, the more she looked at the book, the more she was convinced it needed further investigation.

She climbed up onto the first shelf, and reached out for the book. It was stiff, stuck fast between the two books either side. She leaned up a bit more and tugged at the top of the book. It moved upwards and as it did so, the whole bookcase spun round, with Milly attached to it. A second later she was plunged into darkness as the bookcase clicked into place, now in a different room entirely.

Crap.

If she'd had any foresight she would have at least brought a torch with her. Feeling a bit panicky over what she couldn't see in the darkness with her, she tugged on the book she was still holding in the hope that it would have the same effect but in reverse, taking her back to the study again, but though the book moved upwards, the bookshelf did not.

Her heart thumping a bit uneasily, she stepped down from the case and peered around. She could see nothing; she didn't know if she was in a secret room or the entrance to a passageway.

She blinked in the darkness and could just make out a tiny slither of muted light from around the bookcase, which gave the room a slight grey tinge. She waited patiently for her eyes to become accustomed to the dark. Slowly she could pick out features. She was standing in a stone room about two or three metres wide. On the wall opposite the bookcase, she could just make out a wooden door. Something pale sat in the corner and she shuffled closer to it. Unease and fear spread quickly in her gut and erupted out of her throat in a terrifying bloodcurdling scream that echoed round the chamber.

She couldn't take her eyes off what was clearly the skeleton of a child.

CHAPTER 6

Cameron heard the scream just as he was investigating a suit of armour he'd never even looked twice at before.

It was a sound of pure fear and panic and it didn't stop. He ran from the room and took the stairs two at a time. He hesitated at the top for a second as he tried to ascertain whether the scream and the accompanying thumps were coming from the study or the library, but the noise was so loud, he was left with no doubt.

He burst into the study and it was very obvious which shelf Milly had gone through as the bookshelf was no longer there. In its place was a blank wooden panel. The screams for help and thumps that were coming from the other side of it were also a big clue.

Milly had obviously gone through and got trapped but he was surprised that this would cause her to scream so much, since she was a feisty little thing that didn't seem to get upset by anything.

He ran his hands over the wooden panel to see if there were any switches or buttons that would release her but he couldn't find anything.

'Milly!' he shouted through the door, but he doubted she could hear him over her own screams. He raised his voice. 'Milly!'

'Get me out!' she screamed.

'How did you get in, was there a lever or button somewhere?'

'Get me fucking out of here,' she sobbed.

There was a time for reason and calm and this was not it. The only thing that was going to solve this problem was sheer brute force.

'Stand back.' The thumping and screaming stopped, but the whimpers and sobs did not. 'Stand back, ok?'

He didn't hear any arguments so he threw his whole body weight against the wooden panel. It cracked but didn't move. He took a few steps back and ran forwards and threw himself against the wood again. This time it gave way. It spun on its axis, revealing a room beyond that was in complete darkness. He didn't have time to investigate it as the next moment he was hit hard in the stomach by a tiny blonde figure.

He wrapped his arms round Milly and was stunned to feel her trembling all over. He held her tight against him.

'What happened? Did you see another ghost?'

She was shaking so much, she couldn't speak. He ran his hands down her back, stroking her soothingly.

Eventually she pulled away to look at him and he hated that she had tears in her eyes. He wanted to hold her forever and protect her from anything that might cause that look of anguish again.

'You know you said you saw the ghost of a small boy up here in the study?'

He nodded, his hands still running up and down her back.

'I think I've just found his body.'

His mouth went dry. 'A corpse?'

She nodded. 'His skeleton.'

Fuck.

'I better take a look.'

Her fingers dug into his shirt. 'Don't go in there.'

'If you're right, we'll need to call the police.'

She nodded and stepped back. Shit, he really didn't want to go into a room with a corpse. He was likely to scream and cry like a girl too. But they couldn't exactly leave it there.

Milly was watching him, waiting for him to be brave. He took a deep breath and squeezed through the gap.

Sure enough, propped up against the corner was a small skeleton. He felt sick. He shuffled closer, holding his breath against any smell of rotting flesh. In the light from the study, he could see something metallic on the elbow joint. As he moved closer he realised it was some kind of hinge or spring. There were similar metal joints and hinges on the shoulder, knees and ankles too. This wasn't a real skeleton at all. He reached out to touch it to make sure and could clearly feel that the bones were made from plastic.

He grabbed it by the arm and carried it out.

Milly shrieked when she saw him carrying it, stepping back against the desk.

'It's not real.'

Her face fell with relief as he tentatively stepped forward to show it to her. 'It's not?'

'It's one of those models that doctors or science teachers have.'

She reached out to touch it and her face flamed red as she realised her mistake.

'I'm so sorry, you must think I'm a right idiot.'

'Not at all. It's pitch black in there, what were you supposed to think?'

'Well thank you for not taking the piss out of me for acting like a pathetic girl. You could have handled that very differently.'

He stared at her. 'No I couldn't. No man worth his salt would have taken the piss out of you when you were so terrified. It didn't even cross my mind.'

'Then you're not like most of the men I know. My ex-boy-friend used to chase me round the flat with spiders because he knew I was scared of them. He thought it was hilarious, whilst I was sobbing and blubbing like a baby.'

'Your ex-boyfriend sounds like an ass.'

She smiled and he was relieved to see it. 'He really was.'

She eyed the skeleton in his hand and shuddered.

'I'll get rid of it.'

'It's ok. What was it doing in there?'

'I don't know. I have vague recollections of my parents throwing costumed parties, maybe he was part of a Halloween party.'

She sighed and pushed her hair off her face. 'I'm not doing anything here to help dispel the bimbo image am I? And I bet Castle Heritage is very quickly going down in your opinion.'

'You have nothing to prove to me, your credentials more than speak for themselves.'

'I can get someone else up here, equally as qualified. They could be here by the end of next week. Professor Stone is very efficient, he's a lot older too. He doesn't wear pretty dresses or sparkly trainers, he's probably much more up your street.'

Something twisted inside him at the thought of her going. He didn't like the feeling that thought gave him, which was ridiculous, he barely knew her.

He shuffled closer to her, leaning round her to put the skeleton on the desk behind her. He returned his gaze to her face, to those intense sea blue eyes that seemed to have a hundred different tones to them, specks of green, turquoise and navy blue, intermingled with flecks of gold and grey. He was standing too close to her, much closer than would be deemed polite according to social etiquette. She hadn't moved away either, she was just staring up at him. He tucked a stray blonde curl behind her ear.

'I like having you here.' He stepped back a tiny fraction. 'In a professional capacity, of course.'

She smiled and the smile turned into a giggle, which made his heart leap. He couldn't help but smile too.

'Of course,' she said.

'And this Professor Stone sounds like a right bore. I happen to like your sparkly Converse.'

Her smile grew even bigger and it filled his heart to see it. 'We'll have to see if we can get you a pair.'

He laughed, loudly. 'I'd like that.'

She stared at him for a moment, before looking away, smiling to herself. 'Right, shall we investigate this passageway, now that it seems it's permanently open?'

He looked over to the bookshelf and the wood that had splintered either side when he had thrown himself against it. It was never going to lock again.

'We don't have to do that today, if you're still shaken up by the whole skeleton thing.'

'Are you kidding? We've just found a secret passageway, aren't you dying to know where it leads?'

'Well, yes but … your happiness and wellbeing is far more important to me.'

She looked at him and something seemed to shift between them. Was it a mutual attraction? Did she like him too but was trying really hard not to? Every nerve ending seemed to be standing to attention with her proximity. He was aware of everything about her; the shape of her lips as she smiled, the length of her lashes, the heat he could feel from her body. The faint scent of his shower gel and his shampoo on her skin was still a killer. He wanted her, he couldn't deny it.

He cleared his throat and stepped back away from her. This was bad, very bad.

She walked towards the bookshelf.

He watched her approach the threshold of the new secret room, take a deep breath and step inside into the darkness. He loved her brave, gutsy attitude. He followed her inside and walked straight into her bum as she was bent over, touching the floor. She nearly toppled onto her face, but he grabbed her by the hips to steady her.

Milly burst out laughing.

'So you decided to throw professionalism to the wind.'

He frowned with confusion and suddenly realised how inappropriate their current position was. He quickly released her and stepped back.

'There's something buried here, in the cracks between these two stones,' Milly said, as if he hadn't just inadvertently tried to take her from behind.

He crouched down by her side to see and sure enough, something gold glinted from the cracks. He grabbed his pen knife which he habitually carried around with him and scraped away the soil from the sides.

'It's a coin,' Milly said, excitedly, shuffling closer so their knees were touching.

A few chunks of moss and dirt came away from the crack and the gold coin came with them. He picked it up and wiped it on his jeans, then peered at it. It was about the size of a ten pence piece, but thicker, with some unusual markings on it.

'It's probably a prop, same as the skeleton,' Cameron said, passing it to Milly. 'Finders Keepers.'

But Milly shook her head and passed it back to him, which surprised him. 'It's yours. It might be worth something.'

'I doubt it.'

'It could help to pay for some repairs, and you never know, it might be part of a hidden haul of treasure.'

He laughed and stood up, pushing the coin into his pocket.

'There is supposed to be some lost family treasure somewhere.' He spotted the wooden door at the back of the room and walked over to it.

Milly followed him, examining the handle. 'Really?'

'So say the legends, but there's also supposed to be a sea monster that frequents these parts called the Oogie that takes away and eats any unwanted guests. So if that's the kind of truth the locals believe in, I hardly hold any faith in the legend of the Heartstone treasure.'

Milly turned the handle but the door didn't give. 'Are they a bit odd? The villagers? I've only met one of them, but …'

'You don't have to be polite, they're all weird. Every time I go into the village, they all chant "Oogie" at me, as if they are summoning the monster to come and take me away. They literally stand outside their houses and chant "Oogie", over and over again.'

'And they've told you about the legend of the Heartstone Treasure?'

'Those that speak to me have.'

'What's the legend?'

'The Heartstones have always been filthy rich, but my mad uncle Boris seems to have been richer than most. He was the one that added all the turrets and flags. Well, it was said that he loved precious jewels. All of the remaining fortune not spent on silly turrets, was spent on big diamonds, rubies and sapphires. He had a chest filled with them that he used to get out at parties and dances so everyone could admire his wealth.'

'Nice.'

'Arrogant. Anyway he became obsessed with this chest, he'd carry it around everywhere with him, absolutely paranoid that someone would steal it from him. He was always hiding it in places and then changing his mind and hiding it somewhere else. Legend says that he loaded it into a boat one day, set sail from the cove below the castle and was never seen again.'

'Interesting.' Milly pulled the handle out and gave it a wiggle but still the door stayed resolute.

'A load of bollocks, more like. The only evidence I can find that this chest ever existed is a portrait of mad old Boris in the pub with the chest of jewels by his side. It would not surprise me if Boris had the artist add the chest in whilst painting to make him look wealthier than he was. It seems that, either shortly after the renovations or even during them, Boris sold off several acres of his land to nearby farmers. I think the man was broke and he couldn't even afford to pay for the turrets he so desperately wanted. He lived an extravagant life with big parties but they seemed to stop completely in his later years. He sacked a lot of his staff too. I don't think he had enough money to pay for that life anymore.'

'Or he didn't want anyone around his precious jewels, so he stopped inviting people to the castle.'

'He was a total ladies' man, so my guess is if this chest did exist, one of the women he was with killed him for it, dumped the body over the cliffs and stole all the jewels herself. Wouldn't be the first time a Heartstone man was screwed over by a beautiful woman, nor the last.'

Milly looked up at him but he concentrated his attention on the door. 'There isn't a keyhole, but it appears to be locked,' he said.

'Maybe it can only be opened from the other side.'

He looked back to the bookshelf. 'That wouldn't make sense if the bookshelf can only be opened from the study side.'

'Unless someone breaks it open,' Milly grinned up at him.

He smiled. 'There must be a switch or something that will release it.'

Milly let out another laugh as she reached up and released a bolt at the very top of the door. 'Or a bolt.' She glanced down to the bottom and found another bolt there near the floor. 'Sometimes these things are just not that technical.'

She tried the handle again and this time the door opened easily. In the limited light from the study, Cameron could just make out some stone steps curling away below them.

Milly turned to face him, her eyes alight with excitement.

'Let me get my torch.'

—

Milly stood at the top of the newly found stairs waiting for Cameron to come back. She was glad she was standing in the darkness of the hidden room so Cameron wouldn't see the blush on her cheeks when he came back. She couldn't believe she had reacted like that. It was bad enough that she had been so freaked out over a skeleton, since she had found human remains in archaeological sites before and never been bothered by it, but to then find out it was only plastic, made her reaction all the more shameful. She had hugged Cameron. Well, clung to him would be a more accurate description. He had held her like a child, which was mortifying. She absently wished on her star bracelet that she hadn't behaved like that although she knew it was useless.

There had been something about the way Cameron had stroked his hands down her back to soothe her that had been wonderful and incredibly hot. She just couldn't understand her body's reaction to him. There had been plenty of attractive guys over the years whom she had barely given a second glance because she wasn't interested in a relationship at all. And now she had known Cameron for less than twenty-four hours and she had thrown all her reservations straight out the window. He was grumpy, rude, sweet, funny and sexy as hell. But there was more to their connection than that. She felt like she knew him, which was ridiculous because of course she didn't. She knew nothing about him. But sometimes there was an ease between them that only came from knowing someone your whole life. But regardless of this spark, she wasn't going to do anything about it, she couldn't. She had a professionalism to maintain. Although she knew that was only part of it. Not wanting her heart broken again was probably the bigger part.

She took a deep breath and let it out. She wasn't going to think about her humiliation any more. There was nothing she could do to change it so she would stop dwelling on it. She moved closer to the stairs. It was pitch black down the secret passageway and the limited light from the study just about lit up the first three or four stairs but beyond that she couldn't see anything. She was desperate to explore it but it would be suicide to go down a very old staircase in the dark – half of the stairs could have crumbled away to nothing.

A slight breeze came from below and with it, just for a second, she could hear the faint sound of a child's laughter.

She swallowed and stepped back, bumping into something hard that hadn't been there before. She swung around to see Cameron standing there.

'You ok?'

She nodded, unable to speak.

'This place can creep you out,' Cameron said, softly. 'I hear footsteps, doors slamming, loud bangs, voices. I tell myself that it's just the wind or loose floorboards or old pipes but … knowing what I've seen down in the dungeons …' He trailed off. 'I have locks on the inside of my kitchen, lounge and bedroom, which is silly as ghosts would just walk through the doors whether they're locked or not but it makes me feel better when I sleep at night. I've felt a lot happier since you've arrived. Having someone here with me has been nice, otherwise it's just me rattling around this big old house with all these bumps and bangs, it's enough to send anyone mad.'

'I'll protect you,' Milly said, with a grin.

'Thank you. And who will protect you?'

'I'm quite scrappy,' she threw a few air punches, dodging about on her feet. She saw his smile grow as he watched her and she stopped dancing. 'Are you laughing at me, Cameron Heartstone?'

'Noooo I wouldn't dream of it. I was just thinking I wouldn't want to go against you in a fight. Shall we?' He gestured to the stairs and she nodded. Without asking, he took her hand and strode into the darkness. That ease and familiarity spread through her again and she smiled, despite the promises she had made to herself a few moments before.

Milly could just make out the torch beam as it danced off the stone steps below. The steps were well worn, indicating that they had been used many times over the years. Cameron's hulking frame was a comforting presence in front of her but she didn't like to think about what lurked in the darkness behind her.

There didn't seem to be any end to the stairs as they continued downwards. The study was two flights up from the ground floor and although it was very hard to tell in the darkness, it felt like they were going much deeper than that.

Eventually they reached the bottom and Cameron shone the torch down what appeared to be a very long, straight tunnel that forked into three separate tunnels at the end.

'We need to be really careful; if that other tunnel caved in, this one could be unstable too,' Cameron whispered, as if talking normally would cause it to collapse.

Milly nodded but as she stepped forward, Cameron was at her side, his hand in hers.

As Cameron continued to shine the torch, Milly could see wooden joints and beams holding the roof of the tunnel up at several intervals. The wood wasn't rotting at all, it looked strong and capable of standing for another hundred years. She was desperate to do some tree ring tests on that wood to get an idea of when the tunnel was built, although if the joints had been replaced at some point it might be a bit harder to date the tunnels, but she suspected it was around the same era that mad Uncle Boris was Lord of the castle. The floor was made from stone which looked clean but again, well worn. It all looked very professional and certainly not done in a hurry.

They came to the fork and stopped.

'What do you reckon?' Cameron said, shining his torch over the three openings and the tunnels beyond.

The tunnels couldn't have been more different. The one on the right sloped downwards very steeply, seemingly going into the very bowels of the earth. It was muddy and wet and it didn't look safe at all. The middle tunnel carried straight on with its stone floor and wooden joists, it was probably the original tunnel and the two other forks were added later. In the limited light they could just see a ladder at the end, which seemed to go straight up. The left tunnel veered up and off to the left almost as if it was heading back towards the castle. There appeared to be a few brass lanterns on the walls, unlit of course, and at the very end, steps rising upwards into a bright shaft of sunlight. Moss lined the edges of the tunnel, but it looked almost magical as the sunlight sparkled off the green walls.

'I know which one you want to explore first,' Cameron said.

She looked up at him. 'You do?'

He took her hand and walked down the slightly sinister looking right tunnel.

She laughed. 'How did you know?'

'I've come to realise that with you, I have to expect the un-expected.'

The tunnel zigzagged and twisted and turned until Milly had no idea which direction the castle was, they seemed to be going further and further down. The smooth dirt walls were soon re-placed with jagged rock walls, covered with moss, and it started to get lighter so that Cameron's torch wasn't needed at all. She could hear a roaring that was getting louder and louder and as they rounded the last corner, they were faced with a stunning view of the inky blue sea. The tunnel ended abruptly, opening out into a gaping hole in the cliff face.

Milly and Cameron inched closer to the edge, but Cameron's grip on her hand tightened just in case she slipped and tumbled inadvertently to her death.

'Oh!' Milly exclaimed, as she took in the view. About ten me-tres below the tunnel entrance lay a pretty little secluded cove, about twenty or thirty metres long and lined with golden sand. Milly longed to lie on the castle's own private beach. She smiled hugely, what an incredible discovery.

Large rocks punctuated the sea along the cove, making it almost impossible to get to the beach by boat, this seemed like the only safe way to access the cove.

Cameron nudged her and pointed directly below the hole, where a tiny old wooden boat lay upside down, broken and seem-ingly wedged between the rocks that lined this end of the cove.

'You don't think that was Uncle Boris's boat, do you?' Milly asked.

'I don't know, but it explains a lot about his disappearance if it is.'

'What if … the treasure is down there too?' Milly said.

He smiled. 'If it was, I expect it washed out to sea a long time ago.'

'Can we get down there to explore?' Milly leaned out over the opening but Cameron pulled her back.

'Please be careful, I really don't want you to die.'

He leaned out himself, ever so slightly and then knelt to the floor, picking at the mud to reveal a piece of rope that seemed to be welded to the edge of the ledge with moss. Eventually he managed to pull it free and a rope ladder came away from the cliff face. It was about four metres long and the end had clearly broken off at some point over the years.

'Well I guess that's a no for now, but I reckon the hardware store in the village might sell rope ladders, or at least know where we can get them.'

Milly pulled a face, disappointed that this current adventure had come to such a swift end.

'I promise we'll come back,' Cameron said, as he moved his fingers to her lips, pulling her pout into a smile. She laughed. 'Come on, we have two other tunnels to explore and I guess you want the one that looks like it leads to an enchanted forest next, you being a Disney princess and all.'

He led the way back up the tunnel, still holding her hand, and she couldn't help smiling at his back, feeling a silly giddiness sweep through her. She really liked Cameron and the more time she spent with him, the harder it was to find reasons not to be with him.

—

Cameron switched on his torch as the light from the beach faded the further they went back up the tunnel.

It was an odd thing, holding Milly's hand. It was warm and fitted his hand perfectly, but he hadn't even known her a day and yet it felt like the most natural thing in the world. The boundaries of their professional relationship seemed to be crumbling very quickly.

Suddenly Milly slipped in the mud behind him and although he was holding her hand, she landed on her bum by his side, the mud splashing over her clothes, face and hair.

'Oh God, Milly, are you ok?' She burst out laughing and took his hand as he offered to help her up. 'Your clothes are covered.' Cameron wiped some mud off her top and her laughter went up an octave as he inadvertently nudged against her breasts again.

'So you're a bit of a breast man?' she laughed.

'I'm so sorry.'

She wiped the mud off her face, leaving trails of dirt across her pale skin. She looked adorable. 'Well normally a man would take me out to dinner first, before I let him get that far.'

Realising she found the whole thing hilarious, he didn't feel the need to apologise again. 'I did make you soup yesterday and a pie last night.'

'Oh well in that case, let's forget the tunnels and jump straight into bed now.'

She walked off up the tunnel and Cameron was seriously tempted to take her up on that offer.

He noticed she was limping slightly and he hurried to catch up with her. 'Are you ok, you're limping?'

'Just stubbed my toe, I'm sure it'll be fine in a minute.'

'How about a piggy back?'

'So you can cop a feel of my bum too? No, I don't think so.'

'Well let me know if you change your mind.' He took her hand again and in the torch light he could see her smile. He walked slower so she could take her time, as he tried to resist the temptation to pick her up and carry her.

—

They reached the junction of the fork again and Milly ignored the dull throbbing in her toe.

She stopped and looked up the passage that was covered in moss. Cameron was right, it did look enchanted.

'We should have brought supplies with us, I'm starving,' Cameron said, standing close behind her.

She could feel his heat, smell his intoxicating scent. He was too much.

And even if he did like her, which he seemed to, they couldn't do anything. Castle Heritage would fire her on the spot if they found out she had been kissing or sleeping with a client.

She stepped forward away from him, but his hand was still entwined with hers. She tried to ignore how good it felt there as they walked up the tunnel.

'Why do you think this part is covered in moss too?'

'I think because the tunnel slopes down from the opening, the rain water just runs down here leaving it all moist and wet.'

She bit back a giggle at his choice of words and the sexy way in which he said them. The tunnel was quite a steep incline up towards the stone steps, which were also covered in moss and didn't look like they had been used for years, if they ever had been.

There was a wooden trap door at the top of the steps that was badly damaged, sunlight pouring through the cracks in the wood onto the stairs below. Milly ran up to the top of stairs and pushed on the door. It moved but didn't open. She felt around for a bolt or latch as Cameron came up behind her.

'Is it locked from the other side?'

'I think so.'

'Here, stand back a bit, let's see if I can break it open.'

She turned to him, horrified. 'You can't do that, this door was obviously the original one. It could be over a hundred years old.'

'And if we ever plan to use these tunnels for whatever reason, it would need to be replaced, it's not safe. The amount of water that must pour through is slowly eroding this tunnel. I wouldn't be surprised if it caves in soon. I'd need to fix it if we are going to preserve the tunnels.'

She nodded reluctantly and stepped back.

'I'll try to break it open gently,' Cameron said.

She smiled. 'I've seen you break something open already today. I don't think you and gentle go in the same sentence.'

He knelt on the third step from the top, leaning his back and shoulders against the door and slowly stood up. The door groaned for just a second before it popped open under the strain. The trap door remained intact.

'I'm impressed.'

He stepped out and looked around as Milly ran up the steps to join him.

The intense heat of the day was a stark contrast to the coolness of the tunnel and Milly blinked a few times in the brightness of the sunlight.

'I knew it,' Milly squealed with excitement as she realised where she was.

CHAPTER 7

Milly looked around her in wonder. Standing on top of a white, wooden gazebo, they were surrounded by a tangle of trees and bushes that hid the walls, twists and turns of the huge maze that stood on top of the cliffs. The maze clearly hadn't been used for years either. A carpet of wild flowers surrounded the gazebo, grew up the sides and competed for sunlight amongst the thornier branches of the maze.

'Oh God, it's beautiful. Did you ever play in here as a kid?'

Cameron shook his head. 'I was never allowed. It was too overgrown, mostly with thorny bushes. One of the bushes collapsed anyway so there was no way through. It needs a lot of clearing and tidying.'

'I think it's perfect just the way it is. Sure, the hedges and walls need to be trimmed back a bit and that collapsed bush would need to be moved but this maze is lovely, all these flowers and twisted branches just add to its appeal. This would make such a gorgeous place to get married. Can you imagine the wedding photos? It's just beautiful.'

Cameron was watching her again, a smile on his face. 'You're very sweet.'

She blushed. 'Oh it gets very tiresome after a while, believe me. I'm normally much better at toning it down than this. Come on, we still have that third passage to explore.'

She turned to go back down the steps but he caught her arm. 'Why would you want to tone it down?'

'Ah come on, we've all seen that girl in the Disney movies who sings and dances everywhere and all the birds and animals flock round her. Most people want to punch her in the face for being so sickeningly happy.'

'Only the miserable people.'

'From my experience, that includes most people. My brother's ex-girlfriend said I was like an annoying puppy that thought everything was the best thing ever, permanently wagging my tail and grinning at the world. I didn't realise I came across as so inane before.'

'I think that reflects more on her issues than it does yours,' Cameron said, softly.

'My ex-boyfriend dumped me for the same reason. He'd come home from a bad day at work and I'd be dancing round the flat as I was cleaning, singing songs from Mary Poppins or Disney. He said he'd rather stay at work and deal with the crap than come home to me. I'm really not everyone's cup of tea.'

Why was she opening up to him? She barely knew him and she was telling him everything: the good, the bad and the ugly.

'I like it,' he said.

Her heart leapt. She stared at him and he blinked and took a step back.

'Don't get me wrong. I think you're a nice girl but I'm not looking for a relationship right now.'

'I'm not either.' She really wasn't. Relationships were messy and time consuming and ultimately heart breaking.

'Well that's good,' Cameron said, nodding thoughtfully, though he didn't take his eyes off her.

'Yep, good that we're on the same page.' She continued to stare at him, unable to move. Why did she think that although a relationship had been taken off the table, hot, passionate, no strings attached sex was still firmly up for consideration? She had never had a one night stand before and she wasn't about to start now. But she knew that if he kissed her now, there would be very little she could do to stop it.

'Right, well I need some lunch, so let's see where the third tunnel leads.' Cameron strode past her and down the stairs.

She sighed, partly from relief, partly from disappointment, and followed him.

He closed the trap door over them, switched on the torch, grabbed her hand, which seemed strange, given the conversation they'd just had, and walked back towards the fork. Though Milly had to admit it'd be even stranger if he didn't hold her hand as it seemed that had long become the norm for them.

They turned into the middle tunnel and eventually they came to the end where a ladder went up towards the limited light. It looked like it led up to a door.

Cameron looked up. 'I'll go first, I'm not sure how much weight this ladder holds.'

'Then shouldn't I go first? No offence but I'm probably a little bit lighter than you. It's a long way to fall if it breaks on you at the top.'

'What if it breaks on you?'

'Then you'll catch me,' Milly said, simply, swinging herself up onto the ladder. It felt strong and didn't give under her weight as she made her way slowly up to the top.

With a bit of difficulty she stood on the last rung and pushed on the door. It didn't give. She fumbled around in the darkness and found a handle which she turned and the door swung open. She quickly climbed out and looked around, hearing Cameron's eager footsteps clanging up the ladder after her.

The door was in the gatepost at the bottom of the drive. Although it was painted bottle green, she hadn't noticed it when she had arrived because it was on the inside, facing the castle.

It was a small door and Milly did wonder if Cameron would be able to fit through it. That question was answered a moment later as he wriggled and shuffled and squeezed himself through the opening. He was just so big.

Milly stifled her laughter as he stood up. He looked around him in shock and back at the gatepost.

'I've seen that door several times but I just presumed it was some kind of electrical cupboard for the lights on top of the posts.'

'I love this castle, it continues to surprise me,' Milly said.

Cameron turned to look at her, a flash of warmth in his eyes. 'You're filthy.'

Milly shrugged. 'It's just mud, it will wash off.'

'And you continue to surprise me too.'

With his hand at the small of her back he escorted her back up the drive. His hand was so hot it was like fire against her skin. She tried not to think about it nor the demons that were holding him back, it was none of her business.

Although her actual business seemed to be taking a complete back seat at the moment. She had to find out once and for all whether this would be a project that Castle Heritage would take on.

But now she had stayed the night, she didn't feel inclined to leave anytime soon.

What was it about this castle that drew her in and made her want to stay? The ridiculous turrets, the secret rooms and passageways, the ghosts? She looked at Cameron. Or was it him?

She suddenly remembered what Danny had said when she first arrived in the village. '*Those that stay there will never leave.*' Was there something more sinister at work here, some kind of magic pulling her in, refusing to let her go? She laughed out loud at this ridiculous notion.

'What?' Cameron asked.

'This place, it just ... gets under your skin, doesn't it?'

'Yeah it does. I haven't figured out if that's a good thing or a bad thing yet.' He nudged her gently through the kitchen door. 'Sit down, I'll make us some lunch.'

'Oh let me help.'

'I was just going to do beans on toast, no big deal.' He grabbed a loaf and a carving knife and started cutting great slabs of bread. She grabbed the butter from the fridge and moved closer to him to put the butter on the table.

'Here, grab that pan,' he gestured vaguely, elbowing her in the face at the same time.

She yelped and leapt back, but blood was already pouring out of her nose, soaking the top of her white blouse.

Cameron turned round and went pale when he saw what he had done.

'Why were you standing so close?' he yelled, grabbing her hand and forcing her to sit down.

'I was putting the butter on the table,' Milly yelled back, though her voice was muffled as her hand was holding her nose, trying to stop the blood.

Gregory leapt up from his position in front of the Aga and started barking at them.

The blood was going everywhere despite her best attempts to stop it. Cameron, kneeling in front of her, still with the carving knife in his hand, was getting covered too.

Milly felt a giggle burst from her throat at the sight of him, which clearly surprised him.

'If someone was to walk in now, this wouldn't look good,' Milly said, gesturing to the carving knife.

Cameron hastily put it down. He grabbed a towel, wet it, and brought it back to her. He knelt down in front of her and held it gently over her nose.

'Shit, I'm so sorry. I have never hit a woman before. There have been many things written in the papers about me and women, most of it isn't good but thankfully wife beater isn't one of them. My ex-wife can attest to that. Well, she would if you could find her.'

'You were married?'

'Yes, it was quite a few years ago.' He sighed and looked away as if remembering something painful. 'Eva was my first proper girlfriend. I was very hairy when I was younger, long hair, fluffy beard. I was flattered that she was paying me any attention, she was absolutely gorgeous. I was naive enough to think that she actually loved me. We got married, and she encouraged me to get joint accounts, put everything in both our names. I was besotted with her and would have done anything for her. One day I came home from a week-long business trip to find the whole house had been cleared out, and I mean everything – bed, washing machine, TV, all her clothes. The place was empty. All the joint accounts, which held a cumulative total of several million pounds, were also empty. I couldn't find her, couldn't contact her. My initial anger over her leaving me soon turned to concern that something must have happened to her. I called the police and her disappearance was a complete mystery, no one could find her. I got word several months later that she was in the Caribbean. I'd seen photos of her on a Facebook profile that she had under a different name. She's moved on since then, different name, different identity. I have no idea where she is now. I presume this is something she's done before and probably again after she married me.'

Milly swallowed, feeling so sad for him. 'I'm sorry that you went through that.'

He shrugged nonchalantly, though she could tell he had been hurt by it. 'You live and learn I suppose. I was heartbroken initially but I was angrier at myself that I had been stupid enough to hand my fortune over on a plate. She couldn't take the house or my car and I've made more money since then with book and film royalties, but I never made that money back. The other women I've been with since were more obvious about being after me for my money. We go out for dinner and they want expensive bottles of champagne or nights in luxurious hotels. But I'm very careful about not making the same mistake I did with Eva.'

She stared at him. 'You don't want to get hurt again?'

His eyes were locked on hers and he shook his head.

'I can relate to that. The last four years of my life I've pushed men away for fear of getting hurt again. A broken heart is beyond painful and it's not something I ever want to go through again.'

'I wish I had your resolve. Every time I get involved with a woman, they betray me. When I came here I promised myself and my PA, Olivia, who always has to pick up the pieces, that I was on a sabbatical from women.'

'How's that working out for you?'

He looked down at his hand, resting on her thigh. She glanced down at it too. He looked back up at her, his soft brown eyes darker now. 'Not good.'

'I can relate to that too,' Milly said, quietly.

He stared at her then blinked and cleared his throat. Standing up, he wiped the last of the blood from her nose. 'It doesn't seem like anything is broken. How about you sit over there out of the way whilst I make us some lunch? That way you won't get hurt.'

She moved down the table and found herself touching her star bracelet. She just hoped his resolve was stronger than he thought because hers was certainly crumbling.

—

After lunch, which was conducted in silence, Milly decided to go down to the village. She needed to get all her test equipment from Dick and she needed a break from Cameron, to clear her head and gain some perspective. Maybe she'd chat to some of the villagers for a bit. They might know more about the castle than Cameron did.

There was so much that didn't add up with Cameron. He had written some children's books that had been turned into films and made him millions, though she had never heard of him. Although in all honesty, that wasn't surprising, she barely watched TV and very rarely read newspapers or magazines. But if he was still making money after his ex-wife had left him, enough for a lavish lifestyle of expensive champagnes and luxurious hotels, why did he not have enough money to pay for the repairs on the castle? There was certainly a lot more to him than he was revealing.

She rounded the corner from the castle into the village and smiled. The sun was out in full force now, making the tiny village look like it was in rural France rather than South East England. The village green had a great oak tree standing in the middle, overshadowing a little pond with two white ducks bobbing on the surface. Flowers poked out of gardens and lined the roadside. It was a tranquil haven. The cobbled road stretched down from the castle past five or six whitewashed houses on the right to a large thatched pub in the corner and then away to the left around the green past several more houses and into the woods joining the road she had traversed with Dick the day before. To the side of the pub was a smaller road, curving behind it, and she could see maybe thirty other rooftops scattered in a higgle-dy-piggledy pattern down to the edge of the cliff. She looked around the village, trying to imagine the history this place had seen, but as she looked across the green, she could quite clearly see that Dick, her beloved Triumph, was gone.

Remembering Danny's threat that her car would be towed, she decided to knock on a few doors and find out where it had been taken. She just hoped she wouldn't bump into mad old Danny again.

She knocked on one door and a little granny opened it. She had tight curly grey hair and gold half-moon glasses. Milly had to suppress a laugh, she was like something straight from a story book.

She stepped forward to speak but the old lady beat her to it. 'Oogie, Oogie, Oogie.'

Milly stared at her in shock as she continued to chant. Cameron had warned her about this but she hadn't actually believed him.

'Sorry to bother you,' Milly raised her voice over the chanting. 'I'm Milly Rose, I'm staying with Lord Heartstone and ...'

The chanting got louder and Milly quickly hurried away, fearful of knocking on the next door in case she got the same reaction. Plucking up her courage, Milly tried the next cottage, trying to ignore the little granny who was still chanting on her doorstep.

The door opened and Milly stepped forward to speak.

'Look, before you start chanting "Oogie" at me, I just want to ask one question and I'll leave you alone,' Milly blurted out into the face of the old lady who had answered the door. She stepped back, noticing the curtain of silvery hair that almost touched the floor, making the woman look like an older and wiser version of Rapunzel. She was dressed completely in what appeared to be black cloak and around her feet a black cat weaved, mewing impatiently. There was a waft of herbs and spices from inside the house. Surely she wasn't a witch?

The little granny's chants were getting louder and louder.

'Oh, come in child, ignore the mad old bat.' The witch scooped up the cat and stepped to one side so Milly could go in.

Milly hesitated but the 'Oogies' were getting louder.

'Leave her alone, you daft old cow,' the witch shouted over the fence.

Milly's eyebrows shot up.

'Don't you call me a cow,' yelled the little granny.

'Oh, fuck off,' the witch said.

Milly had never been so shocked in all her life. Of course she had heard swearing before, she had sworn herself several hundred times but to hear profanity bandied about so easily in this cute tranquil village between a witch and a cute old twinkly granny was ridiculous. Had she perhaps travelled into the Twilight Zone when she had driven up that hill, some weird parallel dimension where the local thugs were over the age of seventy?

The witch turned back to Milly. 'Are you coming in, or what?'

Milly hurried past her, too scared to say no.

She heard the door close behind her and she couldn't help wondering if this was where her life would come to an end. If she'd be fattened up and thrown into an oven and eaten. She looked around for any kind of walls made from gingerbread or a breadcrumb trail on the floor from the last two victims.

The witch followed her down the hall and ushered her into the lounge. 'I'm Gladys. Did you want some gingerbread, dear, I've just made it?'

Holy shit.

'I'm kidding, I'm totally kidding! You should see your face! I'm well aware of what I look like. My grandkids love it, they always ask me to turn them into toads whenever they come round.'

Milly swallowed. 'And do you?'

Gladys roared with laughter. 'Of course I don't. I can only turn people into pigs. Sit down.'

Milly did as she was told as Gladys picked up a walkie-talkie and pressed the button to speak. 'This is Black Crow to Blue Lobster, do you read?'

The walkie-talkie crackled to life and a voice said, 'This is Blue Lobster, go ahead.'

'The Visitor has arrived, I repeat, The Visitor has arrived, over.'

Milly could feel her heart thundering against her chest.

The walkie-talkie crackled again. 'Oooh I'll be right over. Erm … Over.'

'Bring Lavender over as well, over.'

'Ok, over.'

Gladys sat down and watched her, a huge grin in her face.

Milly cleared her throat. 'What's with all this Oogie nonsense?'

'It's a silly myth; a sea creature that's supposed to guard over the village and eat unwanted visitors. I'm not sure where it came from. They mostly do it to wind people up, especially your young Cameron. He's not exactly popular round here at the moment.'

'He's not my Cameron.'

'Ha, of course not,' Gladys said, as if she knew differently. 'The Oogie also protects us on our travels when we go out on the sea, we summon him by chanting his name and he watches over us. Well, that's what they used to do hundreds of years ago, it's sort of stuck as a bit of a silly tradition now.'

Milly decided to move the conversation onto safer ground than mythical sea monsters.

'I was just wondering if you knew the whereabouts of my car. It's a white …'

'Triumph TR2. Oh yes, Igor took it. It was parked illegally. But don't worry, we'll get to that later.'

'I don't think those yellow lines are official.'

'You try telling that to Igor, child.'

'I need some things from it.'

'Oh, we can get those for you, but it's not like you'll be needing the car anytime soon. Those that stay at Clover Castle, never leave.'

Milly sat up straight. 'I'll probably be gone by the end of the week.'

Gladys roared with laughter again. 'I don't think so, you wouldn't want to miss the Summer Solstice celebrations this Friday, for a start.'

'I have a lot of work to do, I really don't think I can stay.'

'Nonsense. You wouldn't be working at the weekend anyway, so you might as well stay for the celebrations. Now this young Cameron, he's a hot piece of ass, isn't he? If I was thirty years younger I wouldn't mind having a go at that myself. Please tell me you've slept with him.'

'I'm not his girlfriend, I'm from ...'

'Castle Heritage, yes I know. You're here to see if you can give him a grant for his castle. Which of course you can't, the place looks completely ludicrous. Not his fault of course, bless him. But you knew you couldn't help him as soon as you laid eyes on the place, yet you're still here, so I can only presume it's because you're banging him. Is he good in bed?'

'I ...'

'Oi Gladys, don't ask her those sorts of questions.' A lady with her hair in curlers came bustling through the open back door.

'Of course, we should wait for Lavender first. Milly, this is Constance.'

'How did you know my name?'

'Oh love, nothing happens in this village, nothing at all, apart from the Summer Solstice celebrations. But you arriving, well, it's like fresh blood, see?' Constance said.

'Fresh blood?'

'A new face, someone from the outside. It's exciting.'

A very round, very short old lady squeezed her way through the back door and Milly immediately noticed her purple hair. This wasn't the faded greyish purple synonymous with old ladies, this was bright, Cadbury's purple.

'Did I miss anything?' Lavender asked, squeezing onto the three seater sofa with Constance and Gladys, facing Milly as if they were some bizarre interview panel.

'Milly's having sex with Cameron,' Gladys said.

'I'm not,' Milly protested.

'Well, she wants to.'

'No I don't.'

The three old ladies guffawed loudly.

'Oh honey, every lady in this village wants to have sex with Cameron Heartstone. If you don't, there must be something wrong with you,' Lavender said.

'He is a paying client and it would be very unprofessional of me …'

The ladies laughter interrupted her again.

'I've seen it in my tea leaves,' Lavender said, her voice taking on a tone of wonder and mystique. 'You and he are going to get married before the year is out.'

'It's June!' Milly said in disbelief.

The ladies nodded in unison.

'So I'm going to get married in the next six months? I barely know the man.'

'The wedding happens very soon. When you find the right person, there's no point in hanging around,' Lavender said.

'So are you two coming to the Summer Solstice celebrations on Friday?' Gladys asked.

'I don't know,' Milly said.

'You should, it's a wonderful, liberating evening, lots of entertainment. There's a play that all the men take part in. We asked Cameron if he wanted a role but he said no.'

'He's not really the socialising, acting kind of person,' Milly said.

Gladys leaned forward. 'He should do it. Taking part in the play would make them love him. He really isn't very popular with the villagers at the moment after sacking them all.'

'He has no money to pay them. It seems his mad old uncle Boris spent every penny on big parties, fancy turrets and beautiful jewels.'

'Oooooh ... the Heartstone Treasure,' they collectively whispered.

'I'm sure it doesn't exist,' Milly said.

'It exists, all right,' Lavender said as the black cat leapt on her lap and stared at Milly in what she took to be an evil way.

'Have you seen it?'

'No one has seen it,' Constance said.

Milly sighed with exasperation.

'Legend has it that it's still in the castle, that the ghost of the Grey Lady guards over it.'

Milly sat up straighter. 'You know about the ghost?'

Lavender's eyes widened. 'You've seen her?'

Milly hesitated and nodded.

'She only shows herself to descendants of the Heartstone line,' Lavender said.

'No that's not true. There was that time that travelling merchant came to the castle, supposedly to steal the treasure. The Grey Lady scared him off, it was said he died of fright,' Constance said. 'But yes, other than scaring off thieves, she only appears to the Lord of the castle.'

'Or wives,' Gladys interjected and they all nodded at each other knowingly.

'I'm not getting married to him,' Milly said. 'I was just with him at the time when she appeared. Cameron needs practical help now; money for repairs and the ongoing upkeep, which will hopefully involve hiring the villagers back again. He can't pin his hopes on a chest of treasure that probably doesn't even exist.'

'He needs to get the villagers onside again, he needs their support going forward,' Gladys said, seriously. 'It can't just be down to his wife to come down here occasionally and be nice to us.'

'I'm not his wife. And I really need to get to my car.'

'We need him in this Summer Solstice play. We need both of you to be in it. If you get him to agree to take part, we'll get you your car back,' Gladys said.

Milly sighed.

'He won't have to do a lot, he doesn't even have to say anything. He only comes on in the last five minutes of the play, grabs you and fights off the evil Oogie monster. Then we all cheer and head off to the pub for beer and spiced wine. There'll be snacks and drinks to enjoy before the play, there's fireworks after midnight, it's quite a spectacle. And I promise everyone will stop chanting "Oogie" at you if you join in,' Lavender urged.

'Fine, I'll get him to do it. We'll both do it.'

The old ladies giggled and clapped their hands excitedly and Milly wondered just what she had let herself in for.

CHAPTER 8

Milly dragged her bags up the drive, thankful that she'd had the foresight to buy luggage with wheels on. Her equipment was really heavy and there was a lot of it.

Gladys had allowed her access to her equipment but poor Dick had been clamped and apparently he would only be released once Cameron and Milly had acted in the Summer Solstice play. It was laughable. She had never been blackmailed or coerced to do anything she didn't want to do before but Gladys was clearly the sort of person who always got exactly what she wanted.

She walked through the kitchen door. Cameron was leaning against the side with a mug of tea in his hand. His face lit up in a huge smile when he saw her and it warmed her to see it.

'I've met a few of the villagers,' Milly said, kicking her shoes off and moving to the kettle on the stove.

'Weirdos?'

'Oh yes. One of them chanted "Oogie" at me and refused to say anything else.'

'Yes, there's lots that do that.'

'I also chatted to three old ladies and although they were also weird, they were very nice.'

'Let me guess, Gladys, Constance and Lavender?'

She laughed. 'How did you know?'

'I had the misfortune of meeting them as well. Lavender told me I'd be married by the end of the year. She'd seen it in her tea leaves apparently.'

Milly put the kettle carefully back on the stove, giving this task all of her attention. She didn't dare tell him that Lavender had said the same thing about her marrying Cameron.

'And how do you feel about that?'

'I've been married before, I'm not in any rush to do that again. It depends, though. If it was the right person, I wouldn't be completely opposed to it, but I think it would take a bit longer than six months to know and trust someone enough to walk down the aisle with them.'

'I think so, too.'

He was still smiling as he watched her and it made her smile too. 'What's cheered you up all of a sudden?'

It took him a while to answer and when he did she was still none the wiser. 'Fate surprises you sometimes. I just think you can have a plan in life, a good one, but that plan isn't necessarily what fate has in store for you. Sometimes what fate thinks you need is so much better than what you had planned.'

She stared at him, knowing that somewhere amongst that nonsense was a reference to her.

She had to say something to change the subject. She was getting into trouble here and someone had to be the strong one. As he was in such a good mood, it seemed as good a time as any to bring up the subject of the Summer Solstice play.

She picked up a red apple from the fruit bowl and turned it over absently in her hands as she tried to ignore that he was watching her. How was she going to broach this with him?

'You can eat it, you know, it's not poison,' Cameron said.

She laughed and took a big bite but she knew he could sense that she wanted to say something and was delaying. He stood patiently waiting for her to talk. 'So, it's the Summer Solstice on Friday.'

He rolled his eyes good-naturedly, 'Oh, don't you start with that! I've had enough of that from the villagers; "*Will you be in the play, we need you in the play, you have to be in the play, please be in the play.*"

'Why *won't* you be in the play? It's just a bit of fun. Besides, you need to get the villagers on side, you're not very popular down there at the moment.'

'I know, I sacked them all and now they hate me.'

'Well, this would be an easy way to get back in their favour. If it's that important to them that you're involved, just do it. Apparently you don't have to do a lot.'

'I'm not doing it.'

'Why?'

'I'm just not.'

'It's only going to be half an hour of your time.'

'I'm not making a fool of myself in front of the whole village.'

'But they're all in it too.'

'I'm not doing it.'

'Oh, go on.'

'No, absolutely not.'

'Don't be a bore.'

'No.'

'Look …' Milly was about to protest some more and tell him that they were holding her beloved car ransom when Cameron's phone rang on the table.

He stared at her for a moment before he moved to answer it. 'It's my PA, Olivia, I'd better take the call.'

'I've got some tests to do anyway, so I'll catch you later.'

He was smiling at her as she wheeled her bag out to the banquet hall. She needed something to distract herself and there was nothing better than spending a few hours conducting tests, especially in the old kitchen. And if Cameron continued to smile at her later, with that knowing look, she would just bore him with every little detail of the tests and everything that excited her, from flecks of paint to mortar that was hundreds of years old. That would most likely put him off her for good.

———

Cameron lay in bed staring at the ceiling; insomnia was his faithful friend. He could never turn his mind off. Normally, he would be thinking about his latest story, the twists, the turns, the conversations his characters would have, so he never got a peaceful night. Lately though, his thoughts had been about the castle too, how he could save it – or even if he should. But now his head was full of Milly.

She had spent the afternoon doing various tests and taking different samples. She had returned to the kitchen with a whole box filled with labelled test tubes all containing little flecks of what looked like dirt, but which Milly had explained were samples of paint, mortar and brick work. He had never seen anyone get quite so excited about test tubes of dirt before and he had spent over two hours listening to her as she explained the procedures for collecting the samples and testing them in the lab and what kind of results she expected to get and what it meant for the castle. He had hung on every word. For someone who had almost no interest in history, he found her completely and utterly fascinating. He had never met anyone who had so much passion and enthusiasm for their job and it was infectious.

She had gone off to bed in her room in the tower very excitedly earlier. There was something about her exuberance and love for life that he found so endearing. Just being in the same room as her made him happy and hopeful. He liked having her here.

Suddenly the light came on in the library window that over-looked his room. That was strange. Although he had seen the Grey Lady once or twice outside her dungeon, the ghosts never turned on lights. He rolled over to look at the clock and saw that it was past two in the morning.

He got out of bed and pulled on his robe. Even though the nights were warm from the day's heat, the castle was always cool, especially at night.

He walked through the empty banquet hall and up the stairs. Light streamed through the open doorway and he smiled slightly when he saw Milly curled up in one of the chairs, wrapped in a blanket, reading a book.

'Hey,' he said, softly, not wanting to scare her.

She looked up and smiled at him. 'Hey yourself.'

'Can you not sleep?'

She pulled a face. 'Not really.'

'Is it the bed, is it not comfy? Is the room too cold?'

'The room is fine.'

She looked down at the book she was reading and he suddenly realised why.

'Being trapped in a room with a skeleton, it kind of freaked you out, didn't it?'

She nodded. 'It's silly, the thing wasn't even real. It's just …' She trailed off.

There was more to this than she was saying so he sat down and pulled out a chair in front of her.

'Thought I'd read for a little while, see if it would send me to sleep, but this book isn't doing that.'

He hadn't paid any attention to the books that lined the library walls, they were all very old, probably mostly written in Latin. 'What you reading?'

She showed him the first book he had ever written and his heart flipped in recognition.

'I love his stuff, well, most of it,' Milly said. 'This *Dream Pirates* series was incredible, it was made into the most stunning movies, but *Hidden Faces,* the short spin off novellas he wrote about the shape-shifters, was absolutely shite. I'm hoping for better things from him for his next series.'

He stared at her in shock. No one had ever told him to his face that his shape-shifter series was shit. He knew it was, mostly because that series wasn't actually written by him. His publishers had arranged for a ghost writer to write them whilst he had gone through the worst time in his life. But no one knew that he hadn't written it. And no one had ever been brave enough to say, this is crap, even though all the reviewers had slated him. But Milly knew who he was, he'd seen that look of recognition when they had first met, and he didn't like the way she was pretending she didn't.

'I know you know who I am.' He stood up, all sympathy for her gone.

She looked up at him in complete confusion and then fear. 'Are you not Cameron Heartstone? But you told me you were.'

She looked to the door, clearly wondering if she could make a run for it.

'I am Cameron Heartstone, but I also write under a pseudonym and I know you recognise me.'

There was no way she didn't know who he was. After the movie deal, his publicist had secured an interview with him in a hugely popular magazine and suddenly a ridiculous fan club, mostly made up of teenage girls and bored housewives, had exploded on social media. Every magazine and newspaper in the country wanted a piece of him. He'd hated it, but for a long while his face had been plastered everywhere and unless Milly had spent that time with her head under a rock, she would have seen it.

She stared at him in bewilderment as if he'd just grown a second head. Either she was a very good actress or he'd got it all wrong.

'I'm sorry, I have no idea what you are talking about. Are you really JK Rowling, because that would be a real surprise?'

He grabbed the book from her hand and waved it in her face.

Finally the penny dropped and it was clear to him that it was the first time she had made the connection. Her eyes grew huge. 'You're Phoenix Blaze?'

The fight went out of him. 'You didn't know?'

'No, I had no idea. What made you think I recognised you?'

'When we first met, you gave me this starry-eyed look.'

'Define starry-eyed.'

He replicated the face she had made when she first saw him, with wide eyes and open mouth.

She blushed a deep shade of red. 'That was most likely my, "Shit this guy is freaking hot" face.'

Not for the first time, she had left him speechless. There were no games with Milly, no pretence, just complete and utter honesty. Yet now she knew who he was, any chance of a normal friendship or professional relationship had gone completely out of the window. Let the fawning and gold digging commence.

'I can't believe you're Phoenix Blaze.'

He nodded, embarrassed that he'd even brought it up.

'And I just told you your books were shit.'

'Yes, you did.' He waited for her to back pedal, to tell him they weren't that bad.

'I loved your *Dream Pirates* trilogy, it was amazing.'

He hated it when people fawned all over him, especially women, because he always thought they had an ulterior motive.

'But your *Hidden Faces* trilogy, I can't lie, it was the most awful thing I've ever read.'

He felt his mouth fall open, she wasn't even going to sugar coat it.

'I kept hoping it would get better but it was tripe. All the magic and wonder that poured from the pages in *Dream Pirates*, none of that was there. The shape-shifters in *Dream Pirates* were my favourite characters and you just ruined that. I always wanted to meet you so I could shake you by the shoulders and say, what the hell were you thinking?'

He threw his head back and burst out laughing. He really liked this girl. And she liked him too, she'd made that very clear, though not for his fame or fortune, just because of him.

He sat down. 'I didn't write them.' It felt good to say that secret out loud.

'What? I don't understand. You just said you were Phoenix Blaze.'

'I wrote the *Dream Pirates* series and then I sent my publishers an outline for the shape-shifter spin off which they loved. I wrote the first five chapters and then my mum died and my wife left me. I asked my publishers if we could put publication back for a year but they said no and that if I couldn't deliver on time they'd get a ghost writer to do it for me.'

'You're kidding? Why wouldn't they wait?'

'I have no idea. At that point, the day before my mum's funeral, I couldn't care less, so I told them to get a ghost writer as I wasn't going to write them. So they did. When they came out, I was horrified. They read like a twelve-year-old had written them and apart from the characters' names and the location, nothing was what I had planned. It was shit and the reviewers and my fans absolutely hated it. I wanted to go public and tell everyone that it wasn't me, but my publishers flat refused. They didn't want to come out and say they'd lied to the fans. So they just said I was going through a bad patch, which anyone who knew anything about my life would know, and promised bigger and better things for my next series. I've since ditched them and gone with a new publisher, but those books are still out there with my name on and there's nothing I can do to distance myself from them.'

'I can't believe they would do that, ruin your reputation just because they couldn't wait.'

Cameron shrugged and passed the book back to her. 'It wouldn't be the first time that a publisher used a ghost writer, or the last.' 'But if you're Phoenix Blaze, surely you have enough money to renovate this place. I know you said your ex-wife took a lot of your money but you still must be earning money from the books.'

'I am, but nowhere near as much as you'd think. A lot of the women I've dated since Eva thought that too. I was comfortably off before I inherited this place, now everything I had in savings has gone to pay off some of the debts for here and severance pay for the villagers. Beyond my house, car and a few thousand I have in the bank, I have nothing. I'm hoping I can make some money out of the next series. I feel like I have a lot to prove with this next book and I'm not sure how many of my fans will be loyal enough to buy this series when they were so disappointed with the last one.'

'Word of mouth is a wonderful thing. If it's half as good as *Dream Pirates*, then word will soon get around.'

He smiled at her optimism.

'I can't believe my books are here, in this old library. I never heard from my Dad after we left, I had no clue he knew about my writing career.'

'All the books are there, even the shit ones. He must have been very proud.'

He smiled at that.

She cuddled back into the blanket and yawned.

'Why don't you go back to bed and I'll come and sit with you for a little while until you fall asleep?'

She smiled. 'Underneath this ferocious bear costume, you're actually really sweet.'

She stood up and, for a brief moment, he saw a flash of bare thigh. Good Lord, was she naked under the blanket?

She shuffled up the stairs and he followed her up to the top of the tower. He watched as she climbed onto the bed, still wrapped in the blanket.

It was only then that he noticed how cold the room was.

'It's freezing in here. I'll build the fire back up.'

He walked over to the fireplace and threw a few more logs on the dying embers, padding it out with dry paper and leaves that he hoped would catch fire. He gave it a few rough pokes, anything to keep his mind from Milly, sitting in bed a few feet away.

When the fire finally started to take, he sat next to her on the bed, leaning against the headboard.

'Here, get under the covers.' He lifted the blankets over her and he smiled when she returned the favour for him. They both sat in silence for a moment. He was hoping she would lie down and go to sleep, but sitting in bed together, deliberately not looking at each other and suddenly finding nothing to say was beyond awkward. He stared at a giant red tapestry that depicted some kind of fight with a dragon. He had to keep his eyes away from Milly but she clearly had no intention of going to sleep any time soon.

'Do you want to tell me why the skeleton freaked you out so much?'

She looked up at him and smiled, sadly. 'My mum died when I was five. It was just me and her, my dad had walked out before I was even one. She said goodnight to me on Friday night and when I went in to wake her on Saturday morning she was dead, though I don't think my little five-year-old brain had worked that part out. I lay with her, hoping she would wake up, but she never did. I was trapped in the house, couldn't find the keys. Silly thing had left the phone in the shed, she was always doing that. Our house was quite remote, the only person that ever came near it was the postman. It took four days for someone to find us.'

'You were trapped in a house with a corpse for four days?'

She nodded.

'Christ. I'm so, so sorry, what a horrible thing for you to go through.' He wrapped his arm round her shoulders, pulling her against him before he realised how inappropriate it was for him to do that. But Milly leaned into him, obviously needing the comfort.

'It was. She went grey and green. She smelt funny too.'

His stomach twisted.

'I'm so sorry.' It was inadequate, he knew that, but what else could he say?

She forced a smile onto her face. 'It's ok, it was the subject of many a nightmare but it was a very long time ago. My aunt Belinda raised me after that, she's the most marvellous woman.'

Cameron noted the subject change but let her take the conversation in whatever direction she needed.

'She had such an interest in history, the ancient world more than British history, which is my forte. Her house was filled with pictures and artefacts or replicas from Ancient Greece and Egypt. She used to be an archaeologist and she took me with her on a good many digs. I guess that's where I got my passion for history too. Anyway …' She shook her head, obviously realising she had gone off on a tangent.

He pulled her tighter against him, offering comfort in the only way he could.

He watched her; her blonde hair splayed out over her shoulder, with the candyfloss pink tips that looked both silly and unbelievably sexy at the same time. He felt her body rise and fall with each little breath.

He had to leave, he couldn't stay here like this. But he didn't want to leave her if she needed him. After a while he chanced a look down at her face, but her eyes were closed, her mouth open slightly. She looked so at peace. He tried to relax and not think about the warmth of her body next to his or her sweet scent.

Heat filled the room and he found his eyes closing. Within minutes he was fast asleep.

—

Milly woke the next morning and looked up at Cameron, who was still sleeping. After the nightmares that chased her for the first part of the night, she had slept like a baby since Cameron had joined her. His bare chest was velvety smooth and warm and had provided the perfect pillow for the rest of the night. Both his arms were wrapped around her, holding her tight and there was something very wonderful and very right about waking up with this man, whom she barely knew yet felt so comfortable with. She stretched sleepily, wondering if she should go back to sleep for a while, because right then there was nowhere else she wanted to be.

She suddenly wriggled from his arms and sat up. He stirred but didn't wake.

What the hell was she doing? She had spent the night in bed with a client! She had cuddled up to him like he was a friend or boyfriend. She would be fired on the spot if Castle Heritage found out, reputation was so important to them. What was she thinking? There was a chemistry between them, she couldn't deny that and she knew she was falling for him but she couldn't let anything happen. He was a paying client and she had to remember that, but more than that she couldn't go through the devastating pain of having her heart broken again.

He rolled over towards her, his features soft in sleep. She had seen a very sweet side to him since she arrived. Maybe he would be different to the men that had hurt her in the past.

What was it he had said the day before when he spoke about his ex-wife? That there was lots written about him in the papers and most of it wasn't good.

A thought occurred to her. As a good historian, she had done extensive research into every project she had considered taking on before making a decision. If she was going to give him a chance, after her work here at the castle was done, if she was to give up her ban on men, then she needed to research him, too.

She slid out of bed and pulled on a hoody to protect herself from the cool of the early morning. She pulled her laptop out of her bag and sat down in a chair.

She watched him carefully as she waited for the computer to fire up, touching her star bracelet as she hoped she wouldn't find anything bad. Finally it sprung to life and there was Wi-Fi here which was obviously a good thing.

She googled 'Cameron Heartstone' and there wasn't a lot about him. But when she googled 'Phoenix Blaze' the search engine returned millions of results. A lot of it was about his books, reviews and interviews he had given. He worked hard at his stories and had so much passion for what he did. There were articles about his mum dying four years ago and also about his dad dying and leaving him an unnamed castle last year. The press really could get hold of any information. But what stood out were the stories of him with different women. *Charming,*

sweet, attentive, seductive were all words used by the women he
had bedded to describe their brief relationship with him and
she could vouch for all those qualities. They also said he was
magnificent in bed. Several women had sold their stories to the
papers and Milly's heart bled for Cameron, that he had been betrayed first by his wife and then by these women. She clicked on
Google Images and the screen filled with photo after photo of
Cameron with hundreds of different women at glamorous parties and events. All of them were blonde and tanned with large
boobs. He obviously had a type and although she wasn't tanned
and didn't have big boobs, she still felt she fit into it to some
extent. If she let anything happen between them, she would be
one of many, a face in the crowd and someone he would forget
soon after he'd had her in his bed.

She stared at the screen in disappointment. He had seemed
so different to the men she had been with in the past. He listened to her, he was sweet, attentive, protective but in reality he
was just like all the rest.

Suddenly, amongst the sea of blondes, one photo stuck out.
It was obviously taken on Cameron's wedding day, somehow the
press had managed to get hold of that too. Eva had long brown
hair that cascaded in loose curls over one shoulder. The look
Cameron was giving her was one of pure love. It was so different
to the way he was with the other blonde women, so different to
how he was with Milly too.

She closed the lid on the laptop and looked at him. There
was no way she could ever let anything happen between them.
She would reassert her professionalism. He was her client and
that's as far as it would go.

The room was icy. As the sea wind howled against the castle
walls, the tapestry moved slightly. Either the stone walls were

not built properly and there were gaps, or one of the stones had come loose and there was now a hole in the wall.

She lifted the tapestry and let out a bark of a laugh that had Cameron groaning as he woke up.

He opened one eye and looked at her. He sat bolt up in bed and looked around in confusion and mild panic, clearly realising where he had inadvertently spent the night.

She would shrug it off, pretend that it meant nothing to her and then he could relax about it.

'You might be interested to know I've found another secret passageway.'

He sat up, his eyes wide with shock. 'In your room?'

She lifted the tapestry to reveal an open staircase spiralling down the very edge of the castle. 'No wonder it's so cold in here.'

He shot out of bed and came to stand with her. Muted daylight filled the stairs from tiny little holes that punctuated the walls periodically.

Cameron started to descend the staircase. She grabbed her shoes and made to follow him.

CHAPTER 9

'So each of the four towers appears to have its own fire escape,' Milly said, as Cameron leaned down into the chamber at the foot of the fourth tower they had explored in the last hour and pulled her up onto the driveway.

She smiled at the big biker boots he had pulled on after they had explored the stairwell in the first tower. Paired with the silly dragon print pyjama bottoms, the two didn't seem to go together.

'It makes sense, I suppose. If someone was coming to kill you and you were sleeping in the tower, you'd want an escape route.'

'These passageways from the tower bedrooms were all built around the time that your uncle Boris was here, about a hundred and thirty, hundred and fifty years ago. Your uncle really did have a case of paranoia.' Milly shielded her eyes from the bright sun that was beating down on the castle. The warm sea wind blowing over the cliff tops swirled around her, blowing her hair around her face.

'I can't believe I never noticed these doors in the ground before.'

'Well they were behind these plant troughs, you wouldn't see them unless you were looking for them.'

'It's cool though, isn't it,' Cameron said, excitedly.

'Very.'

'And it all helps in making a case to Castle Heritage for taking this place on, doesn't it? I presume they will be very interested in this kind of thing.'

Milly's face fell, and she stared down at the drive as they walked back towards the kitchen. She really had no idea at this stage if Castle Heritage would accept the project. The tests she had taken the day before needed to be sent to the lab and that would determine the exact date of some of the oldest rooms in the house. If it was clear which rooms were there first and the original structure was of a significant size, Castle Heritage might restore it to how it formerly looked, but in its current condition of fairy tale princess castle, they wouldn't touch it, she knew that. And she had to tell him, sooner rather than later. He would be crushed though and she knew she could help him despite the lack of interest from Castle Heritage.

'What is it you want, just to sell it to Castle Heritage and wash your hands of it?'

He shook his head. 'No, I can't do that. It's been in the family, as far as I can tell, since it was built. I can't just get rid of it. And I've been warming to it in the last few days, I could maybe see myself living here but I can't afford to keep it on my own. I was hoping Castle Heritage would give me some kind of grant to do the renovations. The debts I can handle, especially if, as you suggested, I sell my other house, but the general upkeep of the place will need some ongoing money.'

'You need to make it work for you, open it up as a hotel. Even without the ghosts, people will love to stay in a place like this. It's beautiful and charming. You could hold parties and balls in the banquet hall, just like your family used to, but charge people to come. Get it catered so you don't need to worry about food, you can even hire a team of waiting staff for the night. You have eight bedrooms in the towers and as long as you put a door over the secret passageways, you're ready to open to the public now. Plus we have the bedrooms in the servant quarters we could hire out for a much cheaper price. And we could do tours of the secret passageways and dungeons for a price too.'

'There's that "we" again.'

He was smiling and she knew he was teasing her.

'Sorry, I just get carried away. This place has so much potential and it just makes me so excited about what it could become. You wouldn't have to do a lot to it to get it ready.'

'Your ideas sound wonderful but I haven't the first clue about running a hotel and I really don't want to. It would take up all my time and I love writing too much to want to focus on anything else.'

'You don't have to do it though, you could hire a manager to run all that side of things for you.'

He turned to face her and she stopped to look at him. He smiled. 'You are very sweet and I find your enthusiasm so endearing. I have never met anyone like you. Ever. You are so smart, but you live in a rose-tinted world. I can't just open this place up as a hotel and have paying guests staying over at the weekend. We would have to offer them breakfast and probably dinner and that means having a proper kitchen that would need to meet health and safety standards and a proper qualified chef with a food hygiene certificate. I'd have to have staff that would clean and service the rooms, they would need paying, that makes me an employer and with that comes a whole host of legal responsibilities including wages, pensions, tax and national insurance. There's liability insurance as well which as a customer serving company I would have to have. I would need to do a lot to ensure the dungeons and tunnels and passageways were completely safe, I couldn't have stairways or tunnels collapsing whilst guests were using them. I would be sued for millions.'

'No, I know all that. I know there's a lot more to opening a hotel than just having the rooms. My brother owns a hotel chain that looks after places like this, although I'm sure he has nothing like Clover Castle on his books. All his hotels are unique, historical houses and he is keen to maintain that history and not turn them into something they aren't, but he knows that people love staying in places like this, it's something different from the usual hotels. He runs hotels or holiday rentals out of old churches, windmills, manor houses and castles. If you were to work with him, it would still be yours, but he would run the hotel side of things. He's very successful at what he does, so he must know his stuff. And he's a very honest man, he will tell you if working with him is not in your best interests. You should at least talk to him because even if you didn't want to work with him he would still be able to give you some great advice.'

Cameron stared down at her in that intense way, as if he was still trying to figure her out. 'You have a lot of respect for your brother.'

'He is my most favourite person in the world.'

'Then I'd like to meet him. I think I need all the help I can get at the moment.'

Her heart soared a little at the fact that Cameron was prepared to meet Jamie based solely on her recommendation.

He turned towards the castle and she walked by his side.

'Isn't recommending me to your brother in direct competition with Castle Heritage?'

Oh crap.

'I still need to do some more tests to determine the age of the property, I just think you need to have all the options. While I'm doing these tests and waiting for the results you can speak to Jamie and then you can make up your own mind. I don't think Castle Heritage will keep the castle in its current state. As you've already pointed out, it's not very historical.'

'You said you loved it?' There was an accusatory tone to his voice.

'I do.'

'And do you not speak for Castle Heritage?'

She thought carefully about how to answer. 'When I said it was beautiful, I spoke from the heart, not as an ambassador for Castle Heritage.'

He turned to face her again but there were no smiles on his face now. 'So all this excitement over ghosts and secret passageways during the last few days …'

Oh God, she felt awful, she had fooled him into thinking that she was excited on behalf of Castle Heritage. 'That excitement was just mine.'

Disappointment registered on his face and it hurt that she felt like she had let him down.

'It wasn't my intention to mislead you. I get so excited about old buildings and passionate about history, coupled with my love of fairy tales and magical stories, this place is like a dream come true for me. I feel terrible. I built your hopes up and now I've disappointed you. I'm sorry that I wasn't professional enough that I didn't separate my emotions from Castle Heritage's position. Nothing about my visit has been professional and I don't know what you must think of me or Castle Heritage. It's this place, it brings out the worst in me.'

Cameron turned away and continued walking towards the kitchen. 'Or the best.'

She didn't know what to say to that but she knew she had to draw a line under this now. She wasn't going to let anything happen between them so she would ensure everything about her stay here would be strictly professional from now on.

—

Milly arrived back in the kitchen a short while later wearing her smartest clothes. A navy blue spotted dress underneath a long navy jacket. She had her hair clipped back into a tight French roll and she was wearing her smartest, most sensible, most boring black flat shoes, instead of her ridiculous sparkly Converse trainers. She always packed something smart in case there were any formal meetings during her trips. It had never happened, but she liked to be prepared. She had never felt the need to wear them to impress a client before. But she had to do something to reassert her professionalism, if she had ever showed Cameron any to start with. Reputation was everything to Castle Heritage and she had to leave Cameron with a good impression of them even if they couldn't work with him. Cuddling in bed with a client was stupid and reckless and a million miles away from the professionalism she normally maintained on a site visit.

Cameron stared at the transformation in shock.

'What's this?'

'I'm trying to be professional. I haven't succeeded so far but …' She gestured helplessly as she realised it was going to take a lot more than a suit to walk away from this with any degree of respect from Cameron.

He smiled at her and she hated that he was laughing at her. God, he infuriated her, she just couldn't win.

He stood up and walked towards her, appraising her with heated eyes. He stopped in front of her, too close yet again. This guy clearly had no idea about appropriate personal space. Though she had done nothing to move away from him. She couldn't; his scent, his heat, it was intoxicating. His eyes were almost black as he stared down at her.

He bent to whisper in her ear. 'If this look is supposed to turn me off, it's not working.'

He moved back slightly and she felt her mouth fall open at his blatant flirting.

He continued speaking as if that comment had never happened.

'I've thoroughly enjoyed the last few days, I've smiled and laughed and it's been a long time since I've done either of those things.'

He reached up and unclipped her hair, untangling the knots with his fingers. His touch was electric and she'd forgotten how to breathe.

He moved his hands to the buttons of her jacket and slowly undid each one. Her heart slammed against her ribs.

'I've enjoyed fascinating, intellectual conversations, not only about the castle but about lots of other things too.'

He slid the jacket off her shoulders, his hands skimming over her bare arms. He folded it neatly over the chair without taking his eyes off hers.

'I have loved the energy about the place, and the enthusiasm and love you have for the castle. And I've really enjoyed flirting with a woman who seems to like me for myself, not for my fame and fortune.' He stepped back to look at her. 'Well, apart from the shoes, this is the woman that I've enjoyed all of that with. I will be disappointed if Castle Heritage don't take Clover Castle on, but I don't think I could ever be disappointed with you.'

Silence stretched between them. Neither of them moved.

'You like me?' Milly's voice was choked when she eventually spoke.

'Immensely.'

She had sort of guessed that but to hear it confirmed was both wonderful and terrifying.

She swallowed. 'We can't do anything, you're my client.'

'That's fine.'

'You've paid for my services, sex isn't one of the services on offer.'

'I never thought it was.'

'I need to go to the post office and post my test tubes to the lab.' She had to get away from him as she was about five seconds away from throwing professionalism straight out the window.

'Ok.'

Locked in his hypnotic gaze, she still couldn't move.

'I just need my handbag.'

She reached to grab her bag, he didn't move and she had to lean round him. She picked it up and moved back, looking up into his eyes.

She wasn't sure who kissed whom, but suddenly her bag clattered to the floor and she was leaning up as Cameron's mouth came down on hers, hard.

Without taking his mouth off hers, he lifted her. She automatically wrapped her legs round his waist and he powered her back to the wall.

The taste of him was everything, the feel of his hard body against hers, his intoxicating spicy, woody scent. It was complete sensory overload.

But where her kisses were desperate, urgent, needful, his were calm, slow, methodical, as if he had known that this moment was coming all along. He slowed her down, took his time. It was sexy as hell.

Suddenly his phone burst to life on the table. He didn't break the kiss for a second, as if he hadn't even heard it. But it was enough to snap her out of her moment of madness.

She pulled back and he stopped, searching her eyes. He sighed and gently lowered her to the floor. She was trembling all over. How could a kiss affect her so much?

He grabbed his phone and answered it, his voice low and throaty. It had affected him too.

She bent to grab her bag and the box of test tubes she had packaged up the day before and with his eyes firmly on her, she walked out on unsteady legs.

Milly stumbled down the drive, wondering if he was still watching her. She could barely catch her breath.

She had kissed a client. She was likely to be sacked for that. What on earth had she been thinking? She had never launched herself at a man before. There was something about him that drew her in. Yes, he was attractive and sweet but there was something more than that. A connection so strong it was almost as if they had been linked her whole life.

But that was no excuse for kissing a client. She loved her job at Castle Heritage. Well, part of it, she loved what her job entailed but she didn't love the company so much. They were too fussy about which properties they would take on and they had turned down many beautiful historic places over the years and she hated that. But it looked likely that she was going to be accepted onto the board of directors soon which would give her much more opportunity to have her say about how the company was run. She didn't want to jeopardise that.

It would be better for everyone if she left now before anything else happened. She'd go back to the castle, do a few more tests and then leave. If the results came back with something that would interest Castle Heritage, then she could communicate with Cameron through emails and telephone calls. She would give him her brother's number in case he wanted to pursue that line instead and she would go home. But she had agreed to be in this silly play with him on Friday, although she still needed to persuade him to do that. When was that – another two or three days away? She'd completely lost track of time already, it felt like she had been there for months or years, not just a few days. No, it was silly to stay for the sake of the play. She'd explain to Gladys that she couldn't stop, she'd call a taxi and she could be tucked up in her own bed in her house by tonight.

Alone.

She swallowed back the sadness of leaving Cameron. It was ridiculous to feel this way. He wasn't good for her. If she was stupid enough to let it go any further, he would break her heart when it came to an end.

This wasn't going to work with him, it couldn't.

She sighed as she reached the tranquillity of Clover's Rest. It was so idyllic, like something fresh from a fairy tale. If this really was a fairy tale she would have a fairy godmother to turn to for advice or a little bit of pizazz and sparkle. As fairy tales didn't exist, she would go and talk to the village witch instead.

—

He'd kissed her. Well, he was pretty sure she had made the first move but the end result was the same. And there was nothing gentlemanly about the way it had happened, he had grabbed her and pinned her to the wall. No wonder she'd looked so scared when they had broken apart. He had practically man-handled her.

Cameron could hear Olivia, his PA, chatting down the phone as he sat with his head in his hands, with no idea what she was saying.

The kiss had been incredible though, so much more than he had imagined it would be although it had not led where he had hoped.

There was a note of vulnerability in Milly and he didn't want to hurt her in any way. He wasn't going to pursue this unless she did. God, he hoped she wanted to because it had taken all his

strength to let her walk out of his kitchen and not take her back
to his bedroom.

—

The queue at the post office had been very short, just one other
person stood in front of Milly, but she had already waited over
an hour to be served, because the frail old postmistress – who
looked to be over two hundred years old – had chatted to an
elderly man wearing a bowler hat about *everything*, including
the lack of fish in the sea, the weather, the ducks on the pond
and mostly about the excitement of the Summer Solstice play.

There had even been another old lady that walked into the
post office at one point. She walked straight past Milly, who was
clearly waiting for her turn, joined the chatter whilst she was
served and walked back out again, muttering about the Oogie
as she walked past her. What was it with the residents of this village? Were they all over the age of eighty and completely insane?
Apart from that boy she had seen on his bike on her first day,
she hadn't seen anyone under the age of seventy, and Gladys,
Constance and Lavender, although completely bonkers, seemed
to be the most normal of the lot.

Maybe it was like those villages in horror films where there
were no children. Maybe the Summer Solstice play would be a
sacrificial affair, killing all the children in the village and probably a few virgins too. Thankfully she didn't fall into that bracket.

Finally the old man left. She waited for the chant of 'Oogie'
as he walked past but instead he smiled at her and tipped his hat
as he walked out.

'You must be young Milly,' the postmistress said. 'I'm Agatha.
We are all terribly excited about you and young Cameron being
in the play. You couldn't have come at a better time, the Summer
Solstice play is the most exciting night of the year. The children

have all been practising their songs and dances. Of course the thing they are most excited about is the Great Solstice Hunt.'

Milly frowned. 'What's that, like a fox hunt?'

Agatha laughed. 'No, everyone in the village bakes these chocolate cookies that look like suns, "Solstice cookies", we call them. They are wrapped in pretty paper and hidden all over the village green for the children to find. Like an Easter Egg hunt, dear, but much more fun. One of the paper wrapped cookies is actually made from gold and whoever finds that is mayor of the village for the next year.'

'Your village mayor is a child?'

'Yes dear, Abigail Fletcher is our current mayor, she's seven years old.'

'And what does the mayor do?'

'What does the mayor do in any town? It's a fancy title, nothing more. Where is the parcel going dear?'

'Erm … Cambridge.'

'Ok. Do you want that to go first, second or third class?'

'Third class?'

'Yes dear, is that what you would like?'

'No, first class please.' Milly didn't dare ask for third class, which probably meant it would be delivered by horse and carriage sometime in the next few months.

Milly quickly paid and left but only after she had somehow promised Agatha that she would make a batch of Solstice cookies by Friday.

Wondering how she had been persuaded to do that and how exactly she would go about making a Solstice cookie, she found herself walking in the direction of Gladys's house.

Gladys looked delighted to see her when she opened the door and invited her in for a cup of tea before Milly had even opened her mouth.

'So any progress with our Lord Heartstone, then?' Gladys asked, as she threw some black, red and blue tea leaves into a teapot. Gladys wiggled her eyebrows and Milly laughed.

'No, and there's not likely to be.'

Gladys frowned in confusion. 'But you like him?'

Milly sighed. 'Yes. A lot. But I can't let anything happen.' She couldn't let anything *else* happen.

'Does he like you?'

Milly nodded and because there was something about Gladys that commanded honesty she decided to elaborate. 'We just kissed.'

Gladys's whole face lit up as if Milly had just offered her a million pounds. The tea was forgotten and Gladys sat down opposite her, her eyes shining with excitement.

'I knew it, I knew you two were soul mates, I can feel it.'

'We're not soul mates, it was a kiss.'

'Tell me about the kiss.'

Milly ran her tongue over her lips where she could still taste him. Her heart was still beating wildly at the mere thought of his touch. She had been kissed before but it had never felt like that. 'It was … magical.'

Gladys smiled and reached across the table to hold her hand. 'Why are you holding back?

'He is my client and I would be sacked if my company found out.'

Gladys shook her head. 'Surely no job in the world is more important than true love.'

'It's not true love, I don't know him. That kind of love takes time. You can't fall in love with someone after a few days. Besides, true love and happy endings is a myth. It's not real.'

'Of course it's real, what nonsense.'

'What's nonsense is expecting to be with one person for the rest of your life. Love, it seems, has a shelf life and it's not eternal.'

'You're scared of getting hurt.'

Milly didn't say anything but she didn't have to.

'What if he *doesn't* hurt you? What if he is the one you will grow old and grey with? What if he is your happy ever after? Isn't it worth taking a risk on?'

'There are no happily ever afters, not for me, and I don't want to risk my heart again. I can't.'

'When you get to my time in life you tend to think about how you should have lived and you don't want to look back and have regrets.'

Milly looked at her and saw the sadness in her eyes. 'Do you have regrets?'

Gladys nodded. 'Just one. His name was Billy. I was fifteen when I met him, he was a year older. I fell in love with him from the moment I saw him and he fell in love with me too. My parents, of course, forbade me from having anything to do with him and like a good girl I did exactly as I was told. I loved him so much, he was the sweetest, kindest man I ever met. When I turned sixteen, he asked me to the village dance but my parents still said no. My dad was a formidable man and not someone I could ever disobey. Billy asked me every day if I would go out with him and every day I turned him down even though it broke my heart to do it. A few months later, war broke out in Europe and he was called up to fight. He never came home. I regretted every day that I had never told him that I loved him, that he had died without ever knowing how I felt, but more than that I regretted that we had never shared a kiss, that we could have been happy together for all those months and I never gave him

that chance. If I could do it all again, I'd have taken every beating my dad would have given me in return for being with him.'

'But even if you had been together, it wouldn't have lasted
forever,' Milly protested. 'He would still have gone off to war
and not come home.'

'Life is short and precious and we never know what is around
the corner. So you live for now, seize every moment that comes
your way and if you're going to look back on your life with regret, it's easier to regret the things that you did do, rather than
the things you didn't.'

CHAPTER 10

When Milly walked back into the kitchen a while later, Cameron was sitting at the table in an office chair, tapping away at his laptop. As soon as he saw her he stopped what he was doing, leaned back in his chair and stared at her.

'Hey,' she said, brightly.

'Hey.'

She kicked her shoes off and filled the kettle with water before placing it on the stove, determinedly not looking at Cameron. She wasn't ready to discuss that kiss yet or any part of their non-professional relationship.

She turned round to grab some mugs, picking one off the table near where Cameron was sitting, but he stopped her from moving away with a hand at her waist. Her eyes locked with his; God, his touch on her was electric. He pulled her, gently, to stand in front of him, his other hand cupping her waist on the other side.

He stared up at her, his thumbs gently caressing her hips. 'I really liked that kiss,' he said.

She swallowed. 'I did too.'

'But you don't want to pursue it?'

She wanted to, more than anything she wanted to continue that kiss and see how much chemistry they really had between them. But she knew she couldn't do that.

'I can't.'

'Do you want to share your reasons?'

'You're a client. It would be very unprofessional.'

'Your professionalism means that much to you?'

She hesitated for a moment. 'Yes.'

He nodded thoughtfully and his hands slipped from her sides. Her hips felt cold without his touch. 'I won't harass you about this. You have my word I won't mention it again.'

She stared down at him for the longest moment then turned away to finish making the tea.

'I thought you might be more comfortable in one of the bedrooms down here tonight, it's too cold in that tower,' Cameron said after a while.

'Yes, I was thinking that myself,' Milly replied, still trying not to look at him.

'So I moved your stuff.'

'Oh, which room?'

'My guestroom,' Cameron said, casually.

She whirled round to face him. 'The one that's about three metres from your bedroom door.'

He shrugged. 'I didn't really think about it like that.'

'I bet you didn't.' She couldn't help but smile at the tiny smirk playing on his lips as he returned his attention to his laptop.

'What are you writing? A new book?'

'Yes.'

'Try not to make it shit.'

He laughed. 'I'll try my best. It's nearly finished. You can read it if you like, when it's done. See if it passes the Milly test.'

She smiled hugely. 'I'd like that.'

She turned back and grabbed the mugs of tea, handed one to Cameron and sat down opposite him.

'I might give my brother a call, see if he can arrange a time to come and see you.'

Cameron nodded, his eyes still burning into hers, despite the fact that he had said he would not pursue their relationship.

'He's very busy, but I'm sure he could come and see you in a few weeks,' Milly said, diverting her attention to her mobile phone.

Weirdly there were lots of messages, fifty or more from Facebook, several text messages and a few missed calls. The phone had been on silent and she'd barely even looked at it since she arrived.

She scrolled through her list of contacts, ignoring the messages for now and phoned Jamie.

He answered and almost immediately launched into song, giving her a clue as to what all the messages were about.

'Happy Birthday to you, Happy Birthday to you, Happy Birthday dear Tigger, Happy Birthday to youuuuuuuu.'

She laughed. 'I'd completely forgotten today was my birthday! You sing so beautifully.'

'You'd forgotten it was your birthday? Did the million messages on your Facebook page not give you a clue, or the cards or presents that have been delivered over the last few days?' Jamie laughed.

'I'm not at home, I'm away on business and I've not really looked at my phone. Time just sort of got away from me, I forgot what day it was today.'

How was it Wednesday already? Had she really been there three days? If today was Wednesday then she only had two days to persuade Cameron to be in the play. Though she had no idea how she was going to do that.

'Oh man, no cards or presents, what a sucky birthday,' Jamie said.

She looked across the table at Cameron who was watching her carefully. 'It's not so bad. Listen J, I'm staying at a property you might be interested in.'

'Another of your rejects,' Jamie laughed.

'Jamie.' She eyed Cameron across the table, but she didn't think he could hear. 'This place is beautiful.'

'All your rejects are. I'm not complaining. If it's anything like some of the other Castle Heritage rejects, I'm interested already.'

'Can you come and look at it, talk to the owner about what you could offer?'

'Sure thing, where are you?'

'It's not far from you, maybe half an hour. I know you're busy …'

'I could do tomorrow, if that works. I had a meeting that was cancelled. I could be there about ten?'

'Is tomorrow ok?' Milly whispered across the table. Cameron nodded. 'That's perfect J, thank you. I'll text you directions.'

'Brilliant, it means I can bring your birthday present too. Right, I'd better go, I'm in the middle of a meeting.'

'You sang to me in the middle of a meeting?'

'You're my sister, nothing is more important. Later, Tigs.'

He rang off and she smiled with love for him.

'It's your birthday today?' Cameron asked as soon as she returned the phone to the table.

'Yeah, I just forgot. I actually thought it was Wednesday tomorrow. Time just moves differently here.'

'It does feel like that. Well, we should have a celebration tonight.'

'Oh no, don't worry. It's not a big birthday or anything like that.'

'So you're twenty nine now?'

She nodded.

'Ah, you're a baby.'

'I am not, how old are you?'

'Thirty-four.'

He was watching her carefully, maybe thinking the age gap was too big. Well, if it meant his interest waned and they could get back on to a more professional relationship, that couldn't be a bad thing.

———

Milly looked at the reading on her laser digital tape measure and recorded the length of the banquet hall on her iPad, along with all the other facts she had written down about the building materials used and the methods and styles in place.

It felt a bit redundant as Castle Heritage almost certainly wouldn't take it on in its current fairy tale state, but she had promised Cameron she would do a thorough investigation and there might be some detail somewhere that might make them change their minds. In reality, she needed to do something rather than just sit opposite Cameron and stare into his dark, unrelenting eyes. He had work to do anyway and she definitely didn't want to disturb that.

She took a few more measurements.

If Cameron didn't want to work with Jamie, there were other ways to fund the castle. Ghost tours and tours of the secret passageways would be an obvious choice. Weekends only. Then Cameron could be on his own during the week. It would bring more custom to the pub when all the tourists needed lunch and he could probably hire a few of the villagers to do the tours, so he wouldn't need to get involved. Gladys would be the perfect candidate. Who better than someone who looked like a witch to deliver the ghost tours?

Though the tours could only really be a success if people saw ghosts. What was it Lavender had said? The Grey Lady only showed herself to those that were descendants of the Heartstone line. Was that true? She needed to go down to the dungeons by herself to test that theory and she wasn't keen on that idea.

She walked out to the staircase and eyed the dungeon door underneath the stairs. She had a sudden idea and raced upstairs to the library before she could change her mind.

—

Cameron was getting hungry and after having written over two thousand words since Milly had left to do some measurements, his bum was starting to ache, too.

He got up and tripped over her shoes as he walked out in to the banquet hall. He strode across the room and into the stairwell. He stopped when he saw the dungeon door open and became disturbingly aware of voices coming from below. He moved closer to listen. Not voices, one voice. Milly's. Though he couldn't make out what she was saying, she was too far away for that.

He walked down the stairs. In the passageway, between the cells, Milly was sitting on the cold stone floor, reading out loud from his book. If the ghosts were there, they hadn't showed themselves.

He walked softly towards Milly and she looked up briefly at him as he approached, flashed him a brilliant smile and returned to her reading.

Confused slightly, he sat down next to her. Instinctively she leaned into him as she carried on reading. There was something so beautiful and enticing about hearing his words being spoken by Milly. She brought magic and enthusiasm to his story. He waited patiently for Milly to finish the chapter and then he put his hand over the book to stop her reading any more.

'What are you doing?'

'It occurred to me that it might get quite lonely down here for the ghosts and as most of them are probably your ancestors, I thought they might be interested in seeing what you have achieved. Sadly it seems the ghosts have far better things to do with their time than listen to me read.'

'You wanted to read to the ghosts?' Would he ever stop being surprised by this girl?

'I was thinking more about getting them on our side. This seemed like a good way to do it.'

He stood up and offered her his hand, pulling her up too. 'Why do we need the ghosts on our side?'

'Because if we offer ghost tours, we need people to see ghosts.'

'You're determined to turn this into some kind of tourist attraction, aren't you?' He put his hand on the small of her back, escorting her up the stairs.

'If Castle Heritage take this place on, it's likely they would want to do that too. They are a charity and they rely on tourists paying to visit places like this to fund the renovations and upkeep. They don't have many properties on their books that aren't open to tourists. But I honestly think you'd be better off on your own, then you can control how the place is run and when you're open to the public. You could stay here too. If you wanted. I just don't think you should pin all your hopes on Castle Heritage when there are other options open to you as well. If you want to keep it, you have to make it work for you. I don't think your writing will be enough to sustain this place, especially if you keep churning out shit books.'

She grinned up at him as they walked into the kitchen and he laughed.

'I'll be very interested in what Jamie has to say.'

'You'll like him, everybody does. But his isn't the only hotel chain that would be interested in Clover Castle. There are lots of possibilities. Plus there are other historical preservation associations that might help. Castle Heritage isn't the only one. And you can use all our test results, you wouldn't have to pay for them to come out and conduct the same tests.'

Cameron gestured for her to sit down at the kitchen table while he cut some bread to make some sandwiches.

'My PA, Olivia, did a lot of research into the different historical preservation associations and based on their criteria for which properties they accept and the current properties on their books, she said Castle Heritage was the one most likely to take us on.'

He glanced up in time to see Milly frown.

'What?' he asked.

'Oh, erm ... I'm just surprised that we were the one she recommended. We have really strict rules about the kind of properties we take. Other associations are a bit more relaxed.'

'She assured me that you guys were the only ones that would take the castle on.'

Milly seemed taken aback by this, which confused him.

'And your PA, is she ... normally efficient?'

'She's relatively new, she's been with me a little under a year. But yes, from what I've seen of her work so far, she appears to be. You'll get to meet her Saturday, she's coming over for a few days. She did a load of research into this place and what my options were. I need to look at it all and make a decision but I've been putting it off. She also managed to get me a deal with Palace Hotels. If all else fails, I guess I can sell to them.'

Milly frowned again. He wished he could read her mind, there was so much going on inside that little head of hers. She looked up at him and must have seen his questioning gaze.

'Oh, it's nothing. I don't think Jamie thinks too highly of Palace Hotels.'

'Well they're his competitor, so I imagine there's bound to be a bit of bad feeling between them.'

'I think it's the CEO that Jamie doesn't like. Maxwell is apparently a bit of a twat. There's a rumour that his girlfriend has slept with a few potential clients to persuade them to sign with Palace Hotels or at the very least she's been incredibly flirty and led the clients to believe there was a chance of sex in return for a signature.'

Cameron pulled a face. 'That sounds a bit sleazy. I've not met him but we have had video conference calls and he seems one of those over confident, brash types. He invited me to go and play golf with him at some exclusive resort. I declined.'

'I have no idea whether it's true but that's certainly the rumour that Jamie told me. And he has close relationships with many of his competitors so I know he hasn't made this stuff up to make Maxwell look bad. Jamie has recommended several of his clients to go to his competitors instead of him when he knew they would be able to handle their needs better.'

'That's good of him.'

'He is a very honest man, he won't take you on unless he thinks he is the best person for the job.'

He was liking the sound of Jamie more and more, but she was bound to build him up, he was her brother after all.

'Do you mind if I ask how much Palace Hotels are offering?' Milly asked.

'Two million pounds, it's not great but …'

'It's not anything, that's nowhere near what the castle is worth.' She was angry and he wondered why.

'It's in a bad way.'

'Even so, if you sold it on the housing market, you'd get at least six million for it, probably more like eight or ten million.

Even if you don't want to work with Jamie, there are plenty of companies that would offer a lot more than that.'

'I really need to look at all the research she gave me. Olivia told me that two million was a really generous offer.'

Milly grabbed her phone and pressed a few keys, then held it out for him. 'These are castles that are for sale at the moment, look at the prices of them, five million, nine million, fifteen million. If you really want to sell it, at least get an estate agent round to see what the place is worth. Get a few round to have a look at it.'

'Olivia spoke to an estate agent, she said …'

'Did one come here, have a look around, take measurements? An estate agent can't just pluck a figure out the air when dealing with properties, especially not something as unique as a castle.'

'No, no one came, but … why would Olivia lie?'

'I'm not saying she's lying. Can I ask why you left something as important as this to Olivia to do? This is your family home.'

Cameron sighed. 'I didn't just hand it over for her to make the decision for me. She was just supposed to come back with all the options and information on different companies. The offer from Palace Hotels was a bit of a shock as I didn't expect her to approach companies like that on my behalf. Selling it was one of the options but the offer came through very quickly and I told her I need to take the time to look into all of this, I guess she was just being over efficient. She came to work for me not long after I inherited it. Well, it's taken months for it to be official and she helped me through a lot of that paperwork. I had no clue what to do with it. I never exactly had fond memories of my time here, my parents were always arguing and screaming at each other. But since being back here … These last few days … I've sort of fallen in love with the place. I don't want to sell it off now, I want it to stay in the family in some capacity. I shouldn't have trusted her with this. You're right, it's too important.'

'Maybe … she didn't look into all the factors properly. There is nothing like this property in the whole of the UK and if she was just doing research into castles in general then maybe … her figures might be wrong.'

'I don't pay her to be wrong.'

She quickly stood up and walked towards him, running a hand down his arm in a soothing gesture. 'Don't be angry …'

All thought and reason, all anger, all decisions, went clean out of his head as he stared down at Milly stroking his arm. There was only one thing filling his mind right now and Milly had taken the possibility of finishing that kiss completely off the table that morning. She was still speaking and he tried to tune into it and ignore the feel of her hand on his body.

'… I'll help you and together we can find the best possible solution for you and the castle. I'll do some research for you, and we can get an estate agent up here just so you have all the facts and …' she trailed off, as she could clearly see the look of desire and need in his eyes. It was taking every ounce of strength he had not to grab her, kiss her and throw her across the table, disregarding professionalism once and for all.

She immediately stepped back. 'I'm so sorry, I don't know why I did that.'

He reached forward and grabbed her, needing to feel her body next to his. She didn't even attempt to fight him off.

'Why do you cling to this professionalism so fiercely?'

She moved out of his grasp and he let her go, missing her already.

She sat back down and ran her nails down the heavy grooves of the table. He shouldn't push her about this, he'd promised her he wouldn't. It was quite obvious she wasn't going to tell him, anyway. He started cutting the bread again, needing to do something with his hands.

'My aunt never had much money,' Milly said and he froze to listen. 'She lives in a tiny little house and her job never paid her much. She already had a son to look after and I know she found it a struggle. She took me in without hesitation and I never went without; food, toys, clothes, holidays, she paid for everything. She paid for me to go to university, halls of residence, tuition fees and although I got a part-time job so I wasn't quite so reliant on her, my course also required a lot of volunteering and work experience as credits for the qualification and it didn't leave a lot of time for a job. I couldn't have done it without my aunt, I owe her so much.'

She hesitated, focusing on a crumb of bread as she balled it between her fingers.

'It was a tiny university and the course was very specialised. I was the only girl taking it. Do you know how much attention I got from my classmates?'

'I can imagine,' Cameron said, suddenly insanely jealous.

'I'd never had a boyfriend before. I was a painfully shy, chubby, spotty teenager who loved Disney. I was a right geek too, sat at the front in class so I could absorb everything the teacher said, got all the answers on all the tests correct. People hated me. Suddenly I turned eighteen, somehow lost the puppy fat, went to university and the boys were falling over themselves to be with me.'

'So you had a few boyfriends, no crime in that.'

'I had just one. Patrick. I fell for him hard. He was everything to me and I followed him around like a lovesick puppy. We started cutting class so we could be together. We cut class a lot.'

'You were eighteen, first time away from home, we've all been there. Most people's experience of university is getting as drunk as they possibly can and turning up to the bare minimum of lectures.'

'That wasn't me though. I've always been very studious and I was wasting the opportunity that my aunt was struggling to provide me with. When she found out, she was so disappointed. I was gutted, I had let her down. I turned it round, busted my ass and passed with flying colours. Patrick and I split up long before I finished the course. My diligence to my studies was always annoying for him, he still wanted to go out drinking, whilst I was always sat reading another book. I was gutted at the time but in hindsight I was better off without him. My studies were important to me and he didn't understand that. I wanted to prove to my aunt that she hadn't wasted her money on me.'

'So … you're never going to have a relationship again? Surely you've proved to your aunt by now that her money wasn't wasted, you have this fantastic job …'

'But that's just it. It was her contacts that got me this job. When I came out of university, it didn't matter how qualified or experienced I was, I really struggled to get a job anywhere. It seems that having a beard, tweed jacket and a pair of balls was more important than qualifications for most of the jobs I went for. Castle Heritage were the only ones that would give me a chance and partly – or mainly – it was because of my aunt. I love my job, it's everything to me. If they found out I was sleeping with a client, they would sack me and … I can't do that to my aunt again.'

'So you're never having a relationship again?'

'No, I'm not saying I'm never having a relationship again. I'm saying I wouldn't get involved with someone at work.'

'So … if we were to meet up after you had finished here, that would be ok?'

She smiled but didn't answer. He watched her carefully.

'There's more to this than you're saying. You've been on a man sabbatical for four years, what prompted that? Have there been other men since Patrick?'

'There've been two men. Adam. He was charming and sexy as hell. I fell in love with him very quickly too. We moved in together after just a few months. But my love for Disney and pink and singing obviously grew very tiring. One day, after we'd been together for about ten months, he came home and we had a blazing row over my inadequacies and he dumped me. I was absolutely heartbroken. I figured we were going through a rough patch but I always saw marriage in our future, but he always said he wasn't ready for any of that stuff. Anyway, turns out he was sleeping with someone else whilst he was with me. They're married now with three kids, so I guess he *was* ready for that, just not with me. So, yes, I am wary of falling in love again and getting dumped a few months down the line.'

'And the other man?'

'Tyler.' She swallowed and agony flashed in her eyes.

And in that one word, he knew. Her professionalism was an excuse, a great excuse but he knew Tyler had been the sole reason for the man sabbatical. Patrick and Adam had clearly hurt her, but Tyler had destroyed her. Whatever Tyler had done had ruined her rose-tinted fairy tale existence and made her shy away from love and happy endings. He wanted to kill Tyler. What the hell had he done to her to cause that much pain?

'It was one of those crazy, hedonistic type of love affairs where everything happens so quickly. I was twenty-three. After two weeks we were talking about our future, and where we were going to live and planning holidays together. I have never fallen so hard and so quickly in love with someone before. We had only been together four months when he was killed in a car accident.'

Shit. He hadn't expected that.

'I'm so sorry.'

'It's ok. I mean it isn't, I was devastated at the time … it was a long time ago …' she trailed off, her voice breaking.

He moved to comfort her and then stopped himself. She didn't want a relationship and after that incredible kiss this morning it was unlikely a simple hug would stay as that.

Cameron sighed. She'd had a terrible time with men. And he didn't know why he was pushing it with her. He wasn't after a relationship with her. She'd be gone in a few days, so really he should leave any kind of romantic entanglement well alone, for risk of hurting her again.

'I know what you're thinking,' she said. 'That I shouldn't run away from a relationship just because I've been hurt in the past.'

'I wasn't thinking that. Grief is agonizing. Some people never get over that.'

'Well I'm not completely against being in a relationship again. I'm just going to be very careful about the type of person I do get involved with. As silly and as immature as it sounds, I want marriage and babies and a long and happy life with the person I love. I'm not going to settle for anything else. Being with someone just for sex seems a bit pointless for me. I fall in love very easily and I'd only end up getting hurt.'

She was trying to push him away in order to protect herself and he had to respect that. He turned his attention back to the bread he was slicing.

'Besides, in my limited experience, sex really isn't that great, it's over too quickly and I'm always left sexually frustrated and wanting more.'

Cameron nearly sliced his finger off as he looked up at her in shock.

He leapt back with a shout and quickly sucked his finger. She shot out of her seat.

'Are you ok, let me see?'

He pulled his finger from his mouth and she took it in her hands. God, even that simple touch was such a turn on. He watched her examine his finger gently, wanting her hands on his body in the same way.

'It's ok, where are your plasters?'

He swallowed. 'Over there.'

She left him to get a plaster and then returned to secure it to his finger. She went to move away, but he stopped her, his hand on her arm.

'Milly, are you saying you've never …' He hesitated about talking about sex with her. He'd never had a problem talking about it before but she was so innocent in many ways. 'You've never orgasmed during sex before?'

She blushed slightly. 'Oh come on, all that sex you see in films or read about in books, all that shouting and groaning and toe curling, screaming orgasms, none of that stuff is real. Sex is nice, especially the cuddling afterwards, I always like that, but no, I've never had hot, passionate movie sex before.'

Cameron stared down at her. He had been with many women; women whose names he didn't even know, women whom he hadn't cared for, women he had liked and women he had loved but all of them had come during sex, he was damned sure of that. He knew women faked orgasms, but surely all the women he had been with hadn't faked all that screaming just to feed his ego. He'd never really been into cuddling after sex but he'd never come across a woman who thought that cuddling was the best part of sex before. He thought back to the previous night when he had held Milly in his arms all night. He'd never done that before and he'd had the best sleep he'd had in a very long time. Maybe there was something to be said for cuddling after all, but he didn't think he'd ever rank it higher than sex. She should expect more than a quick fumble and a nice cuddle afterwards. Even if she never slept with him, she should raise the bar a bit higher than that.

'Sex with someone you love should be an incredible experience; not only do you know that person well enough to know how they like it, but their pleasure actually brings you pleasure, plus you have that wonderful emotional connection, too, when you stare into each other's eyes and feel that love between you. But even sex with a stranger should be pleasurable and fulfilling for both partners. Sex with a new partner is always a bit tricky, to find how that person ticks, what they like, where they like to be touched but yes, it should still be toe curling, sheet ripping, headboard-banging amazing sex.'

Milly stared up at him with wide blue eyes and then she laughed. 'You're telling me you have hot movie sex every single time.'

'Yes and I'm not saying that because I want you to jump into bed with me, though that would be an added bonus. I'm saying it because it's true. Sex has always been fantastic.'

Milly shrugged, moving around to the other side of the table. 'For you, maybe. Patrick and Adam always seemed to enjoy themselves too.'

'No, for the women too. Milly, I'm not talking about me here, I'm talking about you. When you find that person you want to spend the rest of your life with, make sure they're a considerate lover. Your pleasure should be their priority. If he doesn't make you scream in bed, if he doesn't make your roar and shake and have multiple orgasms, then he isn't the one for you.'

'Multiple … orgasms!'

'Yes. Don't settle for less than that. Sex should be amazing, it should never ever just be nice.'

She stared at him across the table as he busied himself with making lunch. A huge part of him wanted to take her back to his bedroom now and show her what she had been missing all these years but the stronger, protective, maybe more chivalrous part of him, didn't want her to become another notch on his well-worn bedpost. She deserved someone wonderful and he certainly wasn't it.

CHAPTER 11

Milly was sitting in her old bedroom at the top of the tower, trying to find out as much as she could about Clover Castle. After the conversation about sex, she had wanted to get away from Cameron for a little while.

Extensive research about the place on the usual web sites she visited was turning up nothing. How could a castle, parts of which had clearly been here for over four or five hundred years, and a village with similar aged housing just not exist on any kind of land registry, maps or documents? She had tried to research the castle before she arrived and had come up with nothing time and time again.

There was a knock on the door and she looked up to see Cameron leaning against the door frame. God, even the way he stood, so casually, was sexy.

'There you are, I wondered where you'd got to. I was about to go and search the hole in the grounds in case you had fallen down there again. Can I borrow you for a few minutes, unless you're really busy?'

Milly got off the bed and stretched. 'No, I'm just trying to do some research on the place, but there's not a lot to go on. Well, nothing in fact. Do you have any documents that prove when the castle was built?' Cameron offered out his hand and she instinctively took it.

'No, nothing like that.' Cameron said as they descended the stairs.

'Do you know how big the original estate was before Uncle Boris sold it off? Do you have any kind of maps or documents to show the original land boundaries?'

'No, well maybe. I have a few documents I can show you which relate to the sale of the land around 1868. I think I could show you where the original boundaries were but I'm not one hundred percent sure.'

'And your title, Lord Heartstone, are you really a lord?'

'As far as I know I am, my dad always called himself Lord Heartstone and the villagers did too. When the will was read, it included the title of Lord too, but I've not looked too closely at that side of things. Olivia said there are no hereditary titles anymore and you have to apply to the House of Lords to continue with the title I think. My concern hasn't been with that though, I just wanted to get the castle fixed and secure some kind of funding for it, I wasn't that bothered with a pompous title that held little or no bearing on my future.'

'I've checked Debretts, that shows all the peers dating back hundreds of years and there is no link at all with your family.'

'I don't think we were all Heartstones though, if that helps. Obviously the castle has been passed down through male descendants but when there were no males it would be passed to daughters who married and took other names. Boris was a Heartstone, I know that much, but when we were originally given the title I don't think we were. I don't know much about the family tree though or when the title of lord was awarded or by whom.'

'Ok, maybe I can look into your genealogy, see if I can trace your family back. The whole place is a bit of a mystery if I'm honest. There should be some evidence that Clover Castle and the village exist, but I'm coming up blank at every turn.'

'I don't think this place was all that accessible before the invention of cars. If you were sent by the king to register and record the properties of all the peers and you saw this great steep hill which you had to climb or force your horse up, I imagine it was easier to report back to the king that there was nothing up there.'

'I can't believe that.'

'I know, there's so much that doesn't add up. I'm still trying to get my head round it all myself if I'm honest.'

They had arrived at the bottom of the stairs at this point and Cameron escorted her into the banquet hall. White candles adorned the long banquet table, their flames casting golden light onto the dark wood. Large trays were covered with silver domes, with tantalizing smells coming from underneath.

Milly stopped. 'What's going on?'

'I thought, as it's your birthday, we should have a banquet to celebrate.'

She looked up at him and laughed. 'We're having a banquet?'

'Of course. We have the banquet table, we should put it to good use. I can't speak for the quality of the food though.' He shrugged.

'That's so sweet, thank you so much.'

'Oh no, that's not the best bit.'

He escorted her to a tapestry on the far side of the hall that was hanging off a rail like a curtain. He let go of her hand and pushed the tapestry back to reveal a whole wardrobe of medieval style clothes.

Milly gasped as she ran to examine them.

'They're not real. At least I don't think they are. My parents always used to hold parties and medieval style banquets for their friends. They kept these clothes in here so that people could borrow them for the night. Some of them have labels in and are made from polyester, something that I'm pretty sure wasn't around in medieval times, but I thought … well, that we could have a proper traditional banquet. I'm sure there's something in there that will fit you. So take your pick, get changed and then we can start.'

'Oh God, Cameron, these are beautiful,' Milly said, running her hands over the different clothes.

There were dresses and gowns of every colour; ruby, gold, emerald, sapphire, silver, and magenta, glittering and sparkling from the rails. Although some of the gowns were obviously cheaply made, some were exquisite. They were blatantly not authentic pieces but some had been recreated very skilfully.

Cameron cleared his throat and she looked over at him. He was clearly embarrassed though she didn't know why.

'I shall be wearing this,' he said, lifting a blue velvet doublet off the rail. The doublet was lined with gold and had buttons down the front. It was fitted at the waist and came with or was attached to a pair of blue velvet puffed shorts. It came with a small white ruff, white stockings and a blue and gold velvet hat that had a large feather sticking out from it. Milly wasn't sure which era it was meant to be from as it seemed to be taking little bits from several eras but she couldn't wait to see Cameron in it.

She turned away so he wouldn't see her laugh. 'Well, we should match then.'

She ran her fingers along the different dresses and selected one that was an almost identical shade of blue. It was stunning. A jewelled ribbon adorned the collar, the bodice was fitted to the waist and then flared out into a large skirt that had a large gold, heavily embroidered panel running down the middle. The sleeves were fitted to the elbow then flared out too.

Cameron came up behind her to inspect her choice. 'It's beautiful,' he said, softly. 'There's jewellery too, costume pieces of course. I thought you might like to wear this, it will match your eyes perfectly.'

He secured a necklace round her neck that glittered with an array of large blue crystals all in different hues from the lightest turquoise to the darkest navy. It was obviously made from coloured glass but it was beautiful nonetheless.

'Go and get changed and then we shall dine on a feast fit for kings.'

Milly grabbed her dress and quickly ran up the stairs to get dressed.

It thrilled her to be wearing something so beautiful and luxurious and she did a little experimental twirl and watched with delight as the material spun out around her. She didn't have any appropriate shoes but barefoot was just fine.

She descended the staircase slowly, being really careful not to trip over the long fabric, but she stopped at the top of the last turn of stairs, because Cameron was waiting for her at the bottom wearing his costume. She had thought he would look hilarious, especially in the white stockings, but he looked dashing, sophisticated and still sexy as hell.

'You look great,' she said, coming down the last few stairs to stand in front of him.

'You look incredible,' Cameron said. His voice sounded coarse and her heart soared at the effect she had had on him.

Music was drifting from the banquet hall and Milly was curious where it was coming from. 'Do you have real musicians?'

Cameron smiled as he escorted her into the hall. 'Yes, a great travelling troupe of musicians called iPhone.'

Milly laughed. 'Ah yes, I've heard of them. Very talented. And this song by the medieval band Coldplay I believe is one of the king's favourites.'

Cameron walked her over to the middle of the table and helped her into her seat. One of the silver domes was right in front of her and she couldn't wait to see what she would be eating.

With a great flourish, Cameron removed one of the dome lids and she laughed when she saw two bowls of tomato soup underneath.

'Wait, there's more,' Cameron said, removing another silver dome from a large platter, revealing several slices of cheese on toast. Milly burst out laughing.

'Very traditional.'

'Just wait until you see what's for dessert.'

Cameron handed her a bowl of soup and piled two slices of cheese on toast onto a side plate, then moved round the table to sit opposite her.

'I do however have some fairly decent red wine.' He leaned over and poured some into a heavy gold goblet. He held his up for a toast. 'Happy Birthday.'

She chinked his cup and took a sip, it tasted soft, sweet and fruity.

It was still daylight outside but the glow of the candles in the darkened room was magical, sending flickering shadows across Cameron's face.

'Thank you for this, you really didn't have to go to so much trouble.'

'It's my absolute pleasure,' he smiled across the table at her.

They finished their meal, chatting and laughing and then Cameron came back round her side of the table, offering her his hand again.

She placed her hand in his and he pulled her to her feet. 'No banquet would be complete without a little dancing.'

'And Westlife is very traditional.'

'Well I could probably do a little better than this,' Cameron said, moving to the iPhone and the docking station. He pressed a few buttons and she laughed as 'Tale As Old As Time' drifted out from the speakers.

'How did you know?'

'I can do research too.'

With one hand at her waist and one in her hand, Cameron began to swing her round the room. He wasn't very graceful but she felt like she was dancing on air as he spun her round. She looked up at the crystal chandelier hanging above them, glinting in the semi darkness like a thousand stars. She had never felt so alive, so gloriously happy as she did in that moment. She brought her eyes down to Cameron's and he smiled at her.

She looked away out the windows, scared of the feelings that were crashing through her.

'Look at that sunset,' Milly said and Cameron glanced out of the window too.

'Maybe we should carry on this dance outside.'

He stopped dancing and led her out, unclipping his iPhone from the docking station as they went.

The grass was warm from the day's sun and the sky was a startling rainbow of scarlet, amber, candyfloss and plum.

Cameron set his iPhone down on the rocks, selected a song and as Etta James started belting out 'At Last' he slowly walked back towards her but instead of taking her hand, he put his hands round her waist and pulled her close. She leaned up and wrapped her arms round his neck, leaning her head against his chest. They moved around slowly as day turned to night and one song ended and was replaced with another and another.

Milly knew she was in trouble. She was falling for this man and there was no way to stop it.

—

Cameron felt Milly shiver next to him as they sat on the rocks staring out at the black moon-drenched sea. He quickly whisked off his cloak and draped it over her shoulders, leaving his arm round her back. She leaned into his side and he felt nothing but contentment at having her there.

The sun had long since disappeared and even the iPhone had stopped playing. They had danced and then sat and talked before lapsing into an easy silence. There was a feeling between them that Cameron couldn't put his finger on, something magical, like they were caught in some kind of enchanted bubble and neither one of them seemed willing to break it.

The gentle warm summer breeze drifted over the cliff tops, playing with Milly's hair, sending gentle scents of apple and candyfloss his way.

He leaned into her and before he could stop himself he kissed the top of her head. He winced, hoping she wouldn't notice, but she did.

She pulled away slightly to look at him and he feared the bubble had popped.

'This has been a beautiful night, thank you.'

He looked down into her star filled eyes. 'My pleasure.'

'But if I don't leave you now, I fear we might be continuing this magical night in your bed.'

He swallowed. 'I didn't do any of this in the hope you would suddenly want to jump into bed with me.'

'I know, but I'm finding it almost impossible to cling onto the last scraps of my self-control so I'm going to go to bed before I say to hell with it all and make love to you here under this beautiful moon.'

Cameron rubbed his face, trying to dispel that wondrous image from being burnt into his mind. When he looked up, Milly was already standing. He quickly stood up too.

'I'll walk you back.'

'I'd really rather you didn't. We're going to get back to that kitchen and then we're going to be kissing and there's no way I'm going to be able to stop what happens after that.'

He had nothing to say. She stared up at him for a moment and then stepped up and kissed him on the cheek, lingering there for a moment longer than necessary. He stayed very still, scared to make the wrong move, scared to make the right one.

She stepped back a bit and suddenly let out a laugh of what sounded like defeat.

'I spoke to Gladys today, about you. She said that if you were to have regrets, you should regret what you did, not what you didn't do.'

'What does that mean?'

'It means … when I'm finished here, if I walk away from you, never going further than that incredible kiss we shared this morning, I'm going to regret it for the rest of my life.'

Cameron swallowed, still too scared to move. 'So, should I walk you back?'

'No, I still need to finish all my tests and research here, so I should probably do that first, but I'm on holiday next week.'

'Right.' He had no idea where she was going with this.

'It's lovely here, the view, the food, the rooms.'

'You want to take your holiday here?' He frowned.

'Yes, if that's ok.'

Suddenly, with crystal clarity he could see what she was trying to say.

'In a non-professional capacity?'

She giggled and nodded. 'I could be your first guest at Clover Castle Hotel.'

He put his hands to her waist, pulling her against him and breathing her in. 'I'd really like that.'

'I'd like that, too.'

'It's going to be the longest few days of my life.'

She leaned back and smiled. 'It will give us a chance to finish all the formalities between us.'

He nodded.

'Goodnight Cameron.' She leaned up to kiss him again but this time he moved his head at the last second so she kissed him on the lips.

She stepped back, laughing. 'You have to be patient.'

'I will, I promise.'

They stared at each other, their mutual need sparking off them so intensely that he was surprised he couldn't see little arcs of lightning zipping between them.

'Goodnight,' Milly said, softly and walked off towards the castle.

He watched her go and knew he had the biggest smile on his face.

—

Milly glanced at Cameron across the table as they ate breakfast. Something had passed between them the night before and they both knew it. He was in a good mood and she'd been woken by him singing this morning. She'd quickly got dressed in case Jamie showed up early and when she'd emerged from her bedroom Cameron had already made her breakfast.

She had been thinking about their arrangement all night and hadn't been able to stop smiling about it. Cameron hadn't stopped smiling either. He grinned across the table at her as he ate, looking like the cat that got the cream.

Just then there was a knock on the door.

Cameron got up to answer it and Milly heard her brother introduce himself.

'Hello, I'm Jamie McAllister from Extravagance. I believe you're expecting me.'

Milly squealed and barrelled past Cameron to throw herself into Jamie's arms. Luckily he had heard her coming and quickly dropped his briefcase in preparation for the assault.

'Hey Tigs, how's it going?' Jamie held her tight.

'I've missed you.'

'I missed you too, it's been too long. You need to come round for dinner one night.'

Milly suddenly remembered that this was a business meeting after all, and hugging her brother was hardly professional. She glanced at Cameron who didn't seem to mind. They had long since left professionalism behind, especially with that amazing dance the night before.

'Cameron this is my brother Jamie, Jamie this is Cameron Heartstone.'

With one arm still round her shoulders, Jamie leaned forward to shake Cameron's hand.

'Hi, pleased to meet you. I must say, this place is incredible.'

'Thank you, come in. We had a bit of a late night last night, so we've only just got up and had breakfast. Can I fix you anything to eat?' Cameron asked.

Milly found herself blushing at how intimate Cameron had made that sound, or was she just being paranoid? She glanced at Jamie to see if he'd made anything out of those words but he was sitting down as if there was nothing out of the ordinary in the fact that his sister was having a cosy breakfast with a client. Cameron was dressed, but in torn jeans and a crumpled white shirt, with his hair sticking out everywhere, it did look like last night had been a late one for a whole host of other reasons.

'No, I already ate on the way, thank you. I brought you your birthday present, Tigs.' Jamie rummaged in his bag and pulled out a neatly wrapped gift, covered in Disney wrapping paper. 'It sucks that you had to work on your birthday.'

'Actually, it was one of the best birthdays I've ever had.'

Cameron smiled and blushed and Jamie looked between them, pennies dropping into place.

'Oh. Erm ... right.'

Milly's eyes widened at the way that Jamie's mind was clearly working. 'Um ... we had a medieval banquet and there was dancing afterwards. That's all.'

Jamie's eyes were still flicking between them, but he seemed slightly mollified.

'Well, here's your present.'

Milly took it and gave it a little shake and Jamie laughed.

'Open it.'

Cameron moved off to clear away their breakfast things, leaving them alone for a moment.

She tore at the paper keenly and a beautiful pink scarf fell out, embroidered with a multitude of different coloured sequins and beads.

'Oh J, I love it, thank you.'

'And I saw this at an antique shop yesterday and just thought of you,' Jamie lifted a small black velvet box from the wrapping paper and passed it to her.

Jamie was always so thoughtful with his presents, he never bought anything for the sake of it.

Milly opened it up. Inside was a pale blue cameo brooch, entwined within a gem encrusted frame. She ran her fingers over the pale girl, her hair was tangled with leaves and berries. It was stunning.

'J, it's beautiful, thank you.'

'My pleasure.' He turned to Cameron. 'Why don't you show me round and then we can talk about what I can offer you. I really like what I've seen so far, so I'm sure I can help you.'

Cameron stood up and walked towards the door. Jamie went to follow him and Cameron automatically held out a hand for Milly, which he immediately dropped before Jamie saw.

'You boys go ahead, I need to get a shower anyway whilst you two talk business.'

Cameron seemed a little disappointed that she wasn't coming with them but he quickly recovered. He opened the door and a few moments later they were both gone, their voices fading down the corridor.

She felt a little bad that she wasn't going to go with them, but she didn't want to influence either of their decisions, especially Cameron, the decision to work with Jamie or not had to come from him.

Milly smiled down at the beautiful gifts that Jamie had brought her, closed the lid on the cameo and wandered off to the bathroom.

She turned on the shower and pulled her top off. Waiting for it to heat up, she saw a movement in the reflection of the mirror.

She turned round and came face to face with the Grey Lady.

Milly let out a little scream and backed up into the glass of the shower cubicle.

Silently, the ghost stared at Milly. She was clutching her throat as if she was in pain.

Milly looked around for her towel, feeling very vulnerable standing there half naked, but the towel was on the other side of the room and she would have to walk through the Grey Lady to get to it. Luckily she still had her bra and jeans on, but that still didn't lessen the embarrassment.

The ghost continued to stare and hold her throat, then to Milly's embarrassment her eyes scanned down over Milly's body. The Grey Lady's eyes fastened on her dragon tattoo. For a second, just a brief second, the ghost seemed to smile before she faded into nothing, the last remnants of her swirling with the steam that was slowly filling the bathroom.

What was that about? She had never seen the ghost outside of the dungeons before. Why had she been clutching her throat? Why did she like her tattoo? And why didn't she speak?

Milly shook her head in frustration and got in the shower, hoping that she didn't suddenly have any more unwelcome visitors coming to see her whilst she washed.

CHAPTER 12

Cameron studied Jamie as he took some photos of the exterior of the castle. He looked nothing like Milly at all. Where Milly was blonde, Jamie was dark, with greeny grey eyes instead of Milly's startling blue. He was tall and thin, where Milly was short and had those gorgeous curves. It also hadn't escaped his notice that Jamie had introduced himself as Jamie McAllister, not Jamie Rose.

He liked Jamie a lot. He was relaxed, honest and obviously very good at what he did. He liked that their meeting hadn't been conducted in a formal boardroom or even across the kitchen table, but as Cameron had showed him round. Jamie had talked at length about his company, what they had done in the past for other properties, what he could do for Cameron, how he would make it work. Cameron felt excited just listening to Jamie speak about his plans for the castle, he was a very passionate person. He shared that with Milly, though Cameron was beginning to realise that might be the only thing he shared with her.

Jamie put his camera back in his bag and started walking round towards the kitchen entrance again.

'I really like this place. It has so much potential,' Jamie said.

'I think so too.'

'So I'll get my assistant to draw up an offer, detailing everything we've discussed. I want you to take as long as you need to think about it, get some legal advice if you want, research into my company, research other companies. There is no time limit on the offer. If you come back to me in six months, the offer still stands. I totally understand your concerns but I really do think we can make this into a profitable venture for you, on your terms.'

'Well, thank you for coming out here today. You've given me a lot to think about.'

Jamie stowed his stuff in the back of his car, a small black Peugeot, not anything big or flashy.

He closed the boot and turned to face Cameron. 'Now, about my sister.'

Cameron felt his smile fall from his face.

'I'm not going to ask if there is something going on between you two because it's none of my business and, quite frankly, it's obvious there is. Don't play with her, she's not a game. She has a big heart which has been bruised one too many times.'

'I know.'

Jamie looked surprised at this. 'She told you about her ex-boyfriends?'

'Well yes, but I meant about her mum too.'

Jamie leaned back against the car as if all the wind had been knocked out of him.

'She told you about Emma? She never talks about her mum. Not to me or her aunt or anyone.'

This threw Cameron completely, Milly had told him easily enough.

'It just sort of came up in conversation.'

'Trust me, that sort of thing never comes up in conversation.' Jamie shuddered and then looked at Cameron with some sort of renewed respect. 'She never told any of her exes either. She obviously trusts you. I did a bit of research into you before

I came here, before I knew you were involved with my sister and there are pictures of you on the arm of hundreds of different women.'

Cameron blushed. He had never felt embarrassed about the life he led before and he hated that he suddenly felt the need to prove he was worthy of Milly.

'It's been a long time since I was involved in a serious relationship, but I really like Milly. I can't promise this is going to last forever, but I can promise I'm going to do my utmost not to do anything to hurt her.'

Jamie nodded his approval. 'That's all I can ask for. Now I have another meeting this afternoon so I'll say goodbye to my sister and leave you two to it. I'll be in touch soon.'

Jamie strode off to the kitchen and left Cameron standing on the driveway.

Was it right to get involved with Milly, given his history of bad relationships and one night stands?

He watched her open the kitchen door for Jamie; her blonde hair was blowing in the wind and seeing her enormous smile, he felt his heart fill with her. Nothing was ever going to feel more right than being with this woman.

—

'You won't stop for lunch?' Milly pleaded, as Jamie swigged back a glass of orange juice.

'No, I have a meeting at three so I really need to get going. Will you come for dinner next week?'

'No, I'll still be here but I could do the first weekend in July.'

'Perfect, we'll make it a date. I need to catch up with mum anyway so we'll do dinner round her house. But aren't you on holiday next week?'

Milly blushed and Jamie laughed. He came over to give her a hug. 'Please be careful, Tigs. Don't go falling in love with him, not yet anyway.'

What had Cameron said to him? Or had he guessed there was something between them in the few minutes he had seen them together?

Jamie kissed her on the head and walked out. Milly followed him to his car where Cameron was still standing waiting. Jamie shook his hand and waved at her.

'Bye, Tigs.'

'Where does Tigs come from?' Cameron asked as Jamie moved round to the driver's side and Jamie laughed.

'Erm … because I'm like Tigger from *Winnie the Pooh*, always full of energy.'

'Milly!' Jamie admonished. 'You've told him every part of your life but you haven't told him that?'

Milly blushed as Jamie got in the car and drove away. She waved at him, hoping his departure would be enough to distract Cameron from pursuing it further.

She turned back and he was looking at her expectantly. She sighed. 'My birth name was Mildred Tiggywinkle.'

Cameron tried to suppress the laughter but failed. 'Mildred Tiggywinkle?'

'Stop it, I hate it,' Milly laughed. 'Plus Tiggywinkle was my Dad's name, a man I never knew so I changed it legally as soon as I could to Rose, which is my mum's and aunt's maiden name. Jamie has never let me forget it, though. And now you can tease me mercilessly as well.'

'Of course I wouldn't,' Cameron said, innocently, his eyes twinkling with mischief.

'So what did he say? He likes the place, I know that. Did he give you an offer?' Milly said, trying to change the subject.

Cameron escorted her inside, with his hand on her back. She loved that he did that.

'He did, he made me a very generous offer. He won't buy me out completely, his offer was for equal ownership of the castle, a fifty-fifty share between me and him. He would pay for all renovations and repairs and organise all aspects of the hotel side of things, including staff and insurance, but all profits would be split two ways. I can still live here, if I want. The money he is offering me for half the castle would be enough to pay off all the debts, too.'

'That's fantastic. We can get an estate agent up here to just give you a market value figure to see if Jamie's offer is fair but if Jamie is only going to buy half the castle, his offer won't be near what it's worth.'

'No, he discussed that with me, he thinks the castle is worth between eight or nine million, so he's offered me four and half, but it means that I still have a share of the profits going forward and I still have a say about how some things are run.'

'Yay! That's a brilliant offer, I'm so pleased! And you're going to be rich, you can buy a big house in the Caribbean with that.'

He laughed. 'I'm thinking I'm going to stay here.'

Milly couldn't help smiling. 'You are?'

'Yes, for a while anyway. The hotel might start to piss me off after a bit but I think the castle has something special about it, something that is calling me to stay.'

He stared at her as he said this and Milly wondered if he was referring to her, but that was unlikely, as she wasn't part of the castle.

'So, are you going to accept?'

'I think so.'

'Well, don't rush into any decisions. Think about it carefully, we can always get a few other hotel chains up here to discuss what they could offer.'

'And I'm still waiting on the report from Castle Heritage,' he smiled at her.

'Yes, but a lot of that is going to be dependent on the test results from the lab. And whatever my tests prove, I do think Jamie will suit your needs better.'

'I think so, too. I told him all your wonderful ideas about holding parties and banquets here, doing ghosts tours and utilizing the secret passages and the maze and he loved all that.'

'Did he see the ghost?'

'No, sadly not.'

'That's because she came to see me when I was getting undressed for a shower.'

Cameron eyes widened. 'She came in to our bathroom?'

Our! Milly's heart galloped at that inadvertent sign of togetherness and then she chastised herself for being so silly.

'Yes, she was clutching her throat and then she got very interested in my tattoo.'

'The dragon?'

Milly nodded.

Cameron shook his head in confusion. 'What was she doing here? She's never come down here before. The Heartstone flag has a dragon on it, so I guess that might have something to do with her appreciation for your tattoo.'

'The flag that flies from the middle of the castle?'

'Yes, although it's changed quite a bit over the years, I have a book somewhere that shows the different designs over the last few centuries but it's always been a dragon and a heart.'

'Do you know why?'

Cameron opened the fridge and started pulling out ingredients for what looked like a salad.

'It's a silly story and I'm not sure if any of it has any historical accuracy, especially as the dragon plays such a big part.' He started chopping tomatoes and cucumber, throwing them all into a colander. 'There was a man called Matthew, supposedly my ancestor, though I can find no trace of a Matthew in my family line. He regularly took advice and counsel from a witch who lived here in the village of Clover's Rest. She was beautiful, with long black hair. They would meet for dinner every night and the witch would advise him and make potions for him. She did everything in her power to make him happy, for she had fallen in love with Matthew. Do you want mushrooms with your salad?'

Milly blinked. 'Cameron! You can't interrupt the story with questions about mushrooms.'

He laughed. 'Sorry. Where was I? The witch was in love with Matthew, the kind where you can't sleep or eat or breathe without every thought being of that person. The sort of love that physically hurt when they were apart.'

Milly sat entranced, listening to the magical story, his soft mysterious tone adding weight and wonder to the legend.

'She assumed he felt the same – he would often bring her gifts, animals he had hunted, flowers, jewellery. But he did these things as payment for her services. She was his friend. He did not return her feelings. He loved another, a librarian who lived in the village. She was young and pretty with golden hair and had collected and inherited hundreds of books. Often, Matthew would go to her after visiting the witch just to listen to her read. They were very much in love and they were set to marry at the Summer Solstice celebrations.'

He moved to the sink to wash the salad items he had chopped.

'When the witch found out, she was furious, she felt betrayed. Matthew and the librarian hid in the maze, knowing that if she found them it would almost certainly mean death. They became separated in the maze and couldn't find each other, no matter how many times they called. The witch found them and dealt a hand far worse than death. She cursed them both. She removed Matthew's heart and replaced it with one of stone.'

'That's where the name Heartstone comes from?' Milly asked, bringing her knees up to her chest as she listened.

'Well yes, supposedly. The witch cursed the Heartstone family and said that no man of Heartstone blood would ever find true love. She turned the librarian into a golden dragon, gave her Matthew's heart and banished her from the kingdom for a thousand years. When one thousand years are over, the dragon will return the heart to the castle. But only if the current lord can see past the scales and the breath of fire to the beautiful girl underneath. Only with true love's kiss will the dragon turn back into a girl, the stone heart crumble and the curse be broken forever.'

'True love's kiss,' Milly said, sighing happily.

Cameron smiled at her as he chopped some cooked chicken into cubes. 'Well, it might go some way to explain why the Heartstone men are always so unlucky in love. But it's only a story, there are no such things as dragons, after all.'

'But it's so romantic, soul mates waiting one thousand years to be reunited.'

'Yes an evil, bitter witch, a thousand year old curse, two people in love who will never see each other again. Yes, very romantic.'

'It is, if the lord of the castle spots his soul mate, after all this time, then it really was meant to be.'

'Well that's why the flag flies all day and night – so the dragon can find her way home.'

'I love it. But I've heard this story before. Well, a version of it.'

'I don't doubt it; it's probably a combination of several fairy tales.'

Milly rubbed her head, trying to remember. 'My mum used to tell me something similar, though I can't remember any of it now. She had this necklace, with a golden dragon wrapped around a red heart. It was beautiful and she wore it every day. She used to tell me that we were guarding the heart until I found my true love, when I found him I was to give it to him and he would cherish it forever.'

Cameron was silent for a moment. 'What did the necklace look like?'

'Exactly like my tattoo, that's why I had it done. Trust me though, it's nothing like the flag.'

'Well, as I said, there were very different versions of the flag. Can I see your tattoo?'

'I'd have to get half undressed for you to see it.'

'I don't mind that.' Cameron waggled his eyebrows playfully.

Milly smiled. 'You'll have to wait till Friday when I'm on holiday.'

Cameron stared at her. They hadn't actually spoken about what would happen; whether as of five o'clock on Friday night she would jump straight into bed with him, or whether they were going to date or do something more traditional first. Now the cards had been dealt and it seemed that the horny, hadn't-had-sex-in-years side of her had made the decision.

They sat in silence for a moment staring at each other, before Cameron cleared his throat.

'Do you know what happened to the necklace? Do you still have it?'

Milly shook her head. 'I never saw it again after my mum died. It was just a piece of costume jewellery, I'm sure, but I always loved the story.'

'Well, the legend says that the lord will recognise the girl in three different ways. She will be wearing a dragon heart necklace …'

'Shut up, it does not say that! You just want to get in my pants a few days early by feeding me this story that we're obviously lost soul mates.'

He laughed. 'It's the truth. I'm just telling you the legend, you wanted to know the story. It explains why the Grey Lady was so interested in your tattoo, she may have seen it before. I don't think she was there to admire your boobs, as great as they are.'

'Stop it,' Milly giggled. What had she done? She'd opened the door for him to unashamedly flirt with her for the next few days. 'What are the other two ways?'

He dished up the salad and the chicken onto two plates and offered his hand to her.

'Come on, I'll show you.'

She took his hand and he led her through the banquet hall and up the stairs.

'So, there is a heart of stone in the study. It is said that when the lord holds it in his hand and kisses his one true love, the stone will turn to dust,' Cameron said.

'So the lord has to carry this around with him every time he kisses a pretty lady, that's a bit inconvenient.'

'I know, it is rather. Big, heavy thing it is, too.'

'When was the stone heart made?'

'No idea.'

'Is it a precious stone?'

'No it's just stone, but it was one of the things that was specifically left to me in the will.'

Cameron walked into the study and left her to walk around the other side of the desk. He opened a drawer and pulled out a big box, which was clearly quite heavy. He undid the catch and flipped open the lid, pushing the box across the desk towards her.

Sitting on a blanket of blue velvet was a hand sized stone heart. There was nothing remarkable about it, nothing even very pretty. It looked very old and like it could crumble at any time.

Cameron walked back round the desk and picked it up, weighing it in his hand. He looked up from the stone at her.

'So … we should probably kiss, just to test it out.'

Milly laughed at Cameron's tactics. 'I'm not kissing you just to see if some silly legend is true.'

'A minute ago, the silly legend was very romantic.'

'It is, but it's just a story, besides that rock looks like it would crumble at the slightest touch, even without my kiss.'

'True.' He gave it a hard squeeze but the rock remained intact. He looked up at her hopefully.

Milly sighed. 'Ok, a quick one.'

He grinned and gathered her to him with one arm round her back. He smiled at her as he lowered his lips to hers, kissing her softly and sweetly. Sensations rushed through her as soon as his mouth met hers. A rush of flames ignited her, she felt euphoric and blissfully happy. A soft breeze wrapped round them, a scent of flowers, mingled with gentle laughter. She pulled away in shock and the laughter faded. She stared up at Cameron, wondering if he had felt it too. She couldn't tell from his expression but he had obviously enjoyed the kiss.

She glanced down at the stone heart in his hand, still intact and completely unaffected by their incredible kiss. She felt disappointed but she didn't know why. She had only known Cameron a few days. Of course she wasn't his true love, that kind of love took time. Love at first sight was a fairy tale.

She stepped back a bit out of his embrace. 'Well, we probably needed to be in love to break the spell.'

'Maybe we both needed to hold it while we kissed, or maybe you should have held it,' Cameron suggested. Was he disappointed too?

'Give me that thing,' Milly said, offering out her hand.

'It's heavy.' Cameron warned as he placed it in her hand.

As soon as the stone touched her hand it crumbled into pieces, leaving nothing more than a pile of sand and dust in her palm.

Milly's heart missed a beat. And then another. She didn't dare move or breathe and she certainly couldn't look at Cameron.

Eventually she found her voice. 'It was very old.'

'Yes, probably a thousand years.'

'Stop it,' but Milly could find no humour in it now. This was ridiculous, a fairy tale, nothing more. She didn't believe in fairy tales.

Not knowing what to do with the dust, she let it pour onto the blue velvet in the box and she snapped the lid closed.

'Shall we have lunch?'

She turned and walked from the room but Cameron quickly followed her.

'Do you not want to know what the third way is?'

He clearly thought the whole thing was hilarious.

She sighed and turned round to face him. 'Go on.'

'There is a cameo brooch that …'

'Oh, stop it! You're playing with me, why are you playing with me?' She felt angry and hurt that he would tease her like this. It was all a trick.

Cameron looked shocked at her sudden anger. He put his hands on her shoulders. 'What's wrong?' He was genuinely concerned and she regretted her outburst. He was just joking around with her, he didn't mean any harm.

'You saw the cameo that Jamie bought me for my birthday and now you're weaving it into your legend. I have to give you points, it's one hell of a story.'

'I didn't see it, I swear. I was on the other side of the table.'

Milly shook her head and walked down the stairs. 'Go on, tell me the way that it fits into the story.'

'Well, it's said that Matthew had the cameo made in the librarian's likeness and gave it to her sister with strict instructions to pass it to her daughter and then her daughter's daughter and every daughter after that. Matthew was sure that the girl that came back to break the curse would be a direct relation to the librarian. The girls were supposed to wear it on their wedding day so that their true love would recognise the girl he had lost all those years before.'

Milly rolled her eyes. 'And let me guess, my cameo is exactly the same as the one that Matthew made.'

'I didn't see your cameo, I had no idea Jamie bought you one, but I can show you the one that's part of the legend. Let's go to the portrait gallery above the banquet hall.'

Milly sighed, her stomach rumbling hungrily. But as he'd gone to so much effort to create the story, she didn't see any harm in humouring him for a bit longer.

He took her into the portrait gallery and to a large portrait of a very austere looking woman.

'Twice in the past the lord of the castle married the librarian of the village, I'm not sure whether it was in an attempt to break the curse, or just because they fell in love. This was Alexandra who married Charles Heartstone in 1674. You can see the blue cameo brooch she is wearing.'

Milly squinted at the brooch. It was a cameo but it was impossible to see whether it bore any resemblance to her own, currently sitting in the kitchen.

'She died during childbirth a year after they were wed.'

'Cheery,' Milly said, sarcastically.

Cameron gestured for her to come over to the other side of the room. 'This is Sophia who was my mad old Uncle Boris's first wife. She died just a few weeks after the wedding of scarlet fever. It broke my uncle's heart and that's what sent him mad. The legend says that both women died because the thousand years wasn't up.'

Milly sighed and walked closer to the painting, faltering a bit in her step as she drew nearer.

'That's the Grey Lady.'

Cameron looked at the picture more closely. 'I suppose it is, yes.'

Milly stepped closer and felt her heart thunder against her chest.

'Sophia used to wear her cameo brooch as a choker necklace. I believed she tied a piece of ribbon to the pin,' Cameron explained.

Milly tried to draw in breath but her throat was closed, black spots exploded in her vision and she felt physically sick.

That was why the Grey Lady had appeared to her, clutching her throat. She was trying to tell her she wanted her cameo necklace back. The cameo that was painted in extraordinary detail on the throat of Sophia in this painting was the exact same cameo that was sitting in a black velvet box in Cameron's kitchen.

CHAPTER 13

Cameron had never seen anyone go as white as Milly had up in the portrait gallery. He had thought she was going to pass out. He'd quickly brought her back down to the kitchen and made her eat her lunch and she'd not said another word since.

She was looking a lot better now, the colour had returned to her cheeks. She had finished every bite of the salad and was happily sitting opposite him reading a newspaper. Well, she was going through the motions as if she was reading it, but he strongly suspected she hadn't read a single word.

He was dying to look at the cameo that was sitting at the end of the table, but he hadn't dared. He figured from her reaction it was quite similar to the one in the painting but there were hundreds of blue cameos out there, they had been hugely popular, especially in the eighteenth and nineteenth centuries. There was no way that the cameo in Milly's box was the exact same one. He hadn't seen many cameos in his life but the ones he had seen all looked very similar.

The silence between them was unbearable. They had sat in silence many times since she had arrived but it had never felt like this.

He stood up and she looked up at him warily.

'I need to get some groceries from the village, did you want anything?'

She shook her head. 'No, I'm fine thank you.'

'Right.' Cameron felt awkward and he didn't know why.

He stepped back, taking his time moving Milly's shoes to the side of the room, hoping that she would say something to alleviate this weird feeling between them, but she didn't. He walked out, determined to bring her back a gift, anything that would bring back her normal smile again.

He walked into the village, it was another gorgeously hot day. Preparations for the Summer Solstice play seemed to be underway on the village green. There was bunting being hung from the trees and tiny fairy lights were being strewn from the branches. There was a sense of excitement among the villagers, everyone was getting involved. Milly seemed to want to be a part of it as well, she had even been talking about making some Solstice cookies when she had returned from the village the day before.

A week ago, he would have wanted no part in these celebrations. He liked being anti-social, it suited him fine. But now … everything seemed better, he was happier than he had been in a long time. He still didn't want to make an idiot of himself in front of the whole village but he would at least come down and watch the festivities with Milly.

As he strolled over to the mini supermarket he spotted Lavender, weighed down with her heavy bags on the way back from the shop.

Loath as he was to hear more mystic predictions about his life, he wasn't going to let her struggle.

'Here, let me help you,' Cameron said, hurrying over and taking the bags.

'Such a good boy,' Lavender said, smiling at him as she walked at his side.

Cameron noted that, oddly, the bags seemed to be filled with cans of beans. 'That's nice of you to say, but you're probably the only one who thinks that. Everyone else just chants "Oogie" at me.'

'Well, you upset a lot of people when you sacked everyone.'

'There's no money in the estate, Lavender, and the severance pay I gave them completely cleaned me out personally.'

'I did think you were too generous with that. Most people wouldn't give anything and you were giving away thousands.'

'It wasn't much. I just felt bad. A lot of people had worked at the castle all their lives.'

'And I bet no one thanked you for it.'

'That's not why I did it. And I understand people are upset but there really was no other way round it.'

Lavender pushed open her door and Cameron noted that she didn't even use a key, it was just left unlocked.

'How is your young Milly?' Lavender said.

'She's not mine.'

'She will be. I know she will be.'

'Because you've seen it in the leaves,' Cameron said, with a smirk.

'Yes.' Lavender said, looking at him in confusion as if she didn't understand why he was questioning it.

'And children too?'

'Yes love, two daughters, your first will be here by the end of next year.'

Cameron smiled and shook his head. 'She's a bit sad today, actually. I told her the story of the family curse, she got freaked out by it.'

Lavender rolled her eyes. 'I'm not surprised, you can't just tell someone you're their soul mate when you've only known them for a few days. You have to tread lightly, with Milly especially. She's scared to put her trust in you for her future. You can't just present it to her as a fait accompli.'

'I didn't, that's not why I told the story …'

'The best thing you can do to get her to trust you is agree to be in the Summer Solstice play.'

Cameron stared at her for a moment and then laughed. 'Good try Lavender, but I'm not doing it.'

'Milly has already agreed to be in it. It's important to her and it will show your commitment to her.'

Cameron shook his head in exasperation. He guessed it would be one way to put a smile back on her face but he had been thinking of something along the lines of flowers or chocolates rather than public humiliation.

—

Cameron sat staring at a scene of his new book on the laptop. No matter how many times he tried, he couldn't get the words to say what he wanted them to.

He glanced over at Milly, who was still diligently researching the castle. She had seemed back to her normal cheery self when he had returned with the shopping hours before. She had been singing what sounded like Disney songs as she danced around the kitchen tidying everything up like a proper Cinderella. He had noticed that the cameo box had been removed and he didn't dare ask where it had gone. She had been delighted with the peonies he had picked for her from the castle grounds, which were now displayed proudly in a vase in the middle of the table.

As long as he never mentioned the cameo or the legend of the Heartstone curse again, everything would be fine. Though he had been as shocked as she was when she'd reduced the stone heart to dust.

He returned his attention to the laptop and the words swam before his eyes. It was getting late now and really he should just give up and go to bed, but he didn't want to be faced with sorting this scene out tomorrow. He would clear it up tonight, then he could go to bed.

'Cameron.'

'Hmmm,' he answered, but he was only really half listening.

'This hot movie sex that you always have?'

She had his fullest attention now. He looked across the table at her. 'Yes.'

'Is it really the sort of sex you see in movies, when you tumble through the door, ripping each other's clothes off and do it on the nearest hard surface?'

He thought back to his last few sexual experiences. 'Pretty much.'

She thought about this for a moment. 'I must say, I do like the sound of the whole clothes being ripped off scenario. Adam never ripped my clothes off. We used to undress ourselves and then Adam liked them to be folded neatly on the chair.'

He leaned forward across the table. 'When I make love to you for the first time it will be in my bed, it will be slow and sensuous and I'm really going to take my time getting to know you, to pleasure you. If you want I can tear your clothes off before we get that far but the fun stuff, screwing you on the kitchen table and in every room of the castle, that can come later. I'm going to make love to you first.'

She stared at him, her eyes wide, her mouth slightly open in shock.

'You're going to make love to me?'

'As you're clearly my soul mate, I think it's best we make love first, banish that curse once and for all.'

As soon as he'd said it he wanted to snatch it back. It had been a joke to try to lighten the mood between them, instead he'd just made it a million times worse. She stared at him for a moment and then burst out laughing.

'It's ridiculous, isn't it? The curse, the cameo, the stone heart, the dragon necklace. It's all just one ludicrous coincidence.'

He nodded. 'The story has dragons, evil witches and a family curse in it, of course it can't be true.'

She carried on laughing, shaking her head incredulously.

'Can I see the cameo?'

She nodded, obviously finding the whole thing hilarious, which he was relieved to see. She got up and disappeared into the lounge. A few moments later she returned and passed him the black box. She hovered near him for a moment and he patted the bench next to him. She climbed over and sat by his side.

He opened the box and studied the cameo for a moment, flipping it over to look at the back and then the front again. 'I can see why you would think it's the same one, they're both very similar. But I doubt it is. The cameo was actually supposed to be one of the treasures that Uncle Boris carried around with him in his chest. If Boris and the chest are lost at sea, I doubt the cameo could suddenly turn up here. Besides even if it was the same one, this cameo wasn't yours, it wasn't passed down through the generations, Jamie only bought it for you yesterday.'

She smiled up at him with relief. 'Exactly, it's not really mine. Your soul mate is probably wandering around out there looking for this.'

'Soul mates are such a ridiculous notion anyway; two people who are so intrinsically linked that when they are born again in a new body, they seek each other out because they are destined to be together.'

She laughed. 'Fairy tales don't come true. There are no happy ever afters in life, where everything is perfect. We'll save that for the movies.'

'And the hot movie sex, that should stay in the movies too?'

'Oh I don't know, I'm definitely willing to give that a try.'

'But not the happy ever after?'

'That pot of gold at the end of the rainbow doesn't exist, so there's no point in looking for it. Doesn't mean we can't enjoy the rainbow and have fun splashing in puddles when the sun comes out.'

Cameron didn't really know what she meant by that metaphor but he didn't totally like the sound of it. He closed the lid on the cameo and passed it back to her.

'I really doubt that it's part of some ancient family curse. It's a beautiful piece of jewellery and Jamie bought it for you so you should definitely wear it.'

'I will,' she smiled brightly at him. 'I'm going to bed.'

She kissed him briefly on the cheek and disappeared towards her bedroom.

He stared after her, a huge lump in his throat, and then let his head sink into his hands. He had to sort out his feelings for her. There was an attraction there, an undeniable chemistry that hummed between them but it ran deeper than that and they both knew it. But if he was going to be with her, if he was finally going to let himself fall in love again it had to be for all the right reasons; not because she had broken the thousand year old stone heart, nor because she had a tattoo of a dragon wrapped around a heart and certainly not because she seemingly carried the exact same cameo that his great aunt Sophia had worn on her wedding day. He would not fall in love because fate and legends and curses had decreed that Milly was his soul mate. If she was truly going to capture his heart, he had to get to know her a lot better first.

He thought back to their conversation about hot movie sex and smiled. As Milly said, it would be a lot of fun finding out.

—

Milly was singing in the kitchen as she made breakfast when a very dishevelled looking bear staggered sleepily from his pit.

She giggled when she saw Cameron, his hair sticking out everywhere, his face all creased up. She had an overwhelming urge to go over and straighten his hair for him. He was only wearing his pyjama bottoms again and she couldn't help but stare when he absently scratched his chest. She had a strong desire to go and do that for him too.

'Did I wake you?'

'Yes.'

'Oh … Sorry.'

She walked past him to get a chopping board and he caught her round the waist, pulling her against him.

'Being woken up by your singing is lovely, you have a beautiful voice and I can't think of a nicer way to start each morning. Well, apart from waking up with you in my arms, that would be pretty perfect.'

He leaned in closer for a kiss and she stopped him with her hand on his chest, but even that simple touch sent a twist of desire straight down to her groin.

'Cameron, I'm working.'

'It's not even nine o'clock yet, you can't be working twenty-four hours a day. Besides, I think you have no intention of taking on the castle as a Castle Heritage property. I think you came here, saw my hot little ass and decided you wanted a piece of it and that's why you stayed.'

Milly gaped at him, he had no idea how close to the mark he was with that statement. She had acted unprofessionally. She had known as soon as she saw it that they probably couldn't take it on, but she hadn't wanted to disappoint him. She hadn't even been going to stay the week but then she had got carried away with secret passageways, ghosts and legends of treasure and curses. The castle had pulled her in and so had he. Right now she never wanted to leave and that scared and thrilled her in equal measure.

'It's ok baby, you can have my ass anytime you want it.'

She giggled and he bent his head lower, just brushing her lips with the softest of touches when there was a loud knock on the door.

Before they could move apart, the door opened and Lavender poked her head round. She clapped excitedly when she saw them together.

'Oooh, don't mind us dears,' Lavender said bustling in, leaving the door open for Constance and Gladys who giggled and cooed excitedly seeing them so close. Milly inched apart without straying too far from Cameron's side.

'We just wanted to talk to you about tonight's celebrations,' Gladys said. 'The village is delighted you are taking part.

Cameron sighed. 'We're not doing it.'

'Oh, shush, of course you are. Young Milly here promised you would, we're so pleased,' Gladys said.

'What?' Cameron looked down at her. 'I'm not ...'

Milly wasn't going to have this argument with him here. She had to get Dick back and she wasn't above using Cameron to do it. Out of sight of the old ladies, she ran her hand over his bum and gave it a tight squeeze, silencing any more protests from him.

'The Lord of the castle has always taken part in the Summer Solstice celebrations. It ensures we have good fortune for the next year. It would be bad luck for you not to be involved in some way or another,' Lavender said.

'So, Milly, you're going to wear this,' Constance shook out a floor length, white oversized nightdress that was definitely not flattering in any way. 'And Lord Heartstone, we have a helmet for you.' This resulted in giggles from the other two ladies. 'You both need to be down on the green by ten pm at the latest to be prepared for the play, but of course there's lots of fun and games that go on before it starts. Though they are mostly for the children, we'd be delighted to have you there, too. There'll be plenty of food and drink beforehand and the play will take place just before midnight so the erm … finale can happen as the clock strikes twelve. After that, there'll be more eating and drinking and fireworks too. It's a good night.'

Milly nodded and Cameron didn't say anything, maybe her hand on his bum had rendered him speechless.

'Well, we don't want to keep you two lovebirds from … whatever it was you were doing before we rudely interrupted, so we'll see you later.'

The ladies left, giggling and whispering between them.

The second the door was closed, Cameron turned on her.

'You promised I would do it?'

'Oh, stop being a grump, it's a bit of fun.'

'Why did you promise that?'

'They are holding my car to ransom. If I get you to be in the play they'll give me my car back.'

'They can't do that.'

'Look it's a silly play, why won't you do it?'

'I'm not doing it.'

'Do it for me.'

He faltered in his tirade for a moment as he thought about it, then shook his head. 'No, sorry baby, I'm not doing it.'

'Why not?'

'Because the whole play is done naked, that's why.'

Milly had no words, no words at all.

—

Milly had enjoyed the festivities immensely. She had watched the children run around the green trying to find the Solstice cookies. She had watched the inauguration of four-year-old Seth as he was given the very heavy chains of mayoral office to wear. There had been strawberry bobbing – *because apples aren't in season, dear* – hook a duck, a coconut shy and lots of other fun and games. She had chatted to almost everybody in the village and fallen a little bit in love with their completely bonkers personalities. But the best part of the night was that Cameron hadn't left her side. He had held her hand ever since they had left the castle, which had made them the subject of many a raised eyebrow and he simply didn't care. And he had agreed to be in the play because he wanted to make her happy.

As the sun had set over the sea, there had been cheers of celebration and she and Cameron had drunk hot alcoholic punch which had gone completely to her head. Now, half way through the play, she was finding everything hilarious, especially the sheer amount of willies.

It had started off innocently enough; the children had led her into the arena area on the green, singing, dancing and playing musical instruments. It had been beautiful and charming. And then it had got very weird.

To say the whole play was performed completely naked was a slight exaggeration on Cameron's part but it wasn't far off. As the men poured into the small arena, cartwheeling, twirling and leaping, Milly felt her mouth fall open. Every single man was wearing a full length, skin tight, body stocking. The stockings were coloured in earthy tones of green, brown and grey and were thankfully not see-through, but they left very little to the imagination.

Milly didn't know where to look. From her position, tied to the tree in the middle of the village green, she had a prime view of every willy in the village as they danced and wiggled and bounced up and down in front of her. She stifled another giggle as she forced her eyes away from the inappropriate bulges and tried to focus on her role as damsel in distress. She couldn't stop laughing.

It was a male-only play, with the exception of her part as the sacrificial virgin. Luckily her role did not require nudity. She had been dressed in an oversized white floor length nightie with flowers entwined in her hair. She had had to use the cameo brooch to keep the nightie on her as it was so big it kept falling off.

She had no idea what the play was about as the story was communicated through music, dancing and chanting in some obscure language that sounded like it might be Old Norse. She was only thankful that all the men were wearing masks so she had no idea which bulge belonged to whom, otherwise she'd never be able to look any of the villagers in the eye again. The edges of the self-made stage were lined with every woman in the village, who were eyeing the willies on display with much enthusiasm and cheering. She spotted Lavender, Constance and Gladys all clapping and enjoying the proceedings with much hilarity. The children were seated on the grass, innocently entertained by the play. Some of the men had blatantly stuffed their body stockings as their bulges were abnormally huge and a few of the socks that had been used for padding had travelled from their original position with all the dancing and now looked like mutant growths on their bellies or half way down their legs.

Suddenly all the men dropped to the ground in a bow with their heads touching the grass, leaving a path between her and the fake cave at the far side of the arena.

The men started chanting, 'Oogie, Oogie, Oogie' over and over again and the women and children joined in too.

Ah, the legend of the Oogie monster was about to be explained. Milly looked up at the cave, trying not to focus on the neat rows of scantily clad bottoms that were saluting the moon.

From the back of the cave came a creature who Milly assumed must be the Oogie, as when he appeared the chanting got louder. This was played by a very large man with a huge belly and a long beard that stuck out from underneath his mask, which was painted to make him look like some kind of sea creature with tentacles dripping from his face.

He slowly moved down the pathway towards her and the men stood up behind him, some of them chanting, some of them resuming their drum playing in steady beats like war drums. Milly shifted uneasily, suddenly wishing her hands weren't tied quite so tight.

The Oogie reached her and then turned round to face the audience, rubbing his belly greedily. The audience laughed and many of the children booed. He moved back down towards his cave where two men presented him with a very large knife and a fork.

He laughed manically at the sky and the chanting got louder and louder when suddenly he charged towards her, knife and fork raised.

She had been told to scream at the appropriate time, and now, suddenly fearing for her life, seemed as good a time as any. The scream ripped from her throat when suddenly she was blinded by a flash of fire.

The Oogie fell to the ground and so did the men.

From behind the tree came a fire breather, blowing out great swathes of fire from the sticks he was holding, his body stocking covered entirely in green shimmery scales. Behind him was a man in silver, his stocking made to look like chainmail. His face was hidden behind a silver knight's helmet. Milly was vaguely aware of two more green scaled men behind the knight, one playing the part of the dragon's wings and one playing the part of its tail, but her attention was on the knight in shining armour who was undoubtedly Cameron.

Her mouth was suddenly dry.

He drew his sword from his belt – the only other piece of clothing he was wearing apart from the helmet – and ran towards the Oogie, who stood up to face his attacker whilst Cameron's dragon dealt mercilessly with all the other men. Soon the Oogie and Cameron were the only ones left on the stage as they fought each other in slow motion. Cameron defeated the Oogie, plunging his clearly retractable sword into its belly. The Oogie, obviously mortally wounded, staggered off to its cave and the crowd cheered. The drumming stopped as Cameron turned to face her.

She tried to swallow but there was no moisture in her mouth at all. The thin body stocking showed every muscle in his strong body; his hard chest, his washboard abs, his huge thighs. Her eyes wandered down and she could barely tear her gaze away.

He moved closer, so close she could feel his heat and smell his intoxicating scent, which seemed stronger and more potent out here under the moon. He removed his helmet and stared at her with heated eyes.

Suddenly he kissed her, his hands at her waist pulling her close. The crowd cheered. He was demanding with his mouth, his tongue sliding against hers in one hot, passionate kiss. She could hear fairy-like music getting louder as he kissed her, bells and chimes and what sounded like a harp. His hands skimmed her sides, until he reached her wrists, and he untied her from the tree.

He gathered her close, walking back with her towards the middle of the stage and Milly suddenly realised why he was reluctant to let her out of his arms. If she stepped back now, the village would clearly see how turned on he was after that kiss.

He knelt down on the ground, causing her to quickly kneel too, to save his embarrassment. Another figure appeared, a man dressed in a gold cassock, making him look a bit like a vicar. He put a hand on each of their heads, as Cameron held her close, staring into her eyes. The vicar chanted words neither of them could understand and suddenly everyone was cheering and standing up and throwing petals over them. The clock in the church tower chimed midnight.

And then the vicar said the first English words she had heard since the play began. 'You may kiss the bride.'

Bride?

Cameron didn't need to be told twice though, his mouth came down on hers hard, one hand in her hair, the other round her back. As the last petals fell softly in her hair and on their faces, she closed her eyes and lost herself in the kiss. People cheered again and then as the kiss continued, the voices and laughter became more and more faint.

Milly opened one eye and realised they were completely alone, the pub on the other side of the green a sudden hive of activity.

She pulled away to look at Cameron.

'I think it's over.'

'Tell me again why I protested so strongly about this.'

'Because you didn't want anyone to see your willy,' she giggled.

'Small price to pay,' he kissed her again and she let him, there wasn't a single part of her now that could have stopped him.

Maybe it was the scent of the incense burning on the flares nearby, maybe it was the hot punch, maybe it was just Cameron and his strong arms, his intoxicating scent and his incredible kiss, but she wanted this man more than she had ever wanted anything or anyone.

She pulled away slightly. 'We should get up.'

He groaned softly, leaning his forehead against hers. 'I'm going to need a few more minutes first.'

She dipped her head, pressing her mouth to his throat, layering kisses down his neck to his collarbone.

'Shit, Milly, that's not helping.'

'Good.'

He frowned. 'What do you mean good?'

Feeling silly and brazen she ran her hands down his back and squeezed his bum. 'I'm on holiday which means, as of five o'clock tonight, I'm no longer here in a professional capacity.'

CHAPTER 14

He stared at her for a second, before leaping to his feet. She had a brief moment of seeing him in all his glory before he grabbed a blanket from a nearby chair and wrapped it round his hips. Then he came back for her, almost yanking her to her feet in his enthusiasm and started marching back to the castle, dragging her behind him.

She giggled at this new, wonderful turn of events.

'You sure you don't want to stay for the fireworks?' Cameron asked, walking so quickly that she had to run to catch up with him.

'I'm pretty sure our own fireworks will be pretty spectacular.'

He laughed but didn't break his step.

As soon as they reached the castle gates they both started to run but Milly had to stop a few seconds later.

'Owww the gravel, I need to go back for my shoes.'

Cameron was hopping around too. 'There's no time for that.'

He quickly pulled her to the safety of the soft grass and they ran up the hill towards the castle, giggling and laughing like school kids.

'Perhaps this is what the drawbridge was built for,' Cameron said, pulling her across the wood which covered the gravel into the courtyard and into the old kitchen. As soon as the door closed behind them Cameron pushed her up against the wall, kissing her hard, his lips were soft, the taste of him exquisite as his hands wandered over her body.

'Cameron …'

'It's ok, just a few minutes, baby.'

He grabbed her hand again, striding out of the kitchen into the banquet hall, seemingly much more in control than she was. She wanted him now, even if that meant here on the cold stone floor.

He burst into the corridor that held the staff quarters and into his kitchen, locking the outside door as he almost ran past.

'We don't want to be disturbed again.'

He led her through the lounge into his bedroom and closed the door behind her, staring down at her as if he wanted to eat her. The only light filling the room came from the moon outside. His face was partly in darkness, making him look dangerous.

He kissed her softly, gently this time, his hands at her hips as he slowly inched the material up over her body, breaking the kiss for just a second as he pulled the nightie over her head and let it drop to the floor.

His hands were exploring her body again, but this time his velvety touch against her bare skin was almost too much to bear.

She ran her hands over his back, feeling the muscles taut underneath his skin. Her fingers found the top of the blanket and she pushed it down over his hips. Now the only thing between him and her was his silvery body stocking which sparkled in the light of the moon, but there didn't seem to be any quick way to rid him of it. He suddenly stepped back out of her reach.

'I want to look at you, Milly.' Cameron whispered, as if talking normally might break the spell between them.

She was panting, like she had run a mile, she could hardly breathe. Why was he standing there, not doing anything? Shit, was he turned off?

A bubble of fear, self-doubt and frustration welled in her chest just as Cameron slammed into her, kissing her hard.

'You're so beautiful.'

He quickly removed her bra, groaning against her mouth as he ran tentative hands over her breasts.

Without taking his lips from hers, he scooped her up and carried her to the bed, lying down with her. He continued to kiss her, hungrily, possessively.

His hands slid to her hips and dipped under the waistband of her knickers, slowly sliding them off. He shuffled down the bed slightly, so he could remove them. He gave her a crafty look, before taking her nipple into his mouth.

'Camranemmom …' Milly groaned, and Cameron chuckled against her breast, the vibrations of which travelled straight to her core.

As the last item of her clothing was flung across the room, Cameron's hand moved slowly up between her legs.

He shifted back up the bed, so they were eye to eye as they lay next to each other.

'These last five days have been the longest foreplay ever,' Cameron said, kissing her just briefly.

'I know, so let's just skip that part and go straight for the main event.'

'Not a chance.'

Cameron slid his fingers over the apex of her thighs. It took very little time to coax her to the very edge and suddenly she hurtled over it, her orgasm ripping through her so fast, so unexpectedly, that she cried out, desperate for him to stop and begging him to continue all in the same glorious moment.

Only when her heart and her breathing had slowly returned to normal did he take his hands from her.

'We need to get you out of that ridiculous outfit,' Milly reached for the neck hole and started to pull.

Cameron had a different idea, grabbing the material at the chest and ripping it open like Superman. She helped to push it off his shoulders and he wriggled it off his hips until he was completely and impressively naked next to her.

She watched him fumble in the drawers next to the bed, heard the tear of foil and she lay back as he knelt between her legs.

She eyed the pack of twenty condoms on the top of the drawers and sighed.

'Do you have many girls up here?'

Cameron shifted himself on top of her. 'You're the first. I bought those yesterday after our conversation. You're actually the first in a long time.'

Milly frowned slightly, not sure how to take this. Was he just feeling horny and in desperate need for sex? Did he have any feelings for her at all? How would things be between them tomorrow?

'You ok?' Cameron lay down gently on top of her, wrapping her legs round his hips.

'Just a little nervous.'

He smiled, kissing her so softly and sweetly that all doubts went out the window. Her head lived too much in the future when really she just needed to enjoy the now.

He was still holding back and it must have taken every ounce of strength he had not to just thrust into her.

'We don't have to do this, we can just cuddle instead.'

'You don't like cuddling.'

'That's where you're wrong, I like cuddling with you. Almost as much as I like having sex. But if I had to rank it, making love would come out on the very top.'

She smiled. 'Above all the clothes ripping sex and the sex on the table, on the floor, up against the wall?'

'Without a doubt.'

She stroked his face and pulled him tighter against her.

He didn't need any further encouragement as he pushed gently inside her. She wrapped her arms round him, cradling him against her.

He moved slowly as he stared into her eyes. It was so tender, so sweet, so beautiful, Milly had never experienced anything like it. He bent his head and kissed her, his hunger for her undeniable as he devoured her gasps and moans with his mouth.

Fireworks suddenly lit up the sky outside the window, sending trails of silver and scarlet across the night sky.

Milly closed her eyes and as Cameron moved deeper inside her, increasing slightly in speed, she smiled against his lips as she enjoyed her own private fireworks.

—

Milly woke up with Cameron curled around her back, his hand stroking the outside of her thigh and peppering little kisses over her shoulder and the back of her neck. She could barely open her eyes. They'd done it three times the night before, how was that even possible? She had never done it more than once in a night before. With Adam she was lucky if they did it more than once a week. But with Cameron, every time had been quite simply the best sex she'd ever had.

She sleepily rolled over in his arms and wrapped her hands round his neck. As they lay side by side, she could feel him ready to go again. She was tired and a bit sore but he looked like he could carry on all day.

'You're insatiable.'

He grinned. 'Just ignore it, it'll go in a minute.'

'So last night, did you enjoy it?' Milly asked.

He shifted her a bit closer. 'Immensely.'

'I meant the play, you pervert! I'm in no doubt that you enjoyed yourself in here, if your shouts and moans were anything to go by.'

'Oh, the play. It wasn't really to my taste, too much cock for my liking.'

'Oh yes, there was plenty of that.'

He raised his eyebrows. 'You enjoyed it then? All those half naked men, is that what got you so horny?'

Milly kissed him. 'There was one man, one willy that made me horny. Everything else just made me laugh.'

'So we're husband and wife now,' Cameron said.

'Yes, apparently so. You'll have to take me on a honeymoon so we can have hot sex all day.'

'We can do that here.'

'Yes but if we're on a honeymoon, we can have room service delivered for every meal and we wouldn't have to leave the bed for pesky things like cooking.'

'That's true.'

He nibbled little kisses against her throat. She wrapped her arms and legs around him and rolled him so she was on top. She sat up and looked down at him, marvelling that this beautiful man was hers to play with for at least the next week. How had that happened?

'The view is pretty great here,' Cameron said, reaching up to cup her breasts. 'But I do like the idea of being waited on while we have hot sex all day. How about Bognor Regis? I can stretch to that.'

'Ha. I think we can do better than that.'

He frowned slightly and she leaned forward to kiss him again.

'Where do you want to go?' Cameron asked.

'Norfolk is lovely. Or Scotland?'

His frown faded and he sat up, his hands going to her hips to steady her. 'You don't want much, do you? Fast cars or luxurious holidays, you don't want any of that. You were as impressed with my cheese on toast and tomato soup the other night as you would have been if I'd presented you with lobster and caviar.'

'Not a fan of caviar, tried it once, bit tangy for my liking. And I don't like that you cook the poor lobster whilst it's still alive, so no, that's not for me either.'

He smiled and kissed her as she wrapped her arms round his neck. She pulled back slightly so she could look into his eyes.

'Money can't buy you happiness, not really. You make me happy, you make me feel blissfully content and last night, when you made love to me for the first time, I was happier than I've been for a very long time,' Milly said.

His eyes were soft as he kissed her.

Suddenly there was a loud knocking, probably on the outside kitchen door. Milly jumped.

'What's that?'

He frowned for a moment. 'Crap, I think that's Olivia, my PA. I honestly forgot she was coming, I should have cancelled when you agreed to stay.'

Milly pulled a face, remembering that Cameron had said she was coming today. 'Well I guess the honeymoon is over.' She pulled back slightly but Cameron's hands tightened round her hips, holding her in place.

'She can wait a moment,' Cameron said.

She was about to protest, she wanted to at least be dressed when she met his PA for the first time but as he kissed her, his hands caressing over her body, any more thoughts vanished from her mind.

—

It was nearly fifteen minutes later when Cameron unlocked the kitchen door for Olivia. They had showered together, though Milly had stopped him from having shower sex with her and now he'd left her to get dressed.

He opened the door and saw Olivia sitting on the grass with her laptop open, typing away quite happily. She had removed her jacket in the summer heat and her arms looked tanned in the short sleeved blouse she was wearing. A butterfly fluttered round her head, her chestnut hair gleaming in the sunlight as it billowed in soft waves over one shoulder. She was a pretty woman, although he had never really been attracted to her. She looked up at him, her feline green eyes sparkling with gold flecks as she flashed him a huge smile.

'Hello sleepy head,' she got up, dusting off her trouser suit, closed her laptop and walked towards him, immediately kissing him on the cheek. When had their professional relationship progressed to that? She had been with him for a little less than a year and it had never started that way. But somehow over the months, that greeting had become commonplace. He supposed they had become friends and he certainly had female friends that greeted him that way, even the ones that were married.

'Hi, Liv, sorry to keep you waiting.' Cameron said as she squeezed past him into the kitchen.

'It's no problem, I had some work to do anyway, so it's no hassle. And it was nice sitting out there in the sunshine to do it. This place though, Cam! I don't know whether to laugh or cry for you. It's a bit ridiculous, isn't it?'

'Do you know what, it's starting to grow on me.'

'Really? I can see that with your wonderful imagination it would be a great place to write, but you're not thinking about staying here, are you? It would cost millions to repair and after

Eva bled you dry you're hardly in a position to be paying out for all this stuff.'

'I don't know, I'm thinking about it.' He had to tell her about Milly so it wasn't such a shock when they met, but suddenly it was too late for that. Milly walked into the kitchen wearing her knee length shorts and a bright pink sparkly T-shirt with nothing on her feet. She looked cute and adorable.

Olivia, to her credit, barely batted an eye, although she was used to the influx of women that seemed to flock round him, and the ones she had met the morning after he'd spent the night with them.

Milly looked awkward and nervous and he wanted to say something that would make her laugh. 'This is my wife, Milly.'

Milly blushed so she was the same shade of pink as her T-shirt. He didn't know who looked more shocked by his statement; Milly, because he had just presented the fake marriage the night before as something real, or Olivia, who he'd last seen just before coming to the castle when he swore he was never going near a woman again. He looked between the two of them. His money was on Olivia.

Milly looked absolutely mortified and he regretted having done anything to upset her.

Olivia recovered first, rearranging her features into an expression of complete professionalism. 'You're married? Well congratulations, I'm really happy for you.'

'Nah, not really, we were just involved in some play last night and we got married in that. We were just joking about our honeymoon.'

Olivia laughed with relief. 'You had me going there. So you two are …'

Cameron held out a hand for Milly and she took it. He pulled her into his arms and planted a kiss on her forehead. He wasn't sure which word to use to best describe his relationship with Milly. Girlfriend, lover, business associate. None of those were particularly good. He settled on one that was safest.

'She's my friend.'

Milly looked up at him in confusion and he pressed a sweet kiss to her lips so Olivia would be in no doubt as to what kind of friend she was.

Olivia smiled. She had seen it all before, but somehow he wanted to tell her that Milly was different.

'I'll just get my bags and perhaps you can show me to my room.'

Cameron gave a vague nod but he was looking at Milly who was still blushing furiously.

Olivia stepped outside and Milly pulled out of his arms. 'Why did you do that?'

'What?' Cameron said, smiling at her outrage.

'Introduce me as your wife and then make it very clear we're together.'

'We are together and how would you like me to introduce you?'

'As Milly from Castle Heritage.'

'You wanted to retain your professional image. I can hardly introduce you as the person from Castle Heritage that I'm now sleeping with and maintain any of your integrity.'

'You didn't have to mention that we're sleeping together at all.'

He stepped closer to her, all humour now gone. 'You might be ashamed that you slept with some scruffy writer with no qualifications, but I'm not ashamed of you. If I want to kiss you or touch you or take you to bed and make love to you until you shout out my name, I will. I'm not going to hide it from her.'

Olivia walked through the back door dragging a small suitcase behind her.

'Cameron, if you could show me to my room?'

He stared at Milly for a moment and then turned towards the door that joined the corridor with the other staff quarters.

He opened it and pointed to Olivia. 'The last room on the right hand side. The bed is made up for you.'

If he was any sort of gentleman he would carry her bags down for her, but whilst his tentative relationship with Milly was teetering on shaky legs, he needed to right things with her first.

Olivia shuffled past him into the corridor and he closed the door behind her. He turned back to face Milly.

'Look, you're on holiday for a week. We haven't discussed what will happen after that week, whether you will continue to work here for a few days to complete your tests, but I won't be allowed to kiss you or touch you during that time because you'll be working. Or whether you will leave here with a casual wave and not a backward glance and I'll never get to see you again. I don't think either of us know where this is going and that's what this week was supposed to be about, wasn't it? Finding out whether it is just a sexual attraction or something deeper, something worth fighting for. So if I only have a week, I want to be able to kiss you and touch you whenever the mood arises. Yes, I wanted Olivia to know we are in a relationship because I'm not going to waste a single moment sneaking around and pretending we're not and I wanted to protect your precious reputation by introducing you as my friend rather than the girl from Castle Heritage. I'm sorry if I got that wrong.'

Milly's stance had softened during his speech and he hoped he'd had some effect.

'Ok,' she said, quietly.

'Ok?'

She nodded, coming towards him, wrapping her arms round his back and leaning her head against his chest. 'I'm sorry.'

He sighed with relief.

'And I'm not ashamed of you, not for one second,' she mumbled into his chest.

'Ok.'

'I've always just been Milly from Castle Heritage, it's hard to be just Milly.'

'The girl that I've … that I'm …' He pulled her chin up to face him. 'The girl that I'm sort of falling for is just Milly. Remember that.'

Milly stared at him with wide eyes. 'You're … falling for me?'

He held his thumb and finger about a centimetre apart. 'Maybe a tiny bit.'

She giggled and pushed his thumb and finger further apart. 'That's better. We are husband and wife after all.'

He kissed her on the head just as Olivia walked back into the room.

He turned away from Milly and went to the fridge. 'Do you two lovely girls want breakfast?'

Olivia sat down at the table opposite Milly. 'I'll just have a slice of toast, please.'

'I'll have a full English please, I'm starving,' Milly said.

'Me too. Two full English breakfasts coming up, sure you don't want the full works, Liv?'

'No thank you.' Olivia smiled and then diverted her attention to Milly. 'So, how long have you two known each other?'

Cameron smiled to see that Olivia was at least making an effort, even if she thought that Milly was another of his one night stands.

'It feels like a lifetime,' Milly said and Cameron smirked as he turned away to deal with breakfast.

'And what is it you do?' Olivia asked. She was so sweet sometimes. She somehow knew that Milly was feeling nervous and was trying to put her at ease. Although she had asked the one question that was going to be tricky to answer.

'I … I'm a dendrochronologist.'

'Oh, that sounds interesting, what's that?'

'Milly has been helping me with the castle,' Cameron interrupted, watching the bacon sizzle in the pan. 'You'll have to read my story while you're here, Liv, it's going really well. The words have flowed much easier over the last few days.'

'Yes, I'd love to. I'm sure it's up to the normal high standards of your first series.'

That was a very diplomatic way of saying the second series was shit.

'I've told him not to write anything crap, we don't want a repeat of the utter rubbish that was the *Hidden Faces* series,' Milly said and Cameron smiled to himself.

'Cameron is a very gifted writer, every word he writes is pure gold,' Olivia said, defensively.

'It's all right Liv, Milly knows I didn't write it. Anyway, I'm taking a week's holiday from it now, while Milly is here. I'll feel a lot fresher when I go back to it.'

'I don't think you should let yourself get distracted,' Olivia said. 'You need to meet your deadline.'

'My deadline isn't until the beginning of August, I have plenty of time.'

The kettle boiled and he made three cups of tea and carried them to the table.

'How did it go with Castle Heritage?'

Cameron thought about how to answer that for a moment. 'It's still ongoing.'

'I thought they were coming out last week?'

'They did, we need to wait for the test results.'

'Did they seem keen?'

'I don't know. It's tricky because a lot of the exterior is not part of the original building. But I have a really good offer from Extravagance.'

'I thought you were going to go with Palace Hotels if Castle Heritage couldn't help you?'

'I never said that, I said I would consider it, but the offer from Extravagance is much better, plus I get to stay here too.'

'You're seriously thinking of staying here?'

'The last few days have shown me what I've been missing. I've seen it in a new light.'

'Have you signed anything, agreed to anything?' Olivia asked.

'No, not yet.'

He dished up the two breakfasts onto plates and the piece of toast too and carried them all over to the table.

'Let me look into this Extravagance company first. I've not heard of them, let me do some digging.'

'Go ahead,' Milly said, over the rim of her mug, daring Olivia to find any dirt on her brother. Milly was acting defensive with Olivia and he didn't know why. Olivia missed the underlying threat in Milly's voice completely but for Cameron it was as if she had shouted it.

'I just don't think you should sign with a bunch of cowboys.'

Cameron placed a restraining hand on Milly's shoulder before she could say anything.

'I'm very impressed with Extravagance but some research on them wouldn't hurt. And if Palace Hotels want to come back with a further offer, I'd definitely be open to it.'

He sat down next to Milly and gave her hand a squeeze under the table before he started eating his breakfast.

Milly didn't take her eyes off Olivia as she started to eat hers.

Cameron sighed. This blissful week he had planned was not turning out as well as he had expected.

—

'I need to go down to the village for some things, Milly do you want to come?' Cameron asked after breakfast.

'I'll come with you,' Olivia said, practically shooting out of her seat.

Milly smiled sweetly at him. 'I think I'll stay here.'

'Ok, well I'm having a rope ladder made, it's supposed to be ready to collect today. So when I come back …'

'Yes,' Milly interrupted, her eyes lighting up. She immediately pulled her pink sparkly trainers on. 'I'll get a few things ready.'

He opened the door and let Olivia go ahead of him. There was a white Triumph TR2 on the drive, an old classic car. It obviously wasn't Olivia's as her car, a sporty black BMW, was parked next to it, so it had to belong to Milly. The villagers had been as good as their word.

'Hey Milly, is this yours?' Cameron called back into the kitchen.

Milly peered round the door and then threw herself at the car, leaning her head on the bonnet with her arms wide as if she was actually hugging it. Cameron couldn't help the huge grin from spreading over his face.

'Dick, they brought you back, are you ok?'

She was talking to the car, Cameron didn't think he'd seen anything so adorable before.

'You call your car Dick?' Olivia asked.

'Yes, well my brother called him that and it sort of stuck.' Milly walked round the car, inspecting it from all angles.

'Why would you call your car Dick?'

'Because he looks like a whale shark.' She gestured to the unusual inverted grill underneath the bonnet that did indeed look like a giant mouth with teeth. 'You know, Moby Dick, the great white whale?'

Olivia laughed politely though he wasn't sure she totally got the reference.

'We'll see you soon,' Cameron said. He strode off down the drive, but realising that Olivia was struggling a bit in her heels on the gravel, he took her arm and guided her out the gates until they were on the smooth road outside.

'Milly seems nice,' Olivia said, though Cameron guessed that she was being diplomatic. 'Where did you two meet?'

Cameron knew that Olivia had wanted to come with him so she could talk to him about Milly.

'She's a friend.'

'How long has she been your friend?'

'It feels like a thousand years. Please don't worry about her.'

'Of course I worry, you're my friend and you don't pick wisely when it comes to the girls you choose to sleep with. First Eva screwed you for every penny you had and the last three have sold their stories to the papers.'

Cameron winced at the memory. The girls had all seemed nice, out for a quick shag, nothing serious. Maybe they had got involved with him in the hope they'd get taken to nice restaurants or be given expensive gifts, but none of them had seemed like the type to sell their stories to the papers. It really did go to show that you couldn't trust anyone. Olivia put a hand on his arm and he stopped to look at her. Her green eyes were soft with concern. He trusted Olivia, she was his friend and she only wanted the best for him.

'I don't want you to get hurt again. The last time I saw you, you said you were taking a break from women. And I understand that you get lonely, especially up here, but please be careful. You've already told Milly about the *Hidden Faces* series not being yours, if that sort of thing gets out you could be in a whole heap of trouble. You know most women are only after your money, that sort of information would be worth a fortune in the wrong hands.'

'Milly's not like that, she's different.'

'You said that about the last girlfriend, Stacey, and she screwed you over in the papers. All those lies she told about you, it broke my heart to read them.'

'I know, it hurt me too. I know you're worried but you don't need to be about Milly. Trust me.'

Cameron turned away, walking along the short road towards the green. Stacey had been very sweet, a bit ditzy maybe, but never in a million years had he thought she would ever go to the papers and sell them a complete pack of lies. She had even denied she had done it afterwards, sobbing down the phone to him. Of course he hadn't believed her, all the photos had come from her phone and there were snippets of real information in there that only Stacey and those closest to him would know.

He stepped out onto the village green. All the festivities from the night before had been cleared away, so no one would ever know what had gone on there. He looked at the giant oak tree in the middle which Milly had been tied to and smiled. Best night of his life.

Tucked into the corner of the L-shaped road was the little thatched pub. He wondered how welcome he would be in there now, since he had agreed to be in the play. Would the villagers stop chanting "Oogie" at him every time he walked past?

'Lord Heartstone,' a voice boomed out across the green.

Cameron turned to see the vicar that had married him and Milly the night before striding towards them. He was still wearing his cassock, making Cameron wonder if he was a real vicar.

The vicar shook his hand. 'Congratulations on the happy occasion. I presume, as you and Milly didn't join us for the celebrations last night, that you went home to consummate the marriage.'

Cameron blushed and Olivia stared between them in confusion.

'You did consummate the marriage, didn't you? It's very important.'

'Erm … yes.'

'Good, good, excellent in fact.' The vicar strode off and Cameron stared after him in confusion. The wedding the night before had been part of the play, it wasn't real. It couldn't be real.

He turned back to Olivia. 'Stay here for a second.'

He sprinted after the vicar.

'Wait, wait.' He caught up with him. 'The wedding, last night. That wasn't a real wedding was it?'

CHAPTER 15

Milly was drilling into one of the wooden beams in the banqueting hall when she heard Cameron return.

She heard him call for her.

Not wanting to draw attention to her whereabouts if he was with Olivia, she quickly put the sample from the beam into a bag, labelled it, plopped it into her briefcase with the other three samples she had taken and put the drill away.

'There you are, what are you doing?' Cameron asked as he walked towards her.

'Is Olivia with you?' she whispered.

'No, she's sending some emails in the kitchen.'

'I'm just doing a few tests now I've got the rest of my equipment back.'

'You're on holiday.'

'Believe it or not, this kind of stuff is exciting for me. Don't worry, it won't get in the way of … us. I just thought I'd do some while you were out.'

Cameron looked over her samples with interest. 'Tell me about it.'

Milly looked over Cameron's shoulder to make sure they were alone.

'It's called Dendrochronology, which is tree ring dating. We can tell a lot about the age of these pieces of wood from the rings.'

'One ring per year?'

She shook her head. 'No, it's not that simple, if a year had been particularly rainy then you might get several rings in that year. So we have to compare the samples with samples taken from other local trees that we have dated and the patterns at certain points will match up. It's quite a detailed process but I can show you some samples or photographs of samples I have with me and explain how I come up with an exact date.'

Cameron grinned. 'I'd love that.'

She looked at him and laughed. 'You would not! I'm such a geek and this stuff makes me really excited but you're very sweet for humouring me.'

He moved closer, his hand at her waist. 'I love your passion for stuff like this. It's infectious.'

She smiled. 'I've thought recently about becoming a lecturer and teaching people about it.'

'You would be amazing at that. Trust me when I say I could listen to you talk about it all day long.'

'Well, I'll bore you about it all one day. Not now though, we have a cove to explore. Did you get the rope ladder?'

He nodded.

'I put together a picnic. I know we've just had breakfast but I thought …' she trailed a finger over his chest. 'We could spend a little while down there.'

He smiled. 'I'd like that.'

'Well let's go.'

They walked back to the kitchen and Milly stowed her stuff in the cupboard in her bedroom, just in case Olivia was feeling a bit nosy. When she returned, Cameron had the picnic bag slung over one shoulder and what was probably the rope ladder in another bag.

Olivia was talking on the phone and Cameron waved to get her attention.

'Hold on one second,' Olivia said to whoever was on the other end of the phone and gave Cameron and Milly her undivided attention. Well, probably more Cameron than Milly.

'We're just heading out for a bit, will you be ok on your own for a while?'

'I'll be fine, I have a ton of emails to reply to so I'll be kept very busy. Go and have fun.' She flashed Cameron a huge smile and Milly tried to find a reason to hate her but couldn't. She was such a nice person and Milly regretted that her first impression of Olivia wasn't a good one.

Cameron escorted her out, taking her hand as he walked into the banquet hall.

'I'm sorry, I know it must be a bit weird for you, having Olivia here when we're just getting to know each other, but she's lovely, you'll like her a lot if you give her a chance.'

Remembering how accepting Cameron had been of Jamie just because she had vouched for him made her want to do the same for his friends.

'I will, I'm sorry, I just got the impression that she didn't like me when we first met.'

'Well, I'm sure that's not the case but if it was, it's only because she's looking out for me. She's scared I'm going to get hurt again. And she does a good job of organising me. I haven't got the patience or inclination to organise myself, I can't fault her for that. Look, let's try to enjoy ourselves over the next few days. I'm sure she will love you as much as I do before she goes and then she will know she's leaving me in safe hands.'

Milly nodded, determined to make a good impression on Olivia and to be nice to her too.

They walked quickly up the stairs and into the study. Cameron pushed the bookshelf open, and it swung easily now he had broken the locking mechanism.

As Milly stepped into the little chamber with him, he closed the shelf behind them, plunging them into darkness. Although she couldn't see him, just holding his hand was enough to keep her calm. He switched on his torch and unbolted the door and then closed it again behind them.

They made their way down the stairs in silence, following the tunnel to the fork and taking the right one that slanted steeply into the earth. Eventually, following the sounds of the sea, they came to the entrance in the cliff face.

Milly waited whilst Cameron secured the new rope ladder to the edge, tying the end to several rocks until he was happy. She looked out to the sea, it was a gorgeous sunny day, there wasn't a cloud in sight and the water was as flat as a millpond.

'I'll go first, make sure it's strong enough,' Cameron said as he pulled the picnic bag over his shoulder and swung himself out onto the ladder. Milly held her breath that it would be, it was quite a long way to fall if it broke.

Cameron confidently made his way down the ladder with ease and then shouted up for her to follow when he reached the bottom.

She carefully lowered herself over the edge but became more and more confident as she climbed down and realised the ladder clearly wasn't going to break.

As she neared the bottom, Cameron grabbed her waist and guided her down the last few rungs.

'Careful, these rocks are a bit slippery.'

She hopped down onto the sand and looked around. Her eyes fell on the upside down boat right next to where they stood.

It was wedged on top of the rocks and she wandered over to take a closer look at it.

'I wonder how long it's been here,' Milly said. Cameron dumped the bag on the sand away from the rocks and came to join her.

'Well, I'm no dendrochronologist but judging by the wood I'd say a long time.'

Milly laughed. 'The tide has been in many times which would cause the boat to rot much quicker than if it was on dry land but I suspect that the tide doesn't reach this high or this part of the beach otherwise I don't think there'd be much of the boat left at all.'

'Could explain why it's all broken,' Cameron suggested.

'It could, but I would suggest that the boat hit something big or something heavy fell on it whilst it was upside down.'

She ran her hand over the pale wood, it had been painted at one point but most of the paint had faded away now.

Cameron went around the other side and gasped.

'What?'

She hurried round. In very faded black writing was the name 'Sophia'.

'Do you think this was Uncle Boris's boat?' Milly asked, fingering the letters.

'He loved her, I know that much, it wouldn't be a far stretch that he called his boat after her.'

'It could belong to anyone.'

Cameron nodded. 'You're absolutely right, it could.'

'But … I bet no one comes here apart from the people that live in the castle. The cove itself is protected from the sea with all these rocks in the water. It would be quite difficult to negotiate a passage through them to get here.'

Cameron looked around them thoughtfully.

'There's a ring over there that you'd tie the boat to,' Cameron gestured to the far side of the cove where a rusty ring protruded out of the wall.

'So why is the boat here?' Milly said. 'I think this boat was dragged here and turned upside down for a reason.' She looked up at the cliff face. 'Someone had been trying to reach something.'

'By Jove, my dear Watson, I think I've got it,' Cameron said, putting an imaginary pipe into his mouth and pretending to smoke it.

Milly laughed. 'Pray tell, my dear Holmes.'

Cameron started striding up and down, gesturing with his imaginary pipe.

'Mad Uncle Boris took the treasure chest into his boat and hid it, maybe in a cave down the coast. He returned to the cove as the tide was coming in. He tied the boat up on the hook as he always did and returned to the rope ladder but as he started to climb, the ladder, after years of use, broke. Knowing he needed to be out of the cove before the tide came in, he dragged the boat underneath the ladder, turned it upside down and stood on it so he could reach the remains of the rope ladder. It was still too far, so he jumped, he missed, crashed through the bottom of the boat and fell, smashing his head on the rocks, killing him instantly.'

'You're full of the joys of spring, aren't you? What happened to his body?'

'It was washed out to sea.'

'I see, it's a good theory, but if Boris was stranded in the cove, wouldn't he just get back in the boat and go back out to sea before the tide came in? He could then return to land further down the coast. Why would his last resort be to turn the boat upside down and try to jump for the rope ladder?'

'He was mad, my dear Watson.'

'Ok, if that's the theory we're going with, his treasure is in a nearby cave.'

Cameron puffed on his imaginary pipe. 'I think we need a boat.'

Milly looked out at the sea. It was calm and looked inviting.

'We could swim out a little way, see if we can see any caves in the cliffs.'

'We could but we didn't bring our swimming gear.'

Milly smiled at him mischievously as she pulled her T-shirt off and threw it in the direction of the picnic bag. Cameron stared at her hungrily and she felt so beautiful. She quickly dispensed with the rest of her clothes and as Cameron made a grab for her she ran out into the water. The cold sliced into her skin and she screamed out, but dived quickly into the water, letting the waves glide over her head. She dived down to the bottom, getting used to the temperature quite quickly. It felt cool, not cold, once she had gotten over the initial shock. She surfaced a little way from the beach and turned back to look at Cameron.

'Come on in, it's lovely.'

Cameron pulled off his T-shirt and jeans and Milly gave a loud wolf whistle as he stood on the sand stark naked.

He stepped into the shallows and winced. 'You do realise that certain parts of my body will shrink in the cold.'

'That will make you normal sized then, you monster.'

He walked out a bit further then dived underneath the water, just as she had. He didn't resurface. Just as she was going to dive down to see if he was ok, she felt his mouth trailing kisses up her ankle, over her knee and towards her most sensitive area. But just as he was getting unbearably close, he emerged in front of her, leaving her almost panting.

She looped her arms round his neck and he hoisted her legs round his hips as he treaded water, keeping them both afloat. He didn't kiss her, he just stared at her, almost nose to nose. Her heart was filled with him, almost as if it would burst.

'I think I'm falling for you too,' she whispered.

He grinned. 'You are?'

'A teeny, tiny amount.' She gestured with her thumb and finger touching. 'Miniscule.'

'I'll take miniscule,' he said and kissed her.

Every kiss, every touch from him felt like the first ever kiss. She had been in love before, three times in fact, but this felt so different.

She felt the water swirl around her as he swam them both to a large rock, where he could stand. He pushed her back against the rock face, kissing her hard.

'Owww,' Milly cried out and then laughed.

'What?'

'You just impaled me on a barnacle, it went straight up my bum.'

Cameron tried but failed to keep a straight face.

'Let me have a look.'

'Don't laugh.'

He turned her round and encouraged her to bend over a flat rock. She felt him come up behind her.

'Don't get any ideas, Cameron Heartstone. I'm not having sex with you like this.'

'It hadn't even entered my mind.'

'I'm sure it hadn't.'

She felt his hand caress her bum. 'Your bum looks as perfect as it always does.' He moved his hand over her back, stroking over the tattoo that covered almost the whole of one side as if seeing it for the first time.

'Did you not see the tattoo last night?'

'I was too preoccupied last night to take the time to read all these words.' He started to read it. *'From this slumber, you shall wake, when true love's kiss, the spell shall break.'*

'It's from the film, *Sleeping Beauty*,' Milly explained.

'I see.' He leaned over her back and kissed it.

She rolled over to look at him. 'Try on the mouth instead.'

He smiled and bent over her. Catching her hands and entwining his fingers with hers, he moved her hands above her head, pinning her to the rock with his weight. He kissed her, with one sweet, soft kiss, then pulled back slightly to look at her.

'Are you awake now?'

'Yes.' He moved his mouth to her neck and she looked up at the sun burning brightly in a cloudless sky. She averted her eyes from the glare to look back at Cameron as he kissed across her collar bone. For the first time in years, perhaps in forever, she felt awake and alive, as if she was experiencing the world for the first time. She didn't like feeling like this around him, so completely out of control, but there was nothing she could do to stop it.

—

Milly lay on Cameron's chest on the beach, the hot summer sun warming her back as Cameron played with her hair. There was nothing that could burst her bubble of happiness right now, she just couldn't stop smiling. She glanced at her star bracelet and wished that she could stay there forever, where everything was perfect.

'So, I have something I need to tell you,' Cameron said, stroking up and down her back.

'Mmmm.'

'I don't want you to get freaked out by it.'

She propped herself up on her elbows to look at him, knowing she had a huge, dopey grin on her face.

Cameron took a deep breath. 'The play we took part in last night, with the wedding.'

Milly nodded.

'Turns out that was a real wedding.'

She felt the smile fall off her face. 'What?'

'If a couple wish to get married in the village, they do so by taking part in the Summer Solstice play. The vicar that married us, he's a real vicar.'

Milly sat up. 'So we're actually husband and wife?'

Cameron sat up too. 'No, of course not, it can't possibly be legal, but the villagers believe it is.'

Milly laughed. 'How is that even possible? Neither of us consented to marriage.'

'We consented by being in the play.'

She smiled as she remembered how insistent the old ladies had been about her and Cameron being in the play. 'They tricked us into being part of the play, no one said anything about marriage.'

'I know.'

She supposed she should be worried about being married to a man she had known for a week, even in some farcical capacity, but the whole thing was ridiculous. 'I don't understand how the villagers think it's official? We haven't signed anything.'

'I don't know. The vicar said it was official according to ancient local law.'

Milly laughed. 'That's hilarious.'

'That's what I thought, but every single person in the village came up and congratulated me, so they all believe in it too. And we can't exactly get it annulled. We came back and consummated the hell out of that wedding.'

She rolled her eyes and he laughed.

'Oh God,' Milly laughed. 'I even wore the cameo brooch, the one that Sophia and Alexandra supposedly wore on their wedding days. The nightie was too big and I used it to keep it from sliding off my shoulders.'

'Yeah, that's a bit freaky. So I guess the curse is officially broken.'

'Stop it,' Milly giggled. 'Wow I wore a nightie to my wedding day.'

'You looked beautiful.'

'You know I've imagined my wedding day many times, but I never envisaged it would be like that. There was a big plan.'

'You had a plan? I thought you don't believe in happy endings and marriage,' Cameron teased.

'I suppose I didn't believe in it for me, but it didn't stop me hoping that one day my prince would arrive on a white horse, fight the dragon and my demons and rescue me from the man sabbatical tower.'

'I do have a white horse, if that's any help?' Cameron said.

'You do not.'

'I do. His name's Colin, which is not grand enough for a trusty steed, but he is white. Tell me about the big plan.'

She laughed with embarrassment. 'I know it's cheesy and naff but I always wanted to arrive in a horse-drawn pumpkin carriage just like the one in *Cinderella* and then ... Have you seen *Tangled*?'

Cameron shook his head.

'Of course you haven't. There's a scene where Flynn and Rapunzel are in these boats and people have released Chinese lanterns into the sky and they're floating over the water and it just looks so beautiful … I imagined that one day I'd get married like that, on a boat surrounded by these lanterns.'

'Sounds perfect.'

'And instead I was surrounded by a load of willies,' Milly laughed, shaking her head at the complete craziness of the village.

Cameron laughed at the whole ridiculous situation.

'Why are you so calm about this?' Milly asked. 'You said you were on a sabbatical from women and now, as far as the village is concerned, you're married to one and you don't seem bothered.'

'After Eva left me, my ex-wife, I swore I didn't want to be married ever again. I never wanted to put my trust in a woman again. The women I've been with since then, the ones that were pretty faces to go to parties with and pretty enough to keep my bed warm at the end of the night, they did nothing to restore my faith in women. They either wanted me for my money, my connections, or so they could sell their stories to the papers. Then there's you. I have never been so attracted, so connected, so drawn to a woman before as I am to you. I feel like I've known you my entire life. As weird as it sounds, considering I've only known you for a week, I'm not scared about being married to you, I'm more scared of losing you when this week is over.'

She stared at him. She felt the same way and it scared the hell out of her. She didn't want to fall in love again, because it would only end in heartbreak like it always did. But there was very little she could do to stop it. She leaned forward to kiss him, because when his mouth was on hers, there were no fears, no doubts, there was just him.

He cupped her head with his giant hand, caressing her scalp with gentle fingers as he rolled her back into the sand.

Fear clawed her throat, squeezing her heart but as he kissed her all of that faded away.

—

Cameron walked back along the secret passageway with Milly's hand tightly in his. She hadn't said a lot and he guessed she might be worried. They were just getting to know each other and after one week she had already found out she was supposed to be his soul mate and found herself accidentally married to him. It was too much, especially as she was scared about falling in love again.

He should be scared too. A week ago he hadn't been interested in having any kind of relationship at all, not even a sexual one, then Milly came along with her pink tipped hair and sparkly shoes and this rose-tinted view on life and he'd fallen for her without any warning.

He had no idea if she felt the same.

They walked back into the kitchen and Olivia had obviously been waiting for them.

'Oh, hey. I made lunch for you both, I wasn't sure if you had eaten or not so …' she gestured to the sandwiches.

Cameron instantly felt bad that they had enjoyed a picnic whilst Olivia had been here all alone.

'That's great, thanks Liv, I'm starving.' He sat down in front of one plate and hoped that Milly would be kind enough to do the same. Thankfully she did, tucking into the sandwich with great enthusiasm.

'Thanks Olivia, this was really kind of you,' Milly said.

They ate without talking, whilst Olivia worked. There was a tension in the room and Cameron didn't understand why, though he realised it was mostly coming from Milly as she stared at her plate whilst she ate. Olivia, seemingly oblivious, hummed quietly whilst she worked.

'Cam, we need to go through your diary for the next month or two, you have several commitments coming up in the next few weeks. We also have that Summer Ball next Saturday.'

Cameron pulled a face. 'Ah Liv, you know I don't like those things.'

Olivia laughed. 'It's for charity and besides, it's Gerald's company that are organising it. We went to the one at Christmas and it was a lot of fun. Remember that magician? He was hilarious, I haven't laughed like that in a long time.'

Cameron smiled as he remembered. 'Yeah, it was a good night.'

Olivia blushed. 'It really was.'

Cameron suddenly remembered what else had happened that night and wished she hadn't brought it up.

Milly finished her sandwich, excused herself from the table and went into the lounge.

He frowned after her. Olivia carried on as if she hadn't noticed. 'We also have the film premiere the following Tuesday, do you want me to hire a car for us?'

Cameron stood up. 'Would you mind if we did this later?'

Olivia faltered in her list and then smiled. 'Of course not, go ahead. I don't want to interrupt anything.'

He smiled gratefully at her and followed Milly into the lounge. She wasn't there, but a quick check in his bedroom revealed her sitting on his bed.

He walked in and closed the door behind him.

'What's wrong?'

Milly sighed. 'I don't know. Her, you two …'

'You're jealous! You've got to be kidding me. Nothing has ever happened between me and Olivia. She's my friend and my PA, I have no feelings for her at all. There are loads of parties and functions my publicist makes me attend so that I have a public presence and sometimes I go with Olivia as it's easier than going with a date that only wants me for my fame or fortune. There's no ulterior motive with Liv, she's just my friend.'

'I'm not jealous. I just … I'm scared.'

Cameron swallowed, his anger and exasperation vanishing. 'Of what?'

'Everything.' She laughed hollowly. 'It's all happening so fast. I'm scared of the feelings I have for you, I've never felt anything like this before and I'm terrified of getting hurt. I know your history with women and I thought I would be ok with being a fling but I'm really not. I'm scared because Olivia is nice and sweet and normal with sensible hair and sensible clothes, someone you could be proud to take to functions. You have all this history together, things you've done, people you know. I'm damaged goods and I'm insanely insecure and I have stupid pink hair. There's no comparison. I'm scared I'm going to lose you before we've even begun.'

He sat down next to her, taking her hand. 'I feel scared too, I've never been so scared of a relationship ending before. And you're right, there is no comparison, because I would rather have you with your baggage and gorgeously silly pink hair and your wonderful outlook on life than Olivia or any other woman. I would be honoured to take you to any function, and you could wear whatever you want, I wouldn't care.'

'What if I was to wear bright pink, sparkly high heeled shoes?'

'And nothing else? Now that would be a look I'd be very interested in seeing.' He quickly rolled her on to the bed, pinning her with his weight. 'But I certainly wouldn't let you out the house like that, I'd keep that look all to myself. I'd ditch any function for a night with you dressed only in heels.'

Milly giggled and Cameron was relieved to hear it, the tension had gone. She ran her hands down his back. 'And how exactly would that night go?'

He smiled. 'Let me show you.'

—

Milly woke up to the sun sliding across her face. It was late afternoon and the sky was already turning that gorgeous shade of pink and blue. The view from the window over the sea was stunning but the view lying next to her in bed fast asleep was the best thing she had ever seen. Cameron lying face down on the sheets, stark naked, was something she would never tire of. He was so beautiful, so muscular, so *delicious* she just wanted to bite into his tight little bum.

She was getting into trouble here, she was falling for him and despite the curse that she was somehow linked to, she knew that she was never going to get a happy ending out of this. The perfect Disney happy ending didn't exist for her. She had lost every man she had ever fallen in love with in the past, Cameron would be no different.

And she was no different for Cameron. What was it the women he had slept with had said? That he was charming and attentive. That little stunt he had pulled with the medieval banquet and the dancing on the cliff tops on her birthday was just another charming ploy to secure her place in his bed and it had worked. She wasn't going to regret that she had succumbed to his charms, this was going to be the best week of her life, but she knew that it wouldn't last beyond the week. There was no way that she was the woman that would change his womanising ways.

There was only one woman that he'd had a serious relationship with and that was Eva, his ex-wife. A woman that was the polar opposite of Milly. Eva was a tall, thin, brunette. She was incredibly sophisticated and glamorous and rather annoyingly a lot like Olivia. The pictures she had found of their wedding day showed Cameron absolutely in love with Eva. He had never looked at her like he was looking at Eva in those photos.

He was fond of Milly, she knew that, but to him she was just another blonde to have a bit of fun with. She was a fling, no more than that, but she couldn't hate him for that. She had known all this before she climbed into his bed. A fling was something that was completely out of character for her. She had only had three past boyfriends, all of whom she had been in love and had serious relationships with. But there was something about Cameron that drew her in, that made her come alive. She was different with him, carefree, brazen, addicted and there was no way she could walk away from him before she had taken what was clearly on offer. She was just going to enjoy the next few days and then after the week was over, she'd walk away without a look back. She had to if her heart had any chance of surviving.

She picked her phone off the side and took a picture of Cameron sleeping. She wasn't sure if she would save this keepsake after the week was up or whether she would delete it but it was nice to have it, at least for now. She scooted back a bit so she could capture his full naked glory, from toe, through gorgeous bum to wonderful broad shoulders, to those beautiful lips. She snapped a few shots, just as he woke up.

'Hey, what are you doing?' he asked, rolling over on top of her, snatching the phone from her hand.

'Taking pictures of your gorgeous butt,' Milly giggled, as she ran her hands down his back and stroked his bum.

'It's yours for the taking, anytime you want it baby, you don't have to take pictures.'

She wrestled the phone from his fingers. 'Let's take a selfie.'

'No, I look like a yeti in photos,' Cameron kissed her throat as she tried to position the camera to take some pictures. She fired off a few shots as he trailed kisses over her neck and face.

'Smile, you grumpy sod,' Milly said and Cameron smiled at her, not the camera. She looked up at him and felt her heart soar at the way he looked at her.

Cameron took the phone from her and started taking some shots of her.

'No!' Milly squealed. 'I don't want to see pictures in my phone of me naked.'

'You can text them to me and then delete them.'

'So you can perv over me, you creep.'

'Well hopefully I won't have to, as I'll always have the real thing here, in my bed.'

He tossed the phone to one side and started layering kisses down her body, she stroked his hair fondly. 'You're so full of shit, you've had so many women, I'm not naïve enough to think I'm any different.'

He paused in his kisses and shifted up the bed to look at her, playing with her hair, curling the pink ends round his fingers. 'I resent the fact that you see yourself as just another woman I've shagged. I know there've been a lot but … it's different with us. I knew that from the very first moment I saw you. I thought you understood how much you mean to me.'

'And how many women have you said that to before?'

He pulled her chin up to look at him. 'You're the only one. I never make false promises to the women I'm with. I never promise longevity or tell them I love them when I don't. It's absolutely crazy that I feel this way about you after such a short time, but I feel we have something incredible here, do you not feel that too?'

Milly swallowed, refusing to admit it to herself, let alone to him.

'You say that you want a happy ending, why are you so afraid to give us a chance?' he asked.

Milly moved away from him but he pulled her back, stopping her with a slow, delicious kiss.

He pulled back to stare into her eyes. 'What are you scared of?'

'My heart has been broken three times after I put my trust in someone. After Tyler died … it ruined me.'

'Grief is a horrible thing to get over. I'm so sorry you had to go through that. But it's very different to being dumped, surely?'

'Not really. It's still the pain of not being able to be with the person you love anymore. I'm not sure what hurt the most – that Patrick and Adam didn't want to be with me when I loved them so much or that Tyler was taken from me when I knew he was my happy ever after. The end result was still the same. Me sobbing and in physical pain because my heart had been broken. I don't want to go through that again.'

'Trust me, I never want to do anything to hurt you. Take a risk and I'll do everything I can to make you happy.'

She looked at him and knew she had to take that chance with him. That had been what the week's holiday had really been about, not just about satisfying the sexual attraction between them. She couldn't walk away from him unless she had given it her all.

She nodded, 'I'll try.'

He smiled hugely. 'Besides, there is one main difference between you and those other women,' Cameron said, as he layered kisses down across her chest.

'What's that?'

'I married you.'

She smiled, though where Cameron kissed her next wiped the smile completely off her face.

—

Milly emerged into the kitchen later, leaving Cameron dozing in bed. The man had an insatiable appetite for sex and she was realising she did too, another thing he had awoken in her.

Olivia looked up from her laptop and smiled. Milly smiled back as she poured them both a glass of orange juice. There was something about Olivia she just didn't trust, but she was sweet and nice and completely unfazed by Milly's presence. Cameron had said they were friends, nothing more, so why did she still see Olivia as a threat? It didn't make any sense. She refused to let Olivia's presence drive a wedge between them. If she was paranoid that Olivia didn't like her or worried that Olivia was a better fit for Cameron than she was, she wasn't going to let it show. That would drive Cameron away more than anything else.

She sat down at the table opposite Olivia, passing her the juice.

'Thank you,' Olivia took a delicate sip. 'You two are getting on well.'

'I really like him,' Milly said.

'He must give off so many pheromones or hormones or something, women just flock round him like sharks who can taste blood.'

Milly frowned slightly at that analogy. She studied Olivia across the table, noting the look of concern in her eyes.

Olivia sighed. 'I worry about him. He has been hurt so many times before and I don't want to see it happen again. He's a good man and it breaks my heart every time it happens. It's always me that's left to pick up the pieces.'

Something about the way she said that led Milly to believe that Olivia liked being the one he turned to for comfort.

'You don't need to worry. I'm not going to hurt him, I couldn't, I care about him too much to do that,' Milly said.

Olivia smiled warmly. 'I want this to work for the two of you. He needs someone lovely for a change. I'm going to help you.'

'Thank you, but we're doing great on our own.'

'Let's arrange the perfect date,' Olivia said, clearly getting very enthusiastic about her new project. Milly sighed at the interference but at least having Olivia fight in her corner would be better than having her fight against her. Olivia pressed a few keys on her laptop and Milly wasn't sure if she was returning to her work or using the laptop to help with the perfect date. 'What do you like to do? How about fast things? Motorbikes, fast cars, that sort of thing?'

'Not really, I don't like to feel out of control, I've never really liked rollercoasters either.'

'Pity, Cameron loves all that.' Olivia said, vaguely, making Milly think that she was more interested in what was on the screen than Milly's answers. 'What about flying, hand gliding or helicopter rides?'

'Oh yes, I'd love to do stuff like that.'

'Scuba diving?'

'Yes, I've done that before in France, it was brilliant.'

'Speed boats?'

'Actually yes, I've done that before and loved it.'

'Abseiling, rock climbing?'

'Never done it but yes, it would be great to have a go.'

'Skiing or snowboarding?'

'Not much chance of that round here in the summer but yes, I'd definitely give it a go. Is Cameron into all that adrenaline stuff then?'

Olivia nodded vehemently. 'He loves it, if you're going to be with Cameron then you need to get used to that sort of lifestyle.'

Milly pondered this for a moment. She was much more the stay at home type. She liked meals in and cuddles in front of the

TV, watching a Disney film or some sweet romantic comedy. But a bit of fun like that now and again wouldn't be a bad thing.

'What would your ideal date be?' Olivia asked.

'I'm such a romantic, I'd be happy with a moonlit picnic on the beach or making love in front of that great big log fire in the banquet hall. I don't need grand gestures, I'm happy just spending quiet little moments together.'

'Cameron's not good at the romance side of things. If you want the fairy tale you might be barking up the wrong tree.'

Milly finished her juice thoughtfully. Were they really that mismatched? Did they really know each other at all?

She looked up to see Cameron walk into the kitchen, looking dishevelled and sleepy. She smiled, her heart filling purely at the sight of him. It didn't matter how much or how little they knew about each other, they could learn all that over time. If they were going to work, these differences wouldn't be the thing that broke them. If he wanted to go out every weekend on some adrenaline seeking adventure, she'd go with him and then during the evenings they could cuddle in front of the TV. They could both adapt. She smiled as she realised she was planning for the future, their future, and it wasn't as scary as she had made it out to be.

'Ooh Cameron, we were just talking about you taking Milly out on a date, you two can't just stay here and shag each other's brains out all day.'

'Don't see why not,' Cameron muttered, winking at Milly before he planted a sweet kiss on her lips.

'Milly wants you to take her out on your bike.'

Milly felt her eyes widen. Out of the long list of things she had said she wanted to try, Olivia had just suggested the only thing she had said no to. She glanced across at Olivia to see if she had done it deliberately and Olivia smiled at her encouragingly, giving her two big thumbs up. Had she got confused? It was quite an extensive list and Olivia's attention hadn't really been on it.

She turned back to Cameron to quickly rectify Olivia's mistake only to see that his face had completely lit up into a huge grin. 'Really? I'd love to take you out. We can go now.'

'But it'll be dark soon,' Milly squeaked, sudden terror pulsing through her veins.

'It's brilliant to ride in the dark, you are going to love this, it's such an exhilarating rush.'

'I … but …'

He was smiling so much, she didn't want to be the one that wiped that smile off his face. If he loved motorcycling then it would have to be something she tried at least once.

'Ok.'

'Fantastic. Here, put your fleece on. I know the weather has been gorgeous today but it still gets a bit chilly on the bike.' Cameron held her fleece out for her, she shrugged into it and he zipped it up for her. 'You continue to surprise me, Milly, I love that you want to do this.'

Milly forced a smile on her face, trying not to let her hands shake as she put on her shoes. How hard could it be? She would just hold onto his back and close her eyes the whole time.

He pulled his boots on, grabbed her hand and quickly pulled her out the door. As Milly closed it behind her, she was almost positive that Olivia smiled smugly at her, but it was too fleeting to be sure.

She followed Cameron round the back towards the garage and spotted the electric blue bike that looked as though every angle and curve had been designed to specifically maximise the speed potential.

Cameron passed her a helmet and helped her to put it on, pulling the straps tight under her chin. She felt claustrophobic in it and it felt so heavy, she didn't even think she could hold her head up.

He got on but Milly felt frozen to the spot. She touched her star bracelet, hoping more than anything that now was not the time she was going to die.

'So we'll go slowly first so you can get a feel for it, but basically when I bank, just bank with me.'

'Bank?'

'Lean to the left and right, just do it when I do it.'

She nodded. She was going to die, she knew it. This wasn't like her favourite Disney films, normally there'd be a horse and carriage to ride off into the sunset in. This was a death trap.

'I am feeling a bit tired actually so maybe we can just go out for a short ride.'

Cameron nodded keenly, anything to get her on the bike. He patted the seat behind him and she slid on, wrapping her arms round him as tight as she could. He was so big, so solid, she immediately felt safer by just holding onto him.

He gunned the bike into life and she felt the machine vibrate beneath her, almost as if it was alive and straining to be let loose.

Cameron walked the bike out of the garage and then released the throttle and they shot forward. She clung on tighter, gripping his thighs with her own. They sped out the gates and Milly held on with everything she had. She felt him bank to the right and it was easy to follow suit when she was welded to his back with no space in between. They drove through the village and through the trees to the top of the hill that she and Dick had struggled up a few days before. Dusk was falling but it was light enough to see the steep inclines and twists of the road as it dropped away deeply in front of them.

'Hold on,' Cameron called over the noise of the engine, but it was impossible for her to hold on any tighter.

He gunned the bike faster and they roared down the hill, the darkening countryside rushing past in a blur of green. A scream erupted from her throat, her fear spilling out in one loud wail of terror. Cameron laughed, mistaking her fear for elation. But as the scream came to an end, it unexpectedly turned into a laugh. It bubbled over in her throat so she laughed again and again uncontrollably. It was terrifying but exhilarating and wonderful all at the same time, she wanted to cry and laugh and shout and scream all at once. As they sped round the corners she had never felt such a rush of every possible emotion before in her life, coursing through her veins and ripping from her throat. The more she screamed and whooped and laughed at every one of the bike's movements, she could feel Cameron laughing too at her very bizarre reaction. They sped along the deserted lanes, banking now and then and she just couldn't stop laughing and whooping with delight and fear and joy.

Slowly they started to climb again and before long they had arrived back in the village but by another road that Milly hadn't realised existed, which was much wider and easier to traverse than the curvy one she had struggled up the other day.

Cameron slowed down as they wound their way round the village green, back through the gates and into the garage where he kicked the stand down and killed the engine.

Milly immediately scrambled off and shook her hair free from the helmet. Cameron removed his too as he sat astride the bike.

'How was that?' He grinned.

Milly bounced on the spot, beaming from ear to ear. 'That was the most terrifying, exciting, thrilling, electrifying, most stimulating thing I have ever done in my life.'

Cameron laughed. 'Your reaction was hilarious ...' His words were lost as Milly grabbed a fistful of his T-shirt and kissed him hard. She wanted to feel him against her now. She didn't know how something so exhilarating could be such a turn on, but it was. She felt alive as she had never done before.

Sensing her sudden urgency, he struggled to get off the bike without taking his mouth from hers.

He manoeuvred her backwards down the drive, his hands roaming her body, but they were never going to get back to his room quick enough with her walking backwards. She tore her lips from his and, grabbing his hand, she ran back towards the kitchen door.

'I didn't even want to do this, Olivia suggested it and, bloody hell, I'm so glad she did,' Milly said.

She pushed the door open and Olivia looked up from the laptop, grinning triumphantly.

'You're back quick, didn't you enjoy it …?' she trailed off as she clocked Milly's grin.

'Best thing I've ever done,' Milly said, striding across the room towards Cameron's bedroom and for a brief second she thought she saw a flash of disappointment cross Olivia's face. Had she done it deliberately? If so, she had presumably wanted to set Milly up for failure. But the second the disappointment registered on Olivia's face it was gone, leaving Milly to wonder if she had imagined it. There was no time to think about that now, she needed Cameron while the adrenaline still burned through her blood.

'Best suggestion ever, Liv,' Cameron said, following her into the bedroom and shutting the door.

He kissed her hard, quickly dispensing with all their clothes as his hands explored her body, his weight pinning her to the door.

He tore his mouth from hers. 'Stay there.'

He moved quickly to his drawers, grabbed a condom and came back before she'd barely managed to draw breath. He lifted her, she wrapped her legs round his hips and a few frustrating seconds later he was inside her. She moaned loudly, hoping that Olivia could hear just how successful her little plan had been, but as Cameron pounded against her hard and fast, all thoughts of Olivia were wiped clean from her mind. In mere minutes she was tumbling over the edge, clinging to Cameron as her shouts of pleasure filled the room. As he followed, he kissed her hard, swallowing her last moans.

Finally, when their breathing returned to normal, Cameron pulled away slightly. 'Christ Milly, I'm never going to have enough of you, will you stay with me after this week is over?'

There was no doubt, no fear left in her head anymore. She had been hiding away for years, afraid to fall in love again, afraid to get hurt. But she'd also been terrified of that bike ride and it had been the best thing she had ever done. She knew falling in love with Cameron was going to surpass that if only she was brave enough to take that risk.

'Yes,' she said, before she could change her mind.

Cameron smiled and kissed her again as he carried her over to the bed.

CHAPTER 16

Milly got dressed and left Cameron fast asleep the next morning. She was thankful that Olivia wasn't up either, she didn't know where she stood with her. If she was genuinely concerned for her friend, then she could understand that and accept it. She just hoped the anxiety she felt from Olivia was that and nothing more.

She crept out of the kitchen door, ignoring the one-eyed glare from Gregory, who was snoring in front of the Aga.

She wanted some space from Cameron, just for a few hours. Everything seemed to have changed between them the night before. They both knew this was way more serious than a fling now and she needed some time just to think without being affected by his overwhelming, intoxicating presence.

She walked out of the castle gates, feeling the hot morning sunshine warm her back. She headed towards the village along the little lane, letting the wonderful scent of wildflowers tumble over her as they bobbed their heads on the grassy banks and poked out between the hedges.

It was still early but there were many villagers moving about, tending to their business. They all waved cheerily to her as she passed. What a difference a few days made. At least no one was chanting 'Oogie' at her anymore.

She sat on a bench on the far side of the green away from nosy ears and scrolled through her contacts until she found her Aunt Belinda's number. She quickly called her before she changed her mind.

Belinda answered on the second ring. 'Hello my darling, how are you?'

Milly closed her eyes, feeling the love from her aunt flow down the phone and wrap around her like a soft blanket.

'I'm good Bel, just phoning for a chat.' She wasn't sure whether to tell her about Cameron, she wasn't sure if Belinda would be happy for her or not after the devastation she had witnessed the last three times. Milly always got so emotionally invested in her relationships and she wanted to prove to Belinda that she had matured and entered into a sensible relationship where she was taking her time, but she could hardly do that when it seemed she had accidentally married her client and jumped into bed with him after only knowing him for a week.

'Is this about that nice young man you're seeing?' Belinda asked.

Milly rolled her eyes. She was sure Jamie would have phoned Belinda immediately after leaving them the other day, not to gossip or tell tales, but just because he cared and he would have wanted to talk about it with the one person who loved Milly as much as he did.

'What did Jamie say?'

'He said that Cameron was really nice and that he liked him a lot but that he had a reputation with the women.'

'He certainly has that. Part of me is scared of going into this relationship with him, knowing how much pain I'll be in if it ends, but –'

'Milly, if you know he could hurt you that much if it ends then there's no choice is there?'

Milly frowned. 'What do you mean?' If Belinda told her not to get involved with Cameron, she couldn't do it. There was no way she could walk away now.

'The only person that could hurt you that much is someone you've fallen in love with and if that's the case then he's worth the risk.'

'But you know what I'm like when I'm in love, I dive in, mind, body and soul.'

'And that's exactly what love should be like, it should be all or nothing. Does he feel the same?'

'I don't know. I think so, but … he's not said anything yet. He's been hurt in the past too so I think he's cautious as well.'

'Just take your time, then when you finally confess your love to each other, making love for the first time will be all the more magical.'

Milly winced. Belinda was an old fashioned hopeless romantic. There was no way that she could tell her aunt now that they hadn't waited to declare their love for each other but let lust and passion and desire take over. Her aunt would be very disappointed in Milly's less than wholesome approach to the relationship.

'Bel, I have to go, but I'll call you again soon.'

'Ok, darling, I love you.'

'I love you too.'

Milly ended the call and sighed. She looked across the green towards Gladys's house and saw the curtains twitching. No doubt she or one of the other ladies was watching her.

She got up and walked to the door but Lavender opened it before she had raised her hand to knock.

'Oh come in honey, we were just having breakfast, did you want a bacon sandwich?'

'Oh no, I don't want to put you to any trouble,' Milly said, before remembering that she should be angry with these ladies who had conned her into marrying Cameron in the first place.

But as the wedding was a complete farce and obviously not at all real, she couldn't be too angry.

Lavender ushered her in and Gladys gave her a little wave from the kitchen as she fried several pieces of bacon in the pan. Constance handed Milly a plate with a doorstep bacon sandwich on it and pointed to a seat at the kitchen table.

Milly's stomach gurgled at the wonderful smells and she took a huge bite.

'Now tell us, how is that young Cameron in the sack? I bet he has a huge willy,' Gladys said as she served up some more bacon into a sandwich.

Milly choked, the sandwich lodging itself in her throat. She gasped and wheezed and Constance passed her a big mug of tea. She took a big gulp, washing down the sandwich.

'I'll take that as a yes,' Gladys chuckled.

Milly put her mug down. 'I can't believe you persuaded us to be in the play without telling us that we were supposedly getting married.'

'Ah, we have had a marriage ceremony on that green every year at the Summer Solstice as far back as I can remember. It's terribly unlucky not to have one. This year we had no one who wanted to wed so we had to … hurry things along between the two of you. You would have got married anyway, Lavender saw it in her leaves, we just … accelerated the process a little bit,' Constance said, tucking into her own sandwich.

'It can't possibly be legal,' Milly said and the old ladies looked like she had slapped them.

'Of course it's legal! Good King Stephen granted us permission to wed in this way nearly one thousand years ago and that law has never been revoked. Every person who has been married in this village has done so in this manner. You don't need no fancy bits of paper to make it legal, when you have the King's decree,' Lavender said, rather pompously.

Milly sighed. They were clearly convinced that Cameron and Milly were husband and wife. Milly, on the other hand, was going to need a lot more persuading.

'And how do the villagers get divorced? How can I officially get one of those if I'm not officially married?'

The old ladies look of shock at the slur on their wedding ceremony changed to a look of unbelievable sadness as if Milly had just declared that she regularly drowned kittens in the village pond.

'You want a divorce?' Constance whispered, barely able to believe her ears.

'Well, no, but I might. I barely know him.'

'You have to listen to your heart, child, you'll know if you are meant to be with him,' Gladys said.

Milly suppressed the urge to roll her eyes.

'If you want a divorce, you declare it at the Winter Solstice celebrations. All ties will then be severed and you are both free to pursue other relationships,' Constance said.

The ladies stared at her with huge, sad puppy dog eyes. 'Do you think you will divorce?' Gladys said.

'We've never had one of those before,' Lavender said.

'Well, I bet you've never conned someone into getting married before,' Milly snapped and for the first time the ladies looked apologetic.

'You are meant to be together, you can see that,' Lavender said.

'Do you love him?' Constance asked.

Milly swallowed the huge lump in her throat. Despite her best intentions she had fallen for him.

Constance smiled, obviously seeing the affirmation on Milly's face. 'And he loves you, any idiot can see that.'

'I'm not sure if he does. He has an incredible sexual appetite and I think I'm just handy to have around to satisfy that. He's attracted to me, he's fond of me. I don't think it stretches to love.'

Gladys sat down at the table and they all leaned in towards Milly. 'Tell us more about his *huge* sexual appetite.'

'Are other things huge too?' Lavender asked, wiggling her eyebrows. 'I mean, we saw it at the celebrations and it looked very big but he wasn't …' she gestured with her hand pointing straight and diagonally up, 'ready to perform then.'

'Does he take you from behind?' Constance asked, her sandwich clearly forgotten.

'I'm not talking about my sex life with you,' Milly laughed, biting into her sandwich as a distraction and feeling slightly guilty that she was having this conversation with the three mad old biddies from the village and not her own aunt.

The ladies didn't move as they waited expectantly for some tiny nugget of information.

Milly sighed. 'He's the best sex I've ever had.'

The ladies all clapped excitedly and giggled like school kids.

'Child, tell him you love him. He's been hurt in the past and very cautious with his heart, but you tell him you love him and I promise he'll say it straight back,' Gladys said.

Milly bit her lip, not sure if she could put her heart out on the line again.

'You've been hurt too, I can see,' Lavender said, in her best mystical, all seeing voice. 'But you will heal each other. You will be with child by the next Summer Solstice. There is no greater gift than a baby.'

Milly swallowed down a bite of sandwich with some difficulty, her mouth had gone dry. That was a terrifying thought, was she ready for that?

'Look, I didn't come here to talk about my relationship with Cameron, I'm still trying to figure that part out myself. It happened so quickly and neither of us expected it and we just need some time to figure out how we feel about each other. Plus his PA has arrived and ... I'm just not sure about her, I really don't think she likes me.'

'His PA? Yes, we met her the other day. Don't worry, Gladys has made a voodoo doll of her,' Constance said.

Milly's eyes widened. 'You can't do that. I'm pretty sure her dislike of me comes from wanting to protect Cameron and even if she does have designs on him, I don't want any harm to come to her.'

'She'll get her comeuppance, don't you worry about that.' Constance said.

'If she's a bad apple, the Grey Lady won't let her stay. She's protecting the treasure but she's also protecting Cameron too,' Lavender said.

'You still think the treasure is here?' Milly asked and the three ladies nodded solemnly. 'I wish it was. Cameron needs that money for the castle. He's had a very generous offer from a hotel chain but I still think he'll need it for further renovations.'

'He's turning the castle into a hotel?' Lavender's eyes lit up.

'I thought you'd hate that idea. It will mean visitors to the village. You lot don't like outsiders, you set the Oogie on to them.'

'Almost every single person in the village worked at the castle – with maintenance, gardening, cleaning and cooking. Although Cameron was quite generous with his severance pay, we will all need to look further afield for work soon. Opening it as a hotel will mean employment for us.'

Milly bit her lip, wondering if her brother would really want to hire a bunch of weirdos from the village to work in his hotel. Maybe if he had outside help with the managerial side of things then it wouldn't be so bad.

'Well, the treasure would just give him extra peace of mind. I know he is worried about money. Do you have any idea where it could be?' Milly asked.

'Wherever the Grey Lady is, that's where you need to look.'

The dungeons seemed to be Sophia's favourite place, but there didn't seem to be anything down there.

'Legend has it that Boris took the jewels out in his boat one day and was never seen again. We found his boat on the beach under the castle and Cameron thinks that Boris might have hidden the jewels in a cave somewhere nearby. Do you know of any?'

'There's one under Igor's pub, hundreds of years ago it was used for smuggling. A tunnel leads from his cellar down to the sea. I think he still uses it to go out fishing from rather than travelling to the nearest beach, but I doubt there're any hidden jewels in there, I'm sure any treasure would have been found by now,' Constance said.

'Come on, we'll show you,' Lavender said, getting up, and the other ladies followed suit.

Milly followed them out of Gladys's home and round the green towards the pub.

Lavender knocked on the door.

Igor answered, one of his eyes roaming all over them and the village behind them as if looking for anyone that might have seen them come. Milly glanced down at the length of his beard and was pretty sure that Igor had played the role of the Oogie at the Summer Solstice celebrations. She blushed, knowing she had seen way too much of this man.

'Igor, we need to see the passageway,' Gladys said.

Igor looked Milly up and down a few times, obviously wondering if she could be trusted and then without another word he turned back into the pub. The ladies ushered Milly in after him and then Constance closed the pub door after them with an ominous bang.

Milly noticed the huge portrait of a very opulent looking man presiding over the bar. Dressed in a regal looking gown, he was every inch the pompous lord. In his hands was a large chest of glittering jewels, indicating that this was dear old Boris. If he only knew what trouble he had caused.

They followed Igor through a door at the back of the pub and then down some winding stairs into a dark cellar. It was cold down here and there was a cool wind that seemed to swirl up from the depths of the pub.

Constance switched on the light at the bottom of the stairs, illuminating a huge cellar with several cases of wine, spirits and kegs of beer. Some of the kegs and bottles had French writing on the sides, making Milly wonder if Igor still indulged in a spot of smuggling now.

Igor went to the back of the cellar and moved a large wardrobe out of the way of a gaping hole which clearly led deep into the cliff face.

He flicked a switch and a row of bulbs lit up the tunnel beyond – obviously it was still in regular use. The ground was smooth too.

'Do you mind if I take a look?' she asked Igor.

He nodded and gestured for her to go ahead. For a publican, he was a man of few words.

'We'll stay here dear, it's a bit steep for us,' Gladys said.

Milly started down the tunnel and, like the ones in the castle, she could feel the steep incline as the path took her further into the cliff face and towards the sea. Eventually it opened out directly onto a very small slip of sand. A wooden jetty led from the cave's entrance out into the sea and a little motor-powered fishing boat was beached on the sand, out of the reach of the sea that was lapping on the edges of the jetty.

There was nowhere in the cave where a chest could be hidden, no cracks or crevices. She stepped out onto the jetty and walked to the very end and looked around. Sheer cliff faces stretched into the distance on one side and disappeared round a corner on the other side towards the tiny cove. She could see no other caves at all.

She was about to go back in when she saw a large, deep crack on the edge of the corner of the cliff. No matter how far she leaned out she couldn't tell whether it was just a crack or a cave or another tunnel, but it was definitely something she wanted to investigate. Maybe she and Cameron would have to go for another swim again, or maybe once they were on more friendly terms with Igor, he might take them out on his boat to explore some of the cliffs.

She turned back and headed along the tunnel towards the pub where the ladies were waiting for her. Igor was nowhere to be seen.

'Well thanks for showing me, but I'm still no closer to finding the treasure for Cameron.'

'The Grey Lady guards over it so no one can get their hands on it who isn't part of the Heartstone line. You could try asking her.'

'Well, I doubt she will speak to me, but maybe she might tell Cameron.'

'You're part of the Heartstone line now too,' Lavender said, smiling sweetly. 'She'll tell you.'

Milly looked down the tunnel, listening to the waves crashing on the rocks below. Maybe they could ask the Grey Lady where it was. It couldn't hurt to try.

—

Cameron woke to an empty bed which was beyond frustrating, considering the condition he had woken up in. He needed Milly. He rolled out of bed and opened the door, wondering if she was nearby and he could tempt her back to bed. There was no sound from the kitchen apart from the tapping of keys on a computer. Not wanting to frighten Olivia with his nudity, he quickly got dressed and went out to join her.

She smiled hugely when she saw him.

'Do you want a cup of tea?' She asked, getting up and moving to the kettle.

'That would be great.'

'Will Milly want one?'

'I don't know, she's not in my room. I thought she was out here.'

Olivia shrugged and set about making two cups of tea. Cameron peered out the window, Milly's car was still there. He looked around the kitchen, her shoes were still strewn all over the place, so it was unlikely she had suddenly decided to run away. She was probably doing some more tests somewhere.

'How's it going with you two, getting bored yet?'

Cameron sat down. 'No, I'm crazy about her.'

Olivia turned round, smiling cheekily. 'Come on, Cam, you know you have the attention span of a goldfish. No woman holds your attention longer than a few weeks.'

'It's different with her. I know it sounds stupid but I think she's the one.'

The smile fell from Olivia's face. 'The one?'

'Marriage, babies, she's my happy ever after.' Cameron smiled at the phrase he had obviously stolen from Milly.

Olivia turned back to make the tea and then brought the mugs over and sat opposite him.

'Are you sure about her?'

Cameron nodded. 'More than I've ever been. I can't believe I'm going to say this, but do you believe in soul mates?'

Her eyes widened slightly and he quickly rushed on. He told her briefly about the family curse, the stone heart, the cameo, the dragon necklace and Milly's tattoo and Olivia's face became more and more shocked. He knew it was crazy. He was a rational man, he knew the concept of soul mates didn't actually exist, he didn't believe in the family curse or any of that other stuff that linked Milly to him, it was just a whole load of coincidence but he couldn't escape the feeling that Milly was the other half of his heart.

He let his head fall into his hands. It was insanity to fall this hard and this quickly but he couldn't stop it.

Olivia took his hand and squeezed it. He looked up at her and her shocked expression had gone.

'I'm delighted for you,' Olivia said. 'You deserve to be happy and I think she's lovely.'

Cameron smiled with relief. 'You have no idea how pleased I am to hear you say that.'

'I'm really happy, for both of you.'

Cameron squeezed her hand. 'Thanks Liv.'

Olivia returned her attention to her tea and her laptop for a few minutes.

'Listen, while she isn't around, let's talk business for a moment, especially about Palace Hotels.'

Cameron suppressed the urge to roll his eyes. Olivia was so efficient and organised in every way but why was she so hung up on working with Palace Hotels? Especially when the deal was so bad?

'Maxwell is really keen to work with you. They've come back with a different offer which I think is more than generous under the circumstances, especially given the current condition of the castle. They've offered two and a half million and ...'

'Extravagance have offered four and a half million for fifty percent ownership. I also get fifty percent of any profits and they will handle the repairs. When Palace Hotels come back with an offer like that, then we can talk.'

'We don't know anything about Extravagance. My contacts at Palace Hotels say they're a bunch of cowboys.'

'I've met the CEO, I was very impressed with him and his plans for the castle.'

'Where on earth did you find him? I thought you were leaving all the research to me. Was my work not good enough?'

'Jamie is actually ... Milly's brother. She put me in contact with him,' Cameron said.

Olivia's mouth fell open slightly. 'Cameron, you've known her a week and now you're working with her brother?'

'How do you know I've only known her for a week?'

Olivia sighed, shifted through the papers in front of her and slid Milly's Castle Heritage ID card across the table. 'I found it this morning.'

He felt his jaw clench. 'It doesn't change anything.'

'Of course it does. She comes here, gets you into bed and a few days later you're working with her brother, that's all a bit coincidental for my liking.'

'It's not like that, Milly has helped me to see my options. And a minute ago you were telling me how lovely you thought Milly was, now what? You're accusing her of sleeping with me in order to get me to sign with Extravagance and get some financial kickback from her brother?'

There was a flash of something in her eyes, an emotion he couldn't identify before it was gone.

Olivia sat back in her seat for a moment, eyeing Cameron thoughtfully. 'She does seem really lovely and if you trust her then I do too, but I am worried how much trust you've laid at her feet already, when you barely know her. You've told her about how you didn't write the *Hidden Faces* series, now you're trusting her with the future of the castle. Listen, you know nothing about her except that she is probably good in bed. You ask me to research all these companies before you work with them – Palace Hotels, Extravagance, Castle Heritage – but you've done no research on the woman that you want to spend the rest of your life with. You've known her a week. Don't you think it might be beneficial to do a little bit of digging?'

Cameron bit his lip. He hated to admit it, but she was probably right. If nothing else, Olivia researching Milly and finding out that there was nothing untoward about her would at least get Olivia off his back about her.

'Fine, look her up. Research her. Research Extravagance too. I am one hundred percent confident that you will find nothing dodgy about either of them, but if it will make you feel better then go ahead.'

Olivia sighed with relief. 'I'm sure you're right about her, but a little research won't do any harm.'

Her phone rang on the table next to her. She glanced at the caller ID and snatched it up. 'I'd better take this.'

She opened the back door and stepped outside as she answered the phone, closing the door behind her.

Cameron watched her go. Olivia was right. After what happened with Eva, it paid to be a little cautious. He just hoped that she wouldn't find anything.

—

Milly walked back up the drive and spotted Olivia talking on the phone. She was facing away from her, leaning on the castle wall. Annoyingly, as she drew closer, she could see Olivia absently kicking at some loose brickwork at the very bottom of the wall. The castle was damaged enough as it was, without Olivia making it worse.

She carried on walking past her, but stopped as she caught some of what Olivia was saying.

'Don't worry, he'll sign it. Maxwell, don't worry, I'll get him to sign it. I need this deal as much as you do.'

Maxwell? As in the owner of Palace Hotels?

Olivia shifted slightly and Milly bolted in case she saw her listening. She went into the kitchen and Cameron stuck his head out of the lounge. His smile, when he saw her, lit up his whole face.

'Morning, beautiful.'

She stepped into the lounge, planting a deep kiss on his lips as he pulled her against him.

'I missed you this morning,' Cameron whispered against her lips.

She smiled. 'You missed the hot sex, you mean.'

'That too.'

She pulled him further into the lounge. 'Cameron, listen, how long have you known Olivia?'

He frowned. 'About a year. She came to work for me shortly after my dad died. Why?'

'I think she might be doing some kind of deal with Palace Hotels.'

His frown deepened. 'Jesus Milly, don't you start. I've just had all this with Olivia about you, she thinks you're getting some kind of kickback from your brother.'

'What?'

'I told her Jamie was your brother, wish I hadn't now and I really don't need you going after her too.'

Milly regretted saying anything. Of course he would believe Olivia over her, they were friends and he'd known her a lot longer than he had known Milly. Unless she came to him with some hard proof, she was just going to look petty and silly. And she hardly had anything concrete apart from a few overheard words in a one sided conversation. She could have jumped to completely the wrong conclusion. She had to let it go for now.

She decided to change the subject completely, in an attempt to dispel that frown that was marring his beautiful features.

'Ok, forget I said anything. Listen, I went down to the village and spoke to the ladies. They seem to think the treasure is still here in the castle and that Sophia guards over it.'

This at least managed to wipe the scowl from his face. 'The dungeons?'

'Apparently.'

'I can't see anything being hidden down there.'

'Me neither but we haven't exactly spent prolonged time in the dungeons. There could be lots of nooks and crannies for hiding a chest of treasure. Imagine, if you find it, you wouldn't have to do a deal with Extravagance or Palace Hotels, you might have enough to pay off all your debts and do the renovations yourself. I know that would be your first choice.'

Cameron nodded. 'We'll have to have a look down there.'

There was a noise in the kitchen. Milly poked her head outside and spotted Olivia staring right at her. How much had she heard?

Milly went out into the kitchen and Cameron followed her.

Olivia continued to stare at her and Milly stared straight back. She didn't trust her, but apparently the feeling was entirely mutual.

Cameron sighed as he looked between the two of them. 'I'm going for a shower. Play nicely, girls.'

He walked into the bathroom and shut the door behind him.

Olivia sat down at the table and Milly sat opposite her. Olivia looked at her laptop, apparently ignoring Milly completely. It was time to cut to the chase.

'You don't like me much, do you?'

Olivia looked up, surprised. 'What makes you think that?'

'Lucky guess.'

'Milly, you've got it all wrong. I want Cameron to be happy. You seem really nice and I hope you don't let him down but he is a terrible judge of character and I do worry that after only knowing you for one week that he's possibly jumped without looking again.'

Milly's mouth grew dry. Did Olivia know who she was? Suddenly, like a beacon lighting up the table between them, Milly's eyes fell on her Castle Heritage ID card, sitting just a foot away from Olivia's hand. Milly wanted to snatch it away from Olivia before she saw it, but it was clearly too late for that. Olivia's eyes followed Milly's eyes to the card and her expression didn't change.

'I found that earlier today,' Olivia returned her attention to her laptop. 'I don't blame you at all. You come here, see the big castle, Phoenix Blaze, of course you're going to see pound signs.'

'That's not what this is, I really like him,' Milly hated that Olivia had caused her to raise her voice after only a few minutes. 'I'm not interested in his money at all.'

'Milly, I don't want to upset you, that's the last thing I want,' Olivia said calmly. 'You seem lovely and I really hope that this time I'm wrong, but even if you're not after his money, it's not going to last. Cameron gets bored so easily. I'm sorry but give it a few weeks and you'll be yesterday's news, the same as the rest.'

'You don't know anything about me or us. You have no idea what we feel for each other. And I don't like you coming in here and tarring me with the same brush as all the others.'

Olivia leaned across the table and when she spoke her voice was low and her eyes were as hard as stone. 'You're exactly like the others, some blonde slut out for a good time. Cameron will realise that soon enough and it's me he will return to, like he always has. And if he doesn't realise it, I'll have to help him.'

Milly stood up. 'You fucking bitch.'

'Milly!' Cameron stood in the doorway with a look of thunder on his face. 'What the hell is wrong with you?'

Milly had no words to rectify this situation. He blatantly hadn't heard Olivia's threat or he would be looking furiously at Olivia, not her.

Olivia was already sitting back in her chair, her eyes soft again. 'It's fine, Cameron, it's ok,' she said, calmly.

'It's not ok,' Cameron seethed.

'No really, it's my fault. It's just a huge misunderstanding. Milly asked if I could get another ticket for her for the charity ball. I told her that's it's probably not her sort of thing at all, that it's unbelievably posh and elitist. I think Milly thought that I was saying that she wasn't good enough to go, when nothing could be further from the truth. I was merely saying that it can be terribly pretentious there and she'd probably be bored silly. I know you hate it for that very reason, Cameron. Milly, I can get you a ticket if you really want to go. I really meant no offence.'

Cameron folded his arms across his chest, clearly waiting for Milly to apologise to Olivia. He'd have a long wait.

Olivia stood up. 'I've got to take some photos for Palace Hotels.' She picked up her notepad and pen and walked round the table towards Cameron. 'It's fine, I promise. Don't screw this up by going all bull-in-a-china-shop as you normally do. Milly's lovely and I really don't want to come between the two of you.'

Milly stared at her aghast. The conniving little bitch! But Cameron softened at her words.

Olivia gave his arm a soothing stroke and walked past Milly with a sweet, friendly smile on her face, making Milly wonder if she had imagined the sly comment Olivia had made moments before.

'Liv, stay out of the dungeons,' Cameron said and she nodded and then left them alone in the kitchen.

He stared at her as if he didn't recognise her, waiting for some kind of explanation for which she had none. He was never going to believe her version of events.

Finally Cameron spoke. 'I'm going to get dressed and then I'll take Gregory for a walk. I'm hoping by the time I get back you'll have some kind of explanation for me.'

He walked into the lounge and closed the door behind him.

She pulled a face. As if it wasn't hard enough between them with all their insecurities and baggage, now there was a meddling PA thrown into the mix too. How on earth was she going to get past this? She somehow had to make it up to Cameron but she hadn't actually done anything wrong. She opened the fridge to see what she could make for dinner, annoyed that it would have to be a meal for three and that she would have to feed the evil witch or make herself look petty for not including her. She pulled out some tomatoes, mushrooms and peppers, ready to make some kind of pasta sauce when she heard a loud, low moan that seemed to echo round and fill the whole the castle. She looked around in confusion as the moan continued, but over the top of the moan suddenly came an ear splitting scream.

CHAPTER 17

Milly sped from the kitchen as fast as she could, heading straight for the dungeons. The silly cow had clearly decided not to heed Cameron's warning and investigate the dungeons, probably looking for the lost treasure herself. Sure enough, the door was open and Milly ran through it and down the stairs as fast as she could.

Olivia was cowering on the floor, crying and screaming. Sophia towered over her, her face a picture of pure livid hate and venomous wrath. The moan was definitely coming from here, the walls seemed to shake as Sophia seemingly was trying to summon the dead of a thousand years. Wind tore through the tunnel, banged the cell doors and pulled at Milly's hair as it whipped around Olivia like a mini hurricane. Milly could hear mocking laughter and voices.

If Sophia was only supposed to appear to descendants of the Heartstone line, she obviously made an exception for those who pissed her off.

She ran towards Olivia, quickly creating a barrier between Sophia and Olivia.

'No Sophia, stop it,' Milly shouted, sounding braver than she felt.

Sophia stopped immediately. The wind died, the voices and laughter faded. Sophia gave a courteous little bob, bowing her head at Milly before calmly walking away and fading into the darkness. Olivia was a cow but what the hell had she done to Sophia to piss her off that much?

She turned and put an arm around Olivia, who shrugged it off, still wailing and sobbing.

'It's ok, it's over. The ghosts are gone, come on, let's make you a cup of tea,' Milly used her best soothing voice. Olivia didn't move from her foetal position on the floor and the sobbing didn't relent. Milly knelt next to her, stroking her back, just as Cameron stormed down the stairs.

He looked at Milly and then moved to Olivia's other side.

'Liv? Are you ok?'

Olivia threw herself at Cameron, sobbing and almost knocking him to the floor. He stood up, scooping Olivia into his arms and walked out, leaving Milly kneeling on the floor, jealousy burning through her gut.

—

Milly sat staring at her dinner, she had no appetite at all. The pasta bake that she had made for the three of them had long since gone cold and Cameron still hadn't emerged from Olivia's bedroom, where he had taken her after leaving the dungeon. She supposed she should be grateful that he hadn't taken her to his bedroom, Milly couldn't have stomached that.

She kept telling herself that Cameron wouldn't do anything with Olivia behind her back, but how well did she really know him? The thing that stuck in her gut the most was that Olivia looked like Eva. Was there really an attraction between them? Milly remembered how Cameron had lain in bed with her after she had been scared by the skeleton, was he now doing that with Olivia, holding her and stroking her? That would be worse than if he was shagging her. The ghost incident had come mere minutes after Cameron had heard Milly swear at Olivia, and now she had driven him straight into her beautiful arms.

Cameron walked into the kitchen looking exhausted. He piled some pasta onto a plate, not looking at her.

'Liv says you set the ghosts on her.'

Milly felt her mouth fall open. 'Are you frigging kidding me?'

Cameron shrugged.

'And you believe her?'

'I'm not sure what to believe, to be honest. The Milly that I fell for over the last few days was sweet and kind and the Milly I've seen today has been a bit of a cow.'

Milly felt like he had just slapped her. 'She knows who I am and she doesn't like me. She made that very clear just before you arrived in the kitchen this afternoon.'

There was little point telling him that Olivia planned to split them up. She doubted he would believe her and she'd end up looking like the petty bad guy.

'She's looking out for me. I've been through a lot over the last few months and she's very protective of me.'

'And you think that I would do something as horrible as set the ghosts on her.'

He sighed. 'No I don't.'

He tucked into the pasta and chewed for a few moments.

'Thanks for this, I'd better get back.'

'You're spending the night with her?'

'She's terrified.'

Milly couldn't help thinking that Olivia was playing it up so that Cameron would stay with her. Guilt then twisted in her gut for thinking that and for being jealous. The whole experience had been scary for Milly and she wasn't even the subject of the attack.

Cameron turned to go. 'Don't wait up for me.'

He walked out and the door swung closed behind him.

Milly got changed into her pyjamas and decided to sleep in her own room. It didn't seem right to sleep in Cameron's bed when he probably didn't want her there.

She turned off the light and climbed into bed, feeling lonely without Cameron and annoyed that she felt that way. Even more annoying was that sleep was a long way off.

He'd called her a cow. No one had ever called her that before. The honeymoon was well and truly over. She felt a tear slide across her cheek and plop onto the pillow.

She had only been in bed five minutes when she heard Cameron come back into the lounge and go into his bedroom. A second later, the door on the guest room banged open and Milly sat up in shock.

Cameron switched on the light. 'Why are you in here?'

'I didn't think you'd want me in there.'

'Why would I not want you in my room?'

'Five minutes ago you were going to spend the night with Olivia.'

'She's fast asleep.'

'And you called me a cow. I think I'd rather sleep alone tonight.'

Cameron sighed and moved towards the bed. He pulled back the covers, scooped her up and carried her back to his bed. He lay her down and started undressing.

'I don't think you're a cow, I just … Olivia's my friend and for some reason you don't like her. She has been nothing but nice to you since you arrived and yet I feel like you're going to start pulling each other's hair and slapping each other at any moment. Can you just …'

'Be nice?' She clenched her fists under the covers so he couldn't see her reaction to that thought.

'At least try.' Cameron lay down next to her, pulling her onto his chest as if it was the most natural thing in the world. She closed her eyes for a moment as she breathed him in. Every single part of her was screaming that this was where she belonged. Maybe things would end naturally between them or maybe Cameron would get bored of her eventually like he'd done many of the women before her, but she wasn't going to let him go without a fight and she sure as hell wasn't going to let Olivia be the one to drive them apart.

Her eyes shot open. Suddenly she realised that being nice was the only way she was going to win this battle. Being a bitch to Olivia and staying on the defence was not going to do anything but drive a further wedge between her and Cameron. That's what Olivia wanted, for Cameron to see Milly's rudeness. Olivia wasn't going to win the fight that way.

'I'm going to be super nice from now on, I promise. I'm sorry if I've been a cow today. It's just because I'm scared of losing you, you know that.'

Cameron looked at her in surprise, he probably hadn't expected her to cave so easily. 'I know it's hard for you, we're trying to get to know each other and there's this third person in the relationship. I'm going to make sure we have some quality time together over the next few days. You'll hardly know she's here.'

Milly closed her eyes for a moment as she relished the feel of his hot, velvet skin against her cheek, the intoxicating, sensual, earthy scent.

'She has some things she needs to go through with me and then I can get rid of her, in the nicest possible way. It'll just be a few days and then we can be alone.'

Milly nodded. She could be nice for the next few days but she couldn't help but worry about what other plans Olivia had up her sleeve to try to break them up.

—

Cameron was sitting reading the paper in the kitchen when Olivia walked in. She smiled, sleepily and sat down next to him, leaning her head against his shoulder.

He stood up, not at all comfortable with that level of intimacy from her. He ignored the flash of hurt that crossed her face.

'Want a coffee?' he moved to the kettle.

'What's wrong?'

He turned round to look at her. 'What do you mean?'

'Well last night you were hugging me and now …'

'Last night you were terrified, I was trying to comfort you. Don't read anything more into it than that.'

She moved closer to him, running a hand up his arm. 'Is it Milly? I would never tell her about us.'

His eyes widened. 'There is no us, Liv, you know that.'

'But what about that night, at the Christmas party?'

Jesus, why was she bringing that up? They'd agreed they'd never speak about it again.

'The night where you got drunk, kissed me and then vomited on my shoes? It doesn't exactly hold any special memories for me.'

The hurt that crossed her face was palpable this time and Cameron regretted it immediately. Olivia was a sweet, nice girl but he didn't have any feelings for her and he thought the kiss had just been a drunken thing, she had never mentioned it since.

'You spent the night with me.'

'Jesus, Liv, I took you home because you could barely stand and I stayed with you because I didn't want you choking to death on your own vomit. What do you remember from that night?'

Olivia blushed. 'That we kissed. I woke the next day and you were lying on the bed with me, and I thought …'

'You thought what? We were both fully dressed the next morning. So did you think I took you home, shagged you whilst you were unconscious and put all your clothes back on again? Nothing happened. We agreed the next day that it was just a silly, drunken kiss and that we weren't going to talk about it again.'

Olivia looked down at the floor and Cameron hated that he had hurt her.

'Look, Olivia. You're a very beautiful woman, but I didn't hire you because you're beautiful. I didn't hire you because I wanted to sleep with you. I hired you because I needed someone to handle my meetings and my diary, arrange transportation, filter my emails, a job which you are very good at.'

'I think we should tell Milly.'

'There's no need,' Milly said from the doorway. 'I heard the whole thing.'

Cameron's stomach dropped. Crap.

Olivia finally took her hand off his arm and he regretted not moving away from her earlier. Milly looked mad as hell.

Milly walked round the table and put her shoes on. The silence was worse than her shouting. He wanted her to say something.

'I'm taking Gregory for a walk, are you coming?' She glanced over at Cameron and he quickly nodded.

He pulled his shoes on, whistled for the beast and followed Milly outside.

She walked in silence next to him, until they reached the edge of the cliff. Gregory, completely unaware of the tension between them, sniffed around the rabbit holes near the cliff edge.

Cameron watched the waves swirl around the rocks. The tide was obviously in, as most of the rocks that he had looked down on before were completely covered.

'Why didn't you tell me?'

'I honestly didn't even think about it. It was months ago, at Christmas. She was drunk, she kissed me, threw up and practically passed out. She's never mentioned it since and I just put it down to her being drunk. She has shown no sign of having feelings for me over the last six months. I've never thought of her like that, I promise you. I didn't tell you because that drunken snog meant absolutely nothing to me.'

Milly sighed and leaned into him. He turned and wrapped his arms around her as she rested her head on his chest.

'She's trying to split us up,' Milly said.

'No, I don't think so. She likes you. She's worried that I'm rushing into things, but she genuinely likes you.'

'I don't believe that for one second.'

She pulled back to look at him and suddenly her hands shot to her mouth as she gasped in horror at something that she had seen behind him. He whirled around but he could see nothing.

Milly hurried to the edge of the cliff with tears filling her eyes. She peered over and then bolted back towards the castle.

'Milly, what is it?'

She didn't reply. He looked down at the sea and his heart fell into his stomach. To his horror he saw Gregory desperately swimming against the tide as the waves battered him from all sides. He had quite clearly fallen over the edge whilst sniffing for rabbits. How he had survived the fall was a miracle, now the tide was likely to kill him, throwing him against the rocks. Cameron turned and ran for the castle. If he could get down to the cove, he might be able to swim out and help him. But as he realised with a new horror that Milly had run off to do just that, he suddenly found a speed he didn't know he had. The sea was rough today, Milly would be killed if she went out into the rocky cove. Losing Gregory would be heart breaking but there was no way he could cope with losing her.

CHAPTER 18

He barged into the castle, ignoring Olivia's shocked questions and ran as fast as he could up the stairs to the study. The secret passageway was already open as Milly had clearly been here before him. He ran down the stairs and slipped and tumbled his way down the passageway that that took him to the cove. Milly was already stripping off her T-shirt as he reached the top of the rope ladder. Standing in the knee deep water, the waves swirled angrily around her, almost trying to drag her out to sea.

'MILLY, NO!' he roared as she dived in.

He quickly descended the ladder himself. Now the only thing on his mind was getting to Milly before she was thrown onto the rocks by the incoming tide.

He reached the bottom and waded into the water until it was deep enough to swim. Waves crashed over his head making it difficult to see, but as he looked around frantically Milly was nowhere to be found.

What did she think she was going to do when she found Gregory? She could hardly carry him back to shore, he was too big for that.

Where the hell was Milly? He called her name but there was no answer.

He tried to think about where he was in relation to where they had been standing minutes before. Had Milly gone left or right? He thought he had last seen Gregory towards the left of where he was now, so he swam through the waters, praying that Milly had gone that way too. He called her again. He rounded the rocks so he was now outside of the little cove and in the open sea and that's when he saw her, struggling in the water as she battled to keep both herself and Gregory afloat. Gregory wasn't co-operating at all, in fact the stupid dog was quite clearly panicking. Waves crashed over them both and Milly was clearly in danger. Gregory was going to sink them both in a minute.

Cameron swam quickly towards them. Grabbing Gregory by the collar, he swung him over his shoulder in what was supposed to be a fireman's lift, but he had to keep one arm over Gregory's body to stop him wriggling around when all he really wanted to do was wrap Milly in his arms and make sure she got back to the cove safely.

'Are you ok?'

Milly nodded, clearly shaken up.

'Go ahead of me. Just keep swimming. I'm right behind you,' Cameron said.

Milly swam past him back towards the cove, waves assaulting all of them as they traversed the rocky path back towards the rope ladder.

Cameron winced as Milly made it back to the rocks underneath the rope ladder and slipped, banging her leg quite badly.

She turned around ready to help him get Gregory up the ladder. He gestured for her to go up ahead of him but she shook her head. Bloody exasperating woman.

'Let me help you,' Milly said.

'How do you intend to do that? We can't go up the ladder with all three of us at the same time. Climb up and you can help me when I get to the top.'

Milly reluctantly conceded this and he watched her go up the ladder, breathing a sigh of relief when she made it safely to the top.

Gregory had stopped wriggling so much now, but he clearly wasn't happy about being restrained like this. Climbing the ladder with one hand and such a heavy, uncooperative load over his shoulder was hard and slow going but as he reached the top, Milly helped him to guide Gregory to safety. As soon as Cameron released him, Gregory ran off up the tunnel, wagging his tail, clearly unharmed and finding the whole thing a hilarious game. He wouldn't be surprised if Gregory ran back up to the cliff tops and threw himself back into the sea again shouting woohooooo as he did it.

Cameron sat at the cave opening panting, watching Milly do the same. He wanted to kiss her and shake her in equal measure. Stupid girl had nearly got herself killed over his stupid dog.

He finally got his breath back and glared at her.

'What the hell do you think you were doing? You could have been killed!'

'I was trying to save Gregory.'

'I love that stupid mutt, but there is no way I would choose his life over yours.'

'I couldn't leave him down there to drown.'

He noticed that her leg was bleeding and knelt forward, wiping away the blood gently with his sleeve and then placing a kiss on the cut.

'I'm so angry with you,' he said softly.

She smiled, rolled forwards onto her knees and kissed him. 'You don't look very angry.'

'I'm keeping it inside. You scared the crap out of me.'

She shifted so she was sitting on his lap, resting her head against his chest. He wrapped his arms round her and held her tight. He closed his eyes, breathing her in as he waited for his heart to return to normal.

—

Milly lifted her head from Cameron's chest. They had sat there on the edge of the cave for hours and she hadn't felt the need to move. There was something very peaceful about being in his arms. She looked at him and smiled. He obviously found it peaceful too as he was fast asleep.

She leaned up and kissed him softly on the lips and his eyes fluttered open.

'Hey,' Milly said as Cameron looked around and realised where they were. 'For someone who has trouble sleeping, you sure do sleep a lot.'

'I have slept more in the last few days with you than I ever sleep. Normally I get an hour or two a night. My brain just won't stop thinking, it's wrapped up in stories and character conversations and countless bad decisions I've made. With you … I feel calm.'

Milly smiled. She liked that she had that effect on him. She climbed off his lap and stood up, offering her hand. He took it and pulled himself up.

'When I said I wanted to spend quality time with you, I didn't think I'd be sitting on a muddy cold floor, soaking wet for several hours after rescuing you from the sea.'

'I don't think you rescued me,' Milly said, taking his hand as they walked up the tunnel.

'No but it sounds better in my head that I was some kind of hero and saved my wife from the treacherous waves, rather than that I helped her with my stupid mutt who had leapt off the cliff in the first place.'

'Ok, we can go with your version. When we tell people how we met, instead of the unprofessional gold digger story that Olivia will no doubt share, we can say you saved me from the sea and had to give me mouth to mouth.'

Cameron pulled her into his arms and kissed her, deeply. 'I like the sound of that.'

'And then you carried me back to the shower, where we made love under the hot, pounding water.'

'This story is getting better and better.'

'Ok, and then you made me your delicious tomato soup, because I was ravenous.'

'That I can do. After the hot shower sex.'

Milly smiled. 'Oh, while I was out in the sea, I saw a cave that had steps at the back. I would imagine it leads up to the castle.'

'Well that's interesting, we'll have to explore some more once the sea is a bit calmer.'

'We were supposed to do that the last time we were on the beach and you distracted me with your kisses. You need to learn to control yourself,' Milly teased.

Cameron smiled. 'Ok, I'll try. After the hot shower sex.'

She laughed.

They walked back into the kitchen, sharing sweet glances with each other but Milly's heart sank when she saw Olivia.

'Cameron …' Olivia trailed off when she saw their bedraggled appearance. 'Are you ok?'

Cameron nodded. 'Yes, stupid dog fell in the sea, we're going to take a shower.'

He pulled Milly towards the bathroom.

'Wait, Cam, we need to talk. Alone.'

Cameron stopped to look at her. 'Whatever you want to say, you can say in front of Milly.'

Milly watched Olivia shift awkwardly and she wondered what she could possibly want to say.

'I ... um ... I've done some research on Milly, like you asked, and I found out a few things.'

Milly let her hand fall from Cameron's in shock. He's asked Olivia to do some research on her. He didn't trust her.

Cameron pushed the hair off his face awkwardly. He didn't even deny it.

'Jamie McAllister, CEO of Extravagance, is not Milly's brother.'

'I know, he's her cousin,' Cameron said.

Milly stared up at him in confusion. 'Did Jamie tell you we were cousins?'

'No, I worked it out. He's your aunt's son isn't he? You said that when your Mum died it was just you and her. Plus, he referred to your mum as Emma, not his mum. I just presumed that you call each brother and sister because you were raised together.'

'He's not her cousin, she's no relation at all to him. His name isn't even McAllister, it's Stevens. The only connection that I can find between them is that they lived together for five years, until very recently actually, probably as boyfriend and girlfriend.'

Milly watched Cameron frown and turn his eyes to Milly.

'Do you know how many Castle Heritage rejects she has passed his way since she started working for them?' Olivia said. 'Eight. Eight properties that are part of the Extravagance hotel chain were originally referred to Castle Heritage and were rejected. All of them handled by Milly.'

Cameron stared at her, confusion and anger swirling in his eyes.

'I'm sorry Cameron, she has been playing you from the very start. It's obviously a little scam that she and her boyfriend have cooked up. When a property is referred to Castle Heritage, Milly will come out and find some reason to reject it and then pass on the details to her boyfriend who will swoop in with a deal that will make them both millions.'

Milly knew how it sounded but there was nothing actually wrong with what she had done, she just wished Cameron wasn't looking at her as if she had betrayed him.

Cameron folded his arms, clearly waiting for an explanation which suddenly Milly didn't want to give, certainly not there in front of Olivia.

She waited for Cameron to say that it didn't matter because in reality none of it did. It didn't affect them. She had been nothing but honest with Cameron from the very beginning but he clearly thought she had tricked him somehow.

'I think I'll get a shower somewhere else,' Milly said.

She walked to her bedroom, grabbed some clean clothes and went back into the kitchen again.

'Are we not going to talk about this?' Cameron said.

'There's not a lot to talk about. As far as you're concerned, I've come here for the sole purpose of deceiving you.'

Milly walked past Olivia, resisting the urge to slap her stupid, smug face and out into the corridor. She walked down a few doors and went into one of the other staff rooms that Cameron had shown her on her first day.

Maybe she really would have to get that voodoo doll from Gladys, for Olivia was going to be the thing that broke them, she was sure of it.

—

Milly stared out of the study window over the darkening waves at the bright sunset that filled the sky with great big slashes of scarlet and gold. She hadn't seen Cameron for hours and she was getting hungry. She had hoped he would come after her and apologise but he hadn't. Then again, he didn't really have anything to apologise for. He hadn't accused her of anything, he had just expected some kind of explanation from her which she supposed he was due. But was it too much to ask for him to trust her? She sighed. Was she expecting too much of him? He'd said himself that the kind of trust it would take to marry someone again would take a lot longer than six months. They'd known each other for a week and just because they were somehow weirdly married now didn't mean that he had known her long enough to put his reservations aside.

The fact that he had asked Olivia to do research on her was the thing that hurt the most, he'd asked Milly to have faith in him but he hadn't returned that.

She turned back to the desk and picked up another book. Although Castle Heritage probably wouldn't take the castle on, it didn't mean that she wasn't interested in the place. There were several books on the desk that Cameron had obviously been looking at over the last few weeks which had to do with the castle. Some of them were handwritten with drawings and diagrams, some had been published hundreds of years before. The one she held in her hand was a published one with a soft worn leather cover. Where the title had once been was now just a faded patch of leather.

She opened it up and flicked through a few pages. It was written in Latin. If she wanted to, she could probably just about translate what it said but she didn't have the patience for that at the moment.

She turned the page and saw a picture of a large house called Cleaver Court. It looked vaguely familiar and she was sure it was one that she had been to or seen pictures of before. She looked at the writing directly underneath and roughly translated it.

Cleaver Court had been built on the orders of King Stephen in 1135. She stared at the house again but as she couldn't place it, she closed the book and opened another.

Straight away she saw a diagram of the dragon flag that flew over the castle, although it looked slightly different to the one that flew there now. There were some cursive words surrounding the diagram pointing to different elements but she couldn't make out what language the words were written in, let alone start translating it. One part of the text indicated that this was the design from 1912. She turned the page to see a very different design with the dragon looking more like a giant snake as it curled itself around the heart.

Trembling, she realised that this was the book that Cameron had spoken about when they had first discussed her dragon tattoo, the book that showed how the dragon and heart emblem had changed over the years. She flicked through the pages. There were over twenty different designs but not one of them resembled her tattoo. She leafed through them more carefully, wondering if there were any that shared any attribute with her tattoo but there was nothing even remotely the same. The tattoo hadn't been done from memory. In the few pictures she had of her mum, she had been wearing the necklace in almost all of them. Milly had had the picture blown up and copied the necklace exactly. The fact that there was no match with the Heartstone emblem proved that, even if she still had the necklace, it wasn't the missing family heirloom that would link her with the curse. She stared at the book and unexpectedly felt tears in her eyes. Did that mean she wasn't Cameron's soul mate after all? Was there someone else out there who was?

She shook her head, this was ridiculous. There were no such things as soul mates. Sure, there were people who had wonderful loving relationships, people that were married to the same person their entire lives, but it didn't mean that their souls were destined to meet each other because they had been together in a previous life. Even for Milly, who loved to read about or watch fairy tales and happy ever afters, the concept of real soul mates was a bit too far-fetched.

She looked up and realised that Cameron had been watching her from the doorway.

'I thought you might be hungry,' he said. 'I've put together a few things.'

She didn't move and Cameron sat down.

'I thought I should tell you a bit more about Eva,' he said.

Milly's breath caught in her throat. Did she really want to know about the only woman Cameron had ever loved?

'You know that love that you had with Tyler, that stupid, crazy, fast love? That's what I had with Eva. We met, we fell in love and were married after two months.'

Milly felt her eyebrows shoot up.

'I know, I don't know what I was thinking. It was her idea and I should have seen right through it then. I literally became famous overnight. As you know the *Dream Pirates* series became something of a phenomenon. She found me right at the very beginning of my fame, just after it was announced that *Dream Pirates* was going to be made into a movie. I was such a naïve fool. With you, everything is happening at the same breakneck speed that it did with Eva. I trust you, I really do, but I'm sorry if I seem a bit cautious at times. It was Olivia's idea to do some research on you and I agreed but purely to prove to her that you didn't have any skeletons in your cupboard, to put her mind at ease. I'm sorry.'

Milly watched him carefully and sighed. She was cautious with her heart too although for slightly different reasons. After the ultimate betrayal of his wife she couldn't blame him for being a bit guarded.

She wanted to explain everything to him, rid any shadow of doubt from their relationship.

'Jamie was adopted by my aunt Belinda when he was five. A few months before I came to live with them. My aunt adopted me too so we've never thought of ourselves as cousins and I suppose technically we weren't even that. I told him very early on that I'd always wanted a brother and he said that he'd like to be mine. My aunt even referred to us as brother and sister. McAllister is my uncle's name, my aunt's husband. He died a few years after they adopted me. I'm surprised Olivia didn't manage to dig any of this up in her research.'

Cameron sat staring at her, listening.

'And yes, I've sent many Castle Heritage rejects Jamie's way. Not because I get any kickbacks or because we are trying to screw these property owners out of their money but because I hate rejecting these beautiful places. Many of the owners are desperate like you and are also bound by the rules surrounding listed buildings, the limited renovations you can do to a historic property and the expense of restoring it sympathetically. I give the owners multiple options, just like I did with you. I personally believe Jamie is the best option not because he is my brother but because the renovations he does are always in keeping with the building, he never tries to change the property into something it wasn't before and the owners get a really good deal out of it. All of his clients are happy with what he has done and I could get testimonials of ...' She trailed off as Cameron stood up and offered her his hand.

'I'm hungry, let's go eat.'

'I ... I wasn't finished.'

'I don't need to hear it. I didn't come up here for an explanation. I came to get you to come and eat. And to apologise if it seemed that I didn't trust you earlier. You don't need to justify your actions to me. I thought about what Olivia had said about you passing the rejects to Jamie and I realised there isn't actually anything wrong with what you are doing.'

'Castle Heritage are so strict and I hate that sometimes. They take on so few properties. When I first started working for them I asked if I could help the ones we couldn't take on by giving them the details of people that could help and they were more than happy for me to do that. They are well aware that a lot of our rejects get taken on by Jamie.'

'You've been completely honest with me from the start, I have no reason to doubt you. I'm sorry. Come on, I'm starving.'

Milly eyed the leather book she had just been looking at on the desk. She got up and walked round, wrapping her arms round his waist and leaning against him.

'There's something else you should know. If the whole concept of the curse is true, I don't think I'm your soul mate.'

Cameron kissed the top of her head. 'Why do you think that?'

She picked up the book from the table and quickly thumbed through the pictures. 'None of these match my tattoo.'

'I know. I realised that the first time we made love. Well, probably not the first time as I didn't get much chance to look at it then, but maybe the second or third time.'

'What does that mean?'

'It means bugger all. It means we're together for all the right reasons not the wrong ones. It means we carve our own path in the Heartstone legacy for better or worse.'

Milly smiled.

He took the book out of her hand and tossed it onto the desk. 'Doesn't mean we're not soul mates though.'

Milly rolled her eyes and Cameron laughed.

'Come on, let's eat. It's a beautiful night,' he said, leading her to the entrance of the room.

'It really is, it's so warm.'

'I thought we could eat outside. Here, hold this.' He reached down and handed her a brass lantern with a candle flickering inside.

'What's this?'

'A lantern, what does it look like?'

Milly laughed. 'I meant, why are you giving me a lantern?'

'Well you need to ask better questions. You're a historian, you should be good at asking questions. Hold on to that for two minutes and then come upstairs.'

Cameron kissed her on the cheek and ran up the stairs.

Milly stared at the lantern in confusion as the flame danced and twirled inside the glass walls. What on earth did he have planned?

She peered up the stairs and could see a trail of lanterns curving up the staircase, leaving a path for her to follow.

Unable to contain her curiosity anymore she followed the lanterns up the stairs. The lights created a flickering gold warm glow and cast long shadows over the walls. The staircase curled up towards the bedrooms but half way up the stairs was another door that led out onto the battlements. There were four lanterns in front of this door and as they didn't go up any further, she presumed she was supposed to go through there.

She pushed the door open to see more lanterns lining the walls of the battlements and Cameron, standing at the end waiting for her.

She walked towards him, looking out over the spectacular view; the inky sea, the stars that were just starting to pepper the night sky, the tiny village sleeping peacefully in the semi darkness, their white walls looking ethereal and ghostly against the night that was drifting over the cliff tops like a charcoal fog. It was stunning and right then it felt like she and Cameron were the only people in the world.

She approached him and he offered her his hand.

She took it and he pulled her into his arms.

'I thought we could have a moonlight picnic, the weather is perfect for it.'

Her breath caught. 'That's very romantic.'

'This week is going by so quickly and I just wanted to make it special for you.'

She smiled. 'It already is.'

Behind him there were some blankets with food laid out in the middle. 'More tomato soup?'

He laughed. 'No, I promise.'

She sat down. 'Hey, I'm not knocking it.'

She looked at the baked camembert, bread, grapes and slices of meat. She grabbed a chunk of bread, dipped it into the melted cheese and took a big bite.

'I am sorry about Olivia. Don't take it personally, I don't think she would trust any woman with me after my terrible track record. She cares about me, that's all.'

'It's more than that, she likes you.'

'Maybe?' Cameron said, popping a grape into his mouth as he stretched out on his side. 'Other than that one night when she kissed me and this morning, I've not seen evidence of that.'

'I can't help thinking that she wants to get me out the way so she can make a move herself.'

'I'm not interested in her at all and even if you weren't here, that wouldn't change. Anyway, let's not spend our evening talking about Olivia. I've asked her to leave. We can screw this up on our own with my lack of trust and your fear of getting hurt, we don't need any help from her. She'll be gone by tomorrow night. Listen, tell me more about what the ladies said about the treasure.'

She grabbed another piece of bread and dunked it into the camembert again so it was smothered in thick globules of melted cheese. 'They didn't say a lot, just that wherever the Grey Lady is, that's where it'll be. I think we need to have a really good look around the dungeons tomorrow and that cave that I saw in the sea when I was rescuing Gregory, I think that's the key. I bet there's a tunnel that leads from the dungeons out into that cave. Did you know there's also one from the pub that leads out to the sea? Apparently it was used for smuggling hundreds of years ago.'

'Well, that's interesting, did they say anything else?'

'No, we talked about the wedding.'

'How did that go, did everyone congratulate you?' Cameron said.

Milly smiled. 'It's hilarious, they really do think we are married. It's ridiculous really. As far as they are concerned the wedding is perfectly legal and they took great offence when I suggested that it wasn't. Apparently they have a decree from King Stephen.'

'When did we have a King Stephen?'

'1135 to 1154.' Something jarred in her memory. The picture of that house that was dated 1135. The house that had been built on the orders of King Stephen. Had he been to this village? Had this been the site of the house in the picture? Maybe even parts of the original house were incorporated into the castle. She needed to get those test results back from the lab.

Cameron was talking and she quickly tuned back into what he was saying and ignored the desire to suddenly go and research everything about the reign of King Stephen.

'Wow, so it must be official,' Cameron smirked at her, linking hands. 'We're married.'

Milly laughed. 'Oh, apparently, if we want a divorce we just have to stand up at the Winter Solstice celebrations and declare that we no longer want to be married and that's it, no lawyers, no forms to fill in, we just declare it underneath the oak tree on the village green.'

The smile vanished from his face.

Milly scooted closer to him and he shifted her onto his lap.

'Do you want to get a divorce?' he asked.

She pressed a kiss to his neck, not sure how to explain her feelings for him. She wanted to reassure him that she had fallen in love with him but was too scared to put her heart on the line if he didn't feel the same.

'I have no idea what is in the future for us but I am having way too much fun right now to think about finishing it just yet.'

He studied her face for a moment then broke into a huge smile. 'So we'll just see how it goes after this week.'

She nodded. 'I'd like to carry on seeing you if you want.'

'I'd like that too.'

Milly smiled. Cameron leaned forward to pick up the meat board. He selected a slice of meat and popped it in his mouth. 'Did they say anything else, any more predictions from Mystic Lavender?'

She bit her lip. She supposed this would be the true test to see if Cameron was in this for the long haul or just a bit of fun. 'Well, she said I'm going to be pregnant within a year,' Milly laughed and Cameron did too.

'Well she was right about us being married.' He shrugged as he grabbed some bread and camembert.

Milly looked at him. 'Are you not freaked out by that?'

'Not really. There's no point worrying about something we can't control.'

She reached up to stroke his face.

'You might be a dad this time next year.'

He ran a gentle hand over her stomach. 'I cannot frigging wait.'

Milly couldn't help the huge grin from spreading across her face.

——

Cameron watched Milly fast asleep next to him on the picnic blanket, the early morning sunlight kissing her pale cheeks. He could watch her sleep forever and not grow tired of it. His very own Sleeping Beauty.

They had talked and kissed and talked some more and then they had made love under the stars.

He had never been particularly romantic with women but last night as they lay beneath the moon and the stars, her hair glistening in the silvery glow of the moonlight, the warmth of the summer surrounding them, the scent of the sea mixed with the summer flowers, he couldn't deny it, it had been magical.

He brushed her hair from her cheek and her eyes fluttered open. She smiled when she saw him and cuddled into his chest. He pulled the blanket over her shoulders, protecting her from the early morning chill.

'Thank you for last night, it was incredible. The picnic, the stars, the dessert.' She waggled her eyebrows mischievously.

'Yes that was probably my favourite bit too.'

She sighed, contentedly. 'I love this place, the silly turrets and the blue roofs, that amazing view over the sea. If we stay together, I'd love to live here. We could make love under the stars every night.'

'Might get a bit cold in the winter.'

Milly laughed. 'There is that.'

She stretched out and sat up. He stroked her back. 'Fancy searching for that treasure today?'

'Yes, we should have a look around the dungeons and maybe ask Sophia, if she is around.'

Cameron got up and started getting dressed and Milly followed suit. They packed up all the picnic stuff and walked back down towards the kitchen. It was still early and there was no sign of Olivia, which Cameron was thankful for.

'I'm going for a shower, you want to join me?' Cameron said.

'In a minute, I just want to check my emails first, the test results should be back by now and I didn't get a chance to check yesterday.'

Cameron nodded and went into the bathroom. He had only been in there five or ten minutes when Milly burst in.

'Change your mind, there's plenty of hot water left?'

'Cameron, I got the test results back and …' She reached into the shower, turned the water off and passed him a towel.

'Milly, I still have shampoo in my hair,' Cameron blinked through the soap trails that were trickling down his face.

'This is important.'

He wiped his hair and face and quickly tied the towel around his waist. He gave his fullest attention to Milly who looked like she was ready to burst.

'The oldest room of the castle seemed to be the old kitchen, but I've taken very small samples of mortar and paint from several parts of the castle and sent them off to the lab. They've dated them at 1135.' She hopped from foot to foot and then, seeing the look of incomprehension on his face, she thrust an open leather book into his hands. He took it and looked at the page, which showed a large house labelled 'Cleaver Court'.

'What's this?'

Milly pointed to the date underneath the picture. 1135.

'Are you saying this house was what the castle looked like before it was turned into a castle?'

'Yes. I think this house *was* your castle before all the additions were made. Look at the similarities, the doors and windows. I can't believe I didn't see it before. Plus the name, Cleaver Court, Cleaver Castle, Clover Castle. I think that's why I couldn't find anything on Clover Castle. It started off life as Cleaver Court. Although there might not be anything about Cleaver Court either. This house in the picture was built as part of King Stephen's estate and we know he had quite a few properties in this area. Constance said that the decree for marrying people at the Summer Solstice celebrations came from King Stephen. He may even have stayed here.'

Cameron couldn't help but smile at Milly's enthusiasm, though he had no idea how this affected him.

'What does this mean?'

'It means that Castle Heritage will probably take you on, not only because of the castle's age but because it might have once been part of the royal estates. If they don't, their sister company National Heritage almost certainly will. They'll probably help you to restore it to its former structure, but they will finance most, if not all, of that. It means getting rid of all the turrets and the blue roofs and maybe even the towers and the drawbridge and all the silly stuff I love but it would mean you wouldn't have to sell it on as a hotel, you could keep it in the family.'

Cameron felt the smile fall off his face. After everything he had been through with the castle he didn't know if he wanted to go down the route of stripping it of all its splendour.

Milly registered his look of concern and her smile vanished too. 'Isn't that what you wanted all along? Selling the hotel to Jamie or Palace Hotels was never your first choice.'

'No, but things have changed. I don't know, Milly, I need some time to think about it.'

'Ok,' Milly looked disappointed that her exciting news had fallen so flat.

'It's great news, I'm just not sure I want to revert the castle back to how it was. These turrets and towers are as much a part of its history as King Stephen staying here. Let me just think about it for a few days.'

She nodded, brightening slightly. 'And we have that treasure to find. You never know, we might be knee deep in rubies and sapphires by the end of the day.'

Cameron smiled. Milly never stayed down for long.

'I need a shower too,' she said, quickly undressing. 'And don't look at me like that. You'll have to wait till later.'

Milly stepped into the shower and, resisting the urge to touch her, which would only end in sex again, he quickly rinsed his hair of the last residues of shampoo. He smiled when he felt Milly's hands in his hair, helping him.

He left her and got dressed and a few minutes later she was standing in the kitchen ready to go too.

'So, how are we going to play this? Are we just going to go down to the dungeons and ask Sophia to show us where the treasure is?' Cameron asked.

Milly shrugged. 'I guess.'

'She doesn't even speak and I don't think it's likely that she will be able to draw us a map.'

'What harm will it do? If the treasure is here, then she knows where it is. Besides, I have something to sweeten the deal,' Milly said, plucking the cameo from the box.

'You're giving her your cameo.'

'I think it's more hers than it is mine and I've already worn it on my wedding day, so she can have it back.'

Cameron stared at her for a moment and then grabbed his torch in one hand and her hand in the other. 'Come on then.'

They walked through the banquet hall and down into the dungeon, switching on the lights as they went.

The dungeon was unusually quiet today, no banging or moans and Cameron was disappointed not to see Sophia when she had been down here almost every other time he had visited. They walked down the corridor slowly, checking all the cells and entered the large chamber at the end. Cameron switched on the light but there was no one there.

'Maybe Olivia scared them all off,' Cameron muttered.

'Sophia, are you there?' Milly called out. Cameron wasn't expecting a reply but a gust of wind or a rattle of chains would be something.

'Come on, there's no one here. We can try again later,' Cameron said.

They turned to go and came face to face with Sophia, who was waiting for them in the corridor.

Milly stepped forward slightly. 'Sophia, I thought you might want your cameo back.' She held it out for the ghost to see and Sophia stared down at it. Her pale fingers reached out for it and seemingly touched the surface of the brooch. It was the most interaction that Cameron had ever seen from her. Sophia smiled slightly and then shook her head.

Cameron felt a bit disappointed for Milly that her plan hadn't worked, but then how would Sophia be able to take the brooch even if she did want it?

'Sophia, we wondered if you know where the treasure is, Boris's treasure …' Milly trailed off as Sophia suddenly walked straight through them. An icy feeling sliced through his body and they both shuddered.

'Well, I'm officially freaked out,' Cameron said. 'I may have nightmares tonight.'

'Me too.'

They turned back towards the chamber and Sophia was waiting for them in the corner of the room. They stepped towards her and she turned and walked straight through the wall, vanishing from sight.

'Damn it, I actually thought she was going to show us then,' Cameron said.

Milly stared at the wall where Sophia had disappeared and walked slowly towards it. 'Do you think this could be another secret passage?'

'If it is, I can't see anything that could be a door.'

The wall was made from large stone bricks arranged in a haphazard way, big bricks on top of smaller ones with large cracks in between. She inched closer and reached out to touch the wall but as she did it moved under her fingers. She pushed the wall a bit further and a section of bricks swung out to reveal a dark passageway beyond.

'Ha!' Milly laughed triumphantly.

Cameron rushed to her side. 'How did we not see that?'

'Look at the door, the bricks are all jutting out in different places,' Milly pointed out the jagged edges of the door. 'It just looked like part of the wall.'

Cameron clicked on the torch, grabbed her hand and walked down the passageway. He hoped that Sophia would reappear again to show them the way, but she didn't.

The passageway was muddy and wet and as with the tunnel that led to the cove, the roar of the sea got louder the further down they went.

They came to some steep steps that led downwards and daylight flooded the tunnel from beyond. They went down four steps and had to crawl under the low roof. In front of them the tunnel sloped steeply up a ramp into what looked like a cave. Cameron scrambled up and then turned back and offered Milly his hand, pulling her out into the cave with him.

Cameron looked around. The cave was in two parts, a narrow path that led straight from their tunnel out into the sea and a slightly higher part that was filled with rocks. He couldn't tell if the lower path was a natural occurrence formed by the tide coming in, or whether it had been manmade like the tunnel into the castle. It was quite a low cave; the roof was just a few feet above his head and it wasn't deep, it stretched maybe ten metres from the mouth. The sea lapped at the edges, white waves crashing on to the rocks just inside the cave. The tide was clearly on its way in and already there was a large pool filling the front half of the cave and slowly pouring down the narrow path towards the tunnel entrance. The edges of the cave were rough and jagged and on one side there was some kind of natural shelf that ran along part of the cave wall.

'There's a metal peg here and some rope tied to it. Maybe boats have moored in here whilst their occupants have gone into the castle,' Cameron said, pointing to a rusty pole at the back of the cave.

'Smugglers?' Milly asked.

Cameron shrugged. 'Maybe, or just the people in the castle who wanted to make a quick and discreet getaway.'

A big wave crashed into the cave, splashing them with salt water.

'I can't see anywhere that might be capable of hiding any treasure, no nooks or crannies,' Milly said.

Cameron moved around, exploring the cave. 'Maybe we need to come back once the tide is out, the water could be hiding a multitude of secrets. I bet our tunnel gets partly flooded too once the tide is properly in.'

Cameron looked back at the opening of the tunnel. Based on the water marks and the line of moss on the cave walls, he guessed the tide would fill up at least as high as the shelf and certainly would flood the entrance to their tunnel.

'Look,' Milly suddenly pointed to the other side of the cave where the shelf was. He clambered over the rocks towards it. Milly quickly followed. As he approached, he could see a crevice in the cave wall that had been well hidden from where they had been standing. It was narrow but big enough to take a human. It stretched back a few metres from the cave wall and then disappeared round a corner where a shaft of daylight seemed to fill the void where they couldn't see.

'Let's take a look,' Milly said, already trying to clamber up onto the shelf, but Cameron stopped her.

'The tide is coming in fast and I don't want us to get trapped. We could go back to bed for a bit and come back down here later when the tide is completely out. The crack in the wall will still be there then.'

Milly laughed. 'You just want to go back to bed, do you only think of sex?'

'Pretty much, come on,' he turned to go back to the tunnel.

Cameron stepped carefully over a few rocks and turned back to make sure she was following. He missed his footing, and suddenly stumbled. He fell heavily on his side, his head smacked on a rock and then everything went black.

CHAPTER 19

'CAMERON!' Milly screamed, scrambling quickly to his side. She shook him, and tapped him lightly round the face but he didn't wake up. 'Shit, shit, shit.'

She looked around, desperate for some solution. She had to get help. Waves crashed onto the rocks inside the entrance, the large pool getting bigger and bigger and the narrow path quickly filling with water. Within a few minutes the area where Cameron was lying would be covered. If she ran back up the tunnel now, she could call for help, but would it reach him in time? Would she be able to get back to him before the tide came in? If there was a lifeboat station nearby, they could come and get him before he was washed out to sea. But if there wasn't then that would be useless. Phoning the ambulance and the fire brigade would be equally hopeless as neither would be able to get to him. Maybe someone from the village could help. Igor had a boat, could she get to him in time? She looked at the waves inching closer and knew there wasn't a moment to lose. She was the only help he had. She grabbed hold of his T-shirt and started trying to drag him towards the tunnel entrance. If she could just pull him to safety, then she could get an ambulance after that. He didn't move and she didn't know whether it was because he was wedged between the rocks or because he was so heavy. She grabbed an arm and pulled with all her strength. He didn't move at all. She knelt down next to him, tapping him round the face again.

'Cameron, please wake up, please.' She eyed the water that was lapping at his feet and felt a sob burst from her throat. 'You have to wake up, I broke the curse, remember. I'm your soul mate, we're supposed to be together.'

He didn't move.

She stood up and looked around desperately. Water was already trickling over the edges of the entrance to their tunnel, the narrow path almost completely under water. It was coming in so quickly. She pulled again on his arm, using every ounce of strength she had, but she couldn't move him an inch.

The water was already lapping over his hips now, soaking his clothes.

She quickly scooted round to his head and carefully lifted it onto her lap. She watched as the water sloshed over his stomach, his chest, and started filling up the tunnel, blocking their escape. The water crept over his neck and she leaned his head up, hoping she wasn't doing more damage. It touched his chin and she managed to shift herself further under him so he was half sitting up. Water swirled around them both, soaking their clothes, the cold biting into their skin.

Sophia suddenly appeared on the shelf and she pointed into the crevice. If she had found the treasure, Milly couldn't care less.

Milly's tears mixed with salt water as she cried at the hopelessness of it. She glanced at her star bracelet and wished harder than ever that he would survive this.

She stroked his face. 'Please wake up, you can't die on me. I love you. Please wake up.' She kissed him on the gash on the side of his head. 'I love you.' She kissed his nose. 'I love you.' She kissed his lips and felt his lips move under hers, his hand weakly holding the back of her neck.

She pulled back, tears of relief and joy blinding her. 'You're awake.'

'From this slumber, you shall wake, when true love's kiss, the spell shall break.'

Despite everything, Milly couldn't help but laugh, wiping away her tears. 'Can you stand?'

Cameron looked around blearily and then realised the danger they were in. He sat up but was clearly still feeling the effects of the bang to the head. She pushed him from behind. With a bit of an effort from him and a lot of effort from her, she managed to get him to his feet. He was now up to his knees in water.

The entrance to the tunnel they had come through was completely submerged, and waves continued to crash against the cave entrance.

'We could swim out,' Cameron suggested, holding his head. 'The cove can't be too far from here, if we can get to the rope ladder we'll be ok.'

'It's too rough, we'll get thrown into the rocks.'

Milly glanced up at Sophia on the shelf, still pointing into the crevice. There was only one option; to put their trust in a ghost and hope that the daylight that was filling the end of the crevice might lead to another way out.

Cameron seemed to have the same idea and they both sloshed through the water to the shelf. She helped to get Cameron up onto it and then clambered up herself. Cameron stood up and staggered into the cave wall.

'Come on,' she guided him to the entrance to the crevice, but it was very quickly obvious that Cameron was too big to get through.

'You go, I'll be fine out here,' Cameron muttered, pushing her in.

'No way, the gap is wider at the bottom, just get down on your hands and knees and crawl through.'

Cameron dropped to his knees, he was so woozy he could hardly hold his head up. She walked ahead of him as he slowly crawled behind, following her. The crevice ended in a small chamber that was lit up by a shaft of sunlight from a crack further up the cliff face. There was no way out. But it was dry in here and maybe the tide wouldn't make it this far.

Cameron made it to the chamber and sat against the wall, closing his eyes.

Milly knelt next to him, holding his face. 'Hey, can you try to stay awake for a little while?'

He opened his eyes and looked at her.

She snuggled into his side and he put his arm around her. 'Did you really wake up when I kissed you?'

He smiled. 'No, I woke up to hearing you tell me you loved me, over and over again.'

She blushed and he closed his eyes again. She had to keep him awake. 'Cameron. I do love you. I should have said it before, but I was scared. I've been in love before and it always ended badly, I didn't want to trust that a happy ending was possible with you. And the hardest thing was I loved you more than anyone I've ever been with and so I had so much more to lose. Cameron look at me.'

He opened his eyes. 'Go on, I'm listening.'

'And I want to stay married to you and stay here and raise a family with you, or, if you get fed up with the hotel or you continue writing shit books and make no money at all, you can move into my flat. It's right on the beach and we can walk Gregory along it every day and you can write and I'll look after you, make you nice cooked breakfasts every day and we can have hot sex every night.'

'I like the sound of that.'

Milly rested her head on his shoulder for a moment and as she looked across the chamber she could see a small chest tucked behind some rocks.

'Cameron, look!' She pointed, but as she looked up at him his eyes were closed again, his head leaning back against the wall. She reached up and grabbed his face, his eyes shot open. 'Look, a chest, it might be Uncle Boris's.'

Cameron peered across the chamber, but it was quite obvious that he was having trouble seeing anything.

'Shall I get it?'

He nodded, though clearly he wasn't bothered by it.

She clambered over to the rocks and lifted the chest, surprised by how light it was. She came back and sat next to Cameron, placing it on his lap.

He weakly lifted the clasp and opened the lid. Inside, the red lined interior was filled with jewels of different colours that sparkled in the sunlight. Gleaming rubies, sapphires, emeralds and diamonds shone from inside the chest and sent a rainbow of colours around the dusty chamber.

Cameron peered at them and Milly did too, the moment of wonder and amazement quickly fading. She wasn't an expert on jewels but they all looked like they were made from glass. They were too big, too neat and polished. If these were real they would be worth millions but there was no way that they were. Had Uncle Boris been carrying around a chest of fake jewels all these years and didn't know? Had someone switched the real jewels for fake ones at some point? Or had he always known they were fake and just used them to show off to people about his wealth? But if that was the case, then why go to such great lengths to hide them? Unless his madness and paranoia had eventually led him to believe his fake jewels were real.

Milly chanced a glance at Cameron, wondering if he had spotted their worthlessness too and was disappointed.

'I don't think these are real, Milly, I'm sorry.' He looked at her, sadly.

'I know, but why are you sorry?'

'I know how much you wanted to find them.'

'For you, to help you and the castle.'

He smiled and moved the box off his lap.

'There might be one in there that's worth something,' Milly said.

'Your glass is always half full, isn't it?' Cameron said, fondly.

'You never know, if just one of these jewels is the real deal then that would solve all your financial problems for the rest of your life.'

Cameron leaned against the rock and closed his eyes. She pulled his face back to look at her. 'You have to stay awake, do you hear me?'

'I'm really tired, baby.'

'I know.' She reached up and kissed him, feeling his mouth respond instantly to hers. His kisses were soft and sleepy and she felt his head getting heavy.

'Hey,' she tapped his face lightly and he opened his eyes. 'What can I do to keep you awake?'

'Hot sex.'

'I don't think you're in any fit state for that.'

'Probably not,' he mumbled, his eyes fluttering closed.

She grabbed his face again and he looked at her. 'If you stay awake, I promise that when we get back to the castle and you're feeling better I will give you the best blow job of your life.'

His eyes widened and then he burst out laughing. 'I'm going to hold you to that, Mrs Heartstone.'

—

Milly came back down the crevice to the chamber. 'The tide has started to go out. I reckon it's still a few feet deep out there but it's probably shallow enough for us to get back to the tunnel.'

Cameron nodded sleepily and she struggled to get him up. She had employed every tool in her arsenal to keep him awake over the last hour or two, including flashing her tits, though he hadn't seemed as appreciative of that as he had been on previous occasions.

He bent to pick the chest up.

'Just leave it, we can come back for it another day.'

'We're not coming back here again, I'm not risking your life on these rocks, we'll take it now.'

'Well let me take it then, it's quite light.'

Cameron nodded. He crawled out onto the shelf and she passed him the chest to hold while she slid off into the swirling waters below. The current was still strong but they only had a few feet to traverse to get back into the tunnel. She turned to help him down into the cave but as he slid down next to her he stumbled and the chest flew out of his hands, smashing open on the rocks and spilling the jewels into the murky water.

'No!' Cameron moaned, fumbling around in the water to try to find the missing jewels.

'Leave it Cameron, they're worthless.'

'We don't know that,' he sank to his knees, trying desperately to find them.

She grabbed his hands and stopped him. 'Please. I am really scared that you might have done some serious damage with that blow to the head. I want to get you checked out by a doctor or the hospital. I would rather have you safe than have a million jewels. Please, stop looking. If we are meant to find them, they'll still be here when we come back.'

He stared at her for a moment and then reluctantly conceded. He stood up and with his arm firmly round her shoulders she negotiated their path over the rocks and towards the tunnel. There was still a lot of water in the part before the steps, but it was passable even if it meant they'd be wading up to their waist to get out.

Every step back up the tunnel was slow and laborious and Milly couldn't help but panic over the damage that might have been done to his head.

With Cameron leaning on her heavily, they moved back into the dungeons, along the corridor and up the stairs towards the banquet hall and finally into Cameron's kitchen.

Olivia quickly hung up the phone as they came in, going pale at their bedraggled state.

'What happened?'

'He fell on some rocks and knocked himself out.'

Olivia immediately went into panic mode. 'We need to call someone, who should I call, your publisher or your agent?'

'How about an ambulance?' Milly asked, pointedly.

Cameron groaned as he sat down. 'No don't, I'm fine. Nothing a few paracetamols won't cure.'

Milly stubbornly grabbed her mobile phone and called one anyway, ignoring the glares from Cameron. Finishing the call, she put the phone down and looked back at him. Olivia was still panicking.

'I have papers I need you to sign,' Olivia came over and pushed a document in front of Cameron and tried to force a pen into his hand. Cameron looked at the pen in confusion before Milly snatched it out of his fingers.

'Let's get you into some dry clothes before the ambulance comes.'

She helped Cameron to his feet and he sighed theatrically as if she was making a fuss out of nothing. She led him to his room as Olivia hovered around them.

'Don't let him sleep, it's very important that he stays awake,' she said.

'I know,' Milly snapped.

She helped Cameron get changed and led him back into the kitchen, just as blue flashing lights appeared outside the windows. For a village that didn't seem to exist on any maps and was nearly impossible to get to, the ambulance sure had got there quick enough.

Milly ran outside just as the ambulance was turning around so it was facing the right direction. She quickly told the paramedics what had happened, how long Cameron had been unconscious and how he had been sleepy and dizzy ever since. The paramedics examined him and helped him into the ambulance with Cameron protesting the whole time and Olivia flapping around them all like an oversized bird.

Cameron sat down on the bed inside and Milly moved to get in the ambulance with him.

'Milly, get my phone will you?' Cameron muttered.

Milly raced back inside and looked around for it on the table which was covered in Olivia's stuff. She eventually found it under a pile of papers, grabbed it and raced back outside again, but the ambulance was already pulling out the gate.

Milly chased after it, but it was too far ahead. She sped back to the kitchen and found her car keys. She jumped into Dick and turned the key but though he coughed and spluttered and though she begged and pleaded with him to start, the engine didn't turn over and she knew by that point the ambulance had already left the village, taking Cameron and the evil PA with it.

——

Milly was in a state. She had no idea where Cameron had been taken. She had phoned every hospital in the local area and even the ones further afield and they all denied that Cameron had been admitted there. As a semi famous celebrity, she supposed he was afforded a bit more privacy than other patients.

She had phoned Olivia more times than she could count but she never answered.

She'd phoned his publishers but couldn't find anyone who was willing to talk to her.

It had been nearly twenty-four hours since the ambulance had disappeared. She hadn't slept, she hadn't eaten, she had cried more tears than she knew she had.

She felt sick.

What if he had died? What if she never saw him again?

She felt awful and she knew part of it was from lack of food. She had to eat something but the thought twisted her stomach. She opened up a can of beans and poured the contents into a saucepan but before she could put it on the stove a taxi pulled up on the drive outside.

Her heart soared and sank in equal measure. It could be Cameron, it could just be Olivia.

She watched out the window and as the taxi drove off, she could see Cameron and Olivia walking back up the drive. Cameron looked exhausted but he was alive.

She flew out the door, down the drive and threw her arms around him, sobbing uncontrollably.

'I was so scared, I thought you might have died. Are you ok?'

She leaned back slightly to look at him and only then realised that he wasn't holding her and he was looking at her with absolute hatred.

She stepped back. 'What's wrong?'

He didn't say anything, just shoved a newspaper into her hands and walked past her back to the castle.

Milly stared after him in confusion and then unfolded the newspaper. There, on the front page, was the photo she had taken of her and Cameron in bed together coupled with the headline, '*Phoenix Blaze set my world on fire.*'

Her stomach dropped. She flicked open the newspaper and an account of their love story covered two whole pages. The spread included the photos she had taken of him sleeping; one close up of his face and one naked picture of him lying sprawled out face down on the bed, plus the ones he had taken of her naked and the ones he had taken of them together. These were private intimate photos and someone had exploited them. She felt sick for Cameron and then as she studied the words some more, she realised with horror that this wasn't an account of their love story but an interview with her. There were quotes and huge paragraphs from someone claiming to be Milly giving detailed accounts of her and Cameron's time together.

She ran after Cameron and burst into the kitchen. 'I didn't do this.'

Her suitcase was open on the kitchen table and Cameron was grabbing all her possessions and throwing them in. He didn't even look at her.

'I swear, I didn't do this. I love you, why would I do this if I loved you?'

'I've been asking that question myself,' Cameron said.

Rage ripped through her. 'I can't believe you would think I was capable of this. After everything we've been through …'

Cameron slammed his hand down on the table. 'Yes, after everything we've been through you betray me like this.'

'I didn't do it.'

Cameron shook his head, throwing more of her things into the suitcase. 'I thought you were different, I trusted you.'

'That's bollocks! You never trusted me. I thought you had got past all those fears and had fallen in love with me. But you clearly never loved me at all if you can believe that I would do something like this to you.'

Cameron slammed the lid shut and zipped it up, then stalked past her, opened the door and shoved the suitcase in the back of her car.

'Get out and don't ever come back.'

He strode off to his bedroom without a look back.

Olivia stared at her with disgust. 'Looks like someone's shine has rubbed off.'

Milly had no words. How had this happened?

Cameron came back into the kitchen, wearing only his jeans. Milly gasped at the dark bruise down one side.

'Olivia, I need you in the bedroom,' he said.

Milly watched in horror as Olivia slipped out of her jacket and then walked past Cameron towards his bedroom. Cameron followed her and slammed the door to the lounge.

Milly stared at the door. With angry tears pouring down her cheeks, she walked out. She hoisted her suitcase out of the back of Dick and walked down the drive. She would have to arrange for a garage to come and collect him at some point, if Cameron hadn't burnt him to the ground in some spiteful rage.

Anger boiled inside her as she walked through the gate. It had taken everything she had to let herself trust in a happy ending with him and now he had betrayed her. How could he possibly think she would do that to him?

She was shaking all over and she knew she had to get some food. She walked into the village, a huge lump of emotion and tears clogging in her throat making it difficult to breathe.

She knocked on Gladys's door. When she answered her face lit up at seeing her and then immediately fell when she saw Milly's expression.

'Come in dear, I'll put the kettle on.'

CHAPTER 20

'Has she gone?' Cameron asked as he paced around the bedroom.

Olivia tottered out to check, he heard the lounge door open and then she came back. 'Looks like it.'

'Good.' He flopped back down on the bed. 'I need to sleep, bloody doctors kept me awake all night.'

'I know you've been hurt by this, let me help you.' She ran a hand over his arm but he moved out of her reach.

'Liv, I'm in a really bad mood and I don't want to say something that I'll regret. Will you please just leave me alone for a few hours.'

Olivia sighed. 'Well, can I get you anything?'

'Yes, the newspaper.'

'Cam, I really don't think you should read that now, it isn't going to make you feel any better.'

'I need to know what she said about me.'

Olivia disappeared back into the kitchen and brought the paper back.

She hovered for a moment.

'I can't believe she told the papers that you didn't write the *Hidden Faces* series. I hate to say I told you so, but you should never have trusted her with that.'

'I shouldn't have trusted her with anything, but that secret is going to ruin me.'

'Maybe it isn't. Maybe she's done you a favour with that. You've always said you wanted everyone to know. This might help to get your fans back on side before the release of the next book.'

Cameron had nothing to say, he was so angry. When it was obvious he wasn't going to speak to her, Olivia left, closing the door behind her.

He stared at the picture of him and Milly on the front page. They looked so happy together, so in love. How could she have done this to him?

He opened up the paper and stared at the pictures of him lying fast asleep, stark naked. How could she deny that she had done this when she was the one who had taken these pictures? Why would she take photos of him naked whilst he slept unless she had intended to sell him out all along?

Two pages of his most intimate moments with the woman he loved revealed for everyone to see. When he had been discharged from hospital this morning, he had wanted nothing more than to rush back to Milly, but as they had driven the short ride from the hospital in the taxi, Olivia had handed him the paper and he had been so enraged by what he had seen that he hadn't even been able to read it. Now he needed to know.

He started to read and became more and more confused. The description of his relationship with Milly was a complete pack of lies. Milly's account of how he hadn't been able to keep his hands off her and that they had slept together the first night they had met in the giant four poster bed was utter bullshit. What followed was an account of sex on the banqueting table, sex in the dungeons with Milly manacled to a wall, and sex with Cameron dressed in a full suit of armor. It was a work of fiction and made Cameron out to be a really kinky sex maniac. Why would Milly tell these lies? It was bad enough that she had sold her story to

the papers but to completely make up what had happened between them was just weird. But then his relationship with his last
girlfriend, Stacey, had ended in the same way, with a pack of
lies printed in the papers. He read the part where she explained
about him not writing the *Hidden Faces* series. It killed him
that she had used that for her exclusive. He hadn't told anyone
that before. There were only a handful of people that knew; a few
people from the publishers, his agent and Olivia.

He flicked back to the front page and stared at the photo
of them together again. She loved him, he knew that. She had
shown him she loved him time and time again. The day before
when he had knocked himself unconscious, she sat with him
even when in doing so she was risking her own life. In the moments when she thought he was still unconscious she had kept
telling him she loved him.

He flicked back to the photos on the inside of the paper.
These had been taken with her phone. If it wasn't Milly that had
done this, then who?

His hands shook with rage as he crumpled the paper into
a ball. How had he been so stupid? The bang to the head, the
exhaustion of going without sleep for over twenty-four hours?
There was no excuse.

He stormed from the bedroom into the kitchen where Olivia was on the phone again. She looked at Cameron's face and
quickly ended the call.

'Maxwell, I've got to go.' She hung up the phone.

'You fucking bitch,' Cameron seethed. He waved the screwed
up newspaper at her. 'You fucking did this.'

She scrambled out of her seat suddenly looking very pale.
'What are you talking about?'

'You sold this story to the papers. You did the same with Stacey
too, sold a pack of lies under her name. This wasn't Milly at all.'

'Of course it was her, the photos came from her phone.'

'Which has been in here almost the whole time she's been here.'

He rounded the table towards her and she moved away, keeping the table between them.

'You've hated her from the second you met her. She tried to tell me and I just didn't believe her.'

'No, she wasn't good for you. I was only trying to protect you but I would never do something like this.'

'Why would she still be here, knowing the story would be published today? Why would she do this to me when she loves me? Why would she ruin her reputation when it was so important to her? Why would she make up a complete pack of lies about our relationship?'

'To make it sound more interesting.'

'Why would she need to make it sound more interesting? It was fucking perfect and you screwed it up.'

'She was a money grabbing whore, why can't you see that?'

Olivia's phone lit up with a new call, and Cameron looked at the caller ID to see Maxwell's name flashing next to a photo of Olivia and Maxwell, the CEO of Palace Hotels. It was quite obvious from the photo that they were a couple.

Suddenly everything made sense, her desperation for him to sign with Palace Hotels, trying to find dirt on Extravagance and Milly, he had been so blind.

'You're sleeping with the CEO of Palace Hotels, that's a bit of a conflict of interest there wouldn't you say, Liv?' He glanced down at the table and spotted the contract with Palace Hotels. He recognised the logo at the top. 'This was what you were trying to get me to sign yesterday, when I had banged my head. I could have been seriously brain damaged and the only thing you cared about was this. The only money grabbing whore is you.'

Cameron threw the newspaper across the room in a rage. He moved round the table towards her and she turned and ran, immediately tripping over Milly's shoes that were left lying in the kitchen. Everything happened in slow motion as she grabbed the handle of the saucepan filled with cold baked beans to stop herself from falling, the beans flew through the air, she hit the floor and the beans landed with a splat on top of her head. Gregory leapt up from his position by the stove and proceeded to lick the baked beans from her face as they slowly dripped down her cheeks.

'No, get off me, get him off me,' Olivia sobbed.

He crouched down next to her, ignoring Gregory's ministrations. When he spoke, his voice was quiet. 'You're fired. Get out of my home right now and I never want to see you again.'

He stood up.

'You're firing me? After everything I have done for you?' Olivia cried.

'You've done nothing for me. No, wait, I tell a lie, the one good thing you did for me was put me in touch with one of the best fucking lawyers in the country. If there is any possible way I can stick criminal charges on you for this, I will. Slander, libel. There's also the little case of using private photos without permission, fraud maybe, for acting in Milly's name. I think you're looking at some serious time in prison for this.'

He didn't need any further confirmation that Olivia had been the one that had betrayed him but the fact that she went as white as a sheet when he was talking about prison was the final cherry on the cake.

'Get out now. I swear if you're still here when I get back you're going to see me really angry.'

He grabbed his car keys and stormed out, leaving her crying on the kitchen floor as Gregory continued to lick her clean.

Cameron only hoped the beast would eat her after he had licked all the beans off her, though he severely doubted that Gregory would enjoy the taste of Olivia's bitterness.

He was surprised to see Dick still sitting patiently in front of the house, but he guessed that the car hadn't started when Milly had tried to leave earlier or even the day before when the ambulance had left without her. She couldn't have got that far in the last fifteen or twenty minutes. He ran round to the garage, jumped in his car and tore out of the gates, determined to put this right. He only hoped she would listen to him.

—

Milly stared at the phone in her hand in shock. She'd just been fired. This day couldn't possibly get any worse.

Gladys had fed her up with cake and mugs of tea. Milly had been ranting and screaming at her about Cameron when Castle Heritage had suddenly phoned. She hadn't really heard the words they'd said although she certainly got the gist. She didn't even have anything she could say to defend herself as although she hadn't sold her story to the papers and the bizarre sexual antics weren't true, her relationship with a client was and she knew they were totally justified in sacking her, especially as she had stayed at the castle the week before her holiday on company time purely because she had wanted to stay with Cameron.

The phone rang again and she saw Belinda's name flashing on the screen. Shame and guilt ripped through her. Belinda would be so disappointed.

Thankfully Gladys had left to give her some space when Castle Heritage rang, and she was still banging around in the kitchen now, making cakes or other such delights.

Milly answered the phone.

'Hi Belinda,' Milly said, her voice was choked.

'Milly, I've just seen this awful business in the papers. Are you ok?'

'I didn't sell my story, none of that stuff is true.'

'Of course it isn't. I know you better than that.'

'I'm so sorry, I've let you down again.'

'How have you let me down?'

'Because I let my heart rule my head again.'

She stared at her knees, surprised to see scratches on them, probably from being in the cave the day before. Had that really only been twenty-four hours earlier, when the only thing she was wishing for was for Cameron to be alive. Now all she wished was that she had never met the man in the first place.

'Honey, your heart should always rule your head. Trust in your heart, it knows you a lot better than your head does. I love you so much and all I want is for you to be happy. Don't shy away from love just because you've been hurt in the past. Embrace it and all its wonderful, glorious and horrible moments. I never ever want you to miss out on being in love because you let your head decide rather than your heart.'

'Listening to my heart has just cost me my job.'

'Nonsense. I will speak to Nicholas about this, don't you worry. We go way back.'

'That's ok. I deserve to be sacked,' Milly said, sadly.

'What utter rubbish! You work damn hard at that job and you have done for several years. He was only saying to me the other week what a breath of fresh air you were and how much he loved having you work there. He's a proud man and he won't like that Castle Heritage has been dragged into this mess but he will calm down in a day or two. I will speak with him.'

'Maybe it's time for a change. Maybe I'll lecture in historical architecture instead. I think I might really like that.'

'You would be wonderful at that, you have such passion for what you do.'

Milly sighed. Where she worked hardly seemed important anymore. Her heart was in tatters. The numb anger was starting to fade and the acute pain was finally catching up with her.

'Tell me about Cameron,' Belinda said, softly.

'I love him with everything I have.'

'Then you fight for him.'

'He hates me and I hate him a little bit right now for believing that I would do that.'

'It must have been a shock for him. The pain you're feeling right now because he jumped to the wrong conclusion is the same pain he felt when he thought you had betrayed him. You are a kind, sweet, generous soul. When he apologises, be generous with him.'

'He's not going to apologise.'

'He will. I'm staring at this photo of you two now. The man is completely in love with you. He'll come to his senses. Now where are you?'

'I'm still in the village near the castle. Dick refused to work again so I was just going to call a taxi.'

'I'll send Jamie to come and collect you. It might be an hour or two but then you both can come round for dinner tonight and if you want, you can stay a few days.'

Milly smiled. 'I'd really like that, thank you.'

'I'll see you tonight, my beautiful girl.'

Belinda hung up and Milly smiled at the unconditional love her aunt had for her.

Milly said goodbye to Gladys and decided to wait on the green for Jamie, she needed some space.

She stepped out the front door and walked down onto the road just as Cameron came tearing out the castle gates in his car. He looked furious. He saw her and the car screeched to a halt a few metres away. He got out the car and ran towards her. He looked like he wanted to kill someone, preferably her. She turned and ran across the green away from him.

'Milly wait, I need to talk to you,' he yelled.

'Get away from me.'

'Milly, stop!'

She looked back to see how close he was, he reached out a hand to grab her and suddenly her world turned upside down. Ice cold water soaked her from head to toe as she fell head first into the village pond.

She quickly surfaced, coughing and spluttering and looked up at Cameron standing on the bank with nothing but concern in his eyes.

'Are you ok?' He offered out a hand to help her but she stepped back, stubbornly refusing to take it. He clearly wasn't going to kill her but right then he was the last person she wanted to see.

'Come back to the castle with me, we need to talk.'

Milly folded her arms across her chest. 'I don't want to talk to you.'

Cameron sighed. 'I'll come to you, then.'

He slid into the pond in front of her and she almost laughed as he winced at the cold.

'It was Olivia, she must have stolen the pictures from your phone and sold your story to the paper.'

'No shit, Sherlock. I could have told you that had you not thrown me out. How could you have even thought it was me?'

'I didn't read it.'

'You didn't have to. You were so quick to believe it was me. You asked me to trust you but you never trusted me, not for one minute.'

'I'm sorry, I don't know what I was thinking. Put it down to complete exhaustion or the bang on the head. I'm so sorry. Let me make it up to you.'

She turned away from him and sloshed towards the bank. 'It's never going to work between us.'

'Why are you so keen to throw what we have away?'

'Oh don't put this on me, you threw away what we had all by yourself.'

She tried to heave herself out onto the bank but it was too slippery and she fell back in. She tried again, hating that Cameron was watching her. Why couldn't she leave him with some excellent witty put down and her head held high? Instead she was soaked to the skin, pond weed clinging to her hair and trying to scramble out of a pond in the most ungraceful manner possible. She was sure she heard Cameron stifle a laugh as she tried her best to get some kind of handhold on the side of the bank.

'Here let me help you,' Cameron said, his hands going to her waist. She elbowed him in the stomach to get him to let go of her and he leapt back with a groan of pain.

She turned back with concern, she hadn't hit him that hard.

'Not the ribs, please Milly. I badly bruised them when I fell. Punch me in the face if you want, but not the ribs.'

'I'm sorry.' She scowled. How was she now apologising to him? She had done nothing wrong. He had betrayed her by believing she could do something as underhand as selling her story to the paper and then he had kicked her out.

'Don't be. I deserve it.'

She shook her head and looked away from the wet shirt that was clinging to his body. Was lust the only thing they had between them? But it hadn't been for her. It hurt how much she had fallen for him. Her heart felt painfully full and she knew she would never stop loving him. But he couldn't trust her, there was no way back from this. Tears coursed down her cheeks and there was nothing she could do to stop them.

'Please don't cry.' He moved tentatively towards her and cupped her face, stroking the tears away. 'I'm really sorry. I love you so much. When I left the hospital this morning all I wanted was to come back here and tell you that I loved you. I hated that you sat in the cave with me yesterday telling me how much you loved me and I never said it back. I was so groggy and dizzy but as all that wore off in the hospital last night, I realised that I never said it back to you and it killed me. I should have said it days ago when I knew. I've only been in love once before and I was betrayed so I was scared about falling in love only to have my heart broken again. So to see the story in the paper, I couldn't bear to see it happening all over again.'

Her heart was thundering against her chest. He loved her.

He leaned his forehead against hers and sighed. He waded to the bank and climbed out with ease then turned and held out his hand for her. She took it readily. He loved her. There was a tiny slither of hope filling her heart now too. Could they work through his issues of trust? Could they really have that perfect happy ending that she had dreamed of for so long?

Without relinquishing his hold on her hand, he led her over to the giant oak in the middle of the green. He leaned her against the wide trunk which he had rescued her from just a few days before. The gentle sea breeze fluttered the leaves above them and Milly looked up, wondering how many couples in love had said their wedding vows under the boughs of this great tree. How many of them grew old and grey with their loved one and how many had returned a few months or years later to announce their divorce? Was there really such a thing as a happy ever after?

'When you said yesterday about Castle Heritage taking the castle on and I said I didn't want to change it, it was because of you, because you love it here, you love the silly turrets and the blue roofs. Because you love it, I love it now, too. I'm signing with Jamie tomorrow because he wants to keep it exactly as it is.'

Milly smiled.

'I know you got scared too,' Cameron said and she lowered her eyes from the leaves to stare into his soft brown ones. 'You got freaked out about being my soul mate, about putting your trust in me for a perfect happy ending. And you're right, I can't give you that.'

She swallowed down the pain. 'You can't?'

He shook his head. 'It's never going to be perfect. No relationship is. Disney always end the films on the couple getting married with big inane grins on their faces. They never show what happens after. We will argue and fight over the silliest things. You'll get annoyed with me when I'm writing and I'll get grumpy when you have to leave for work for several days. My farts smell bad, especially when I've eaten mushrooms. If I've drunk a lot of red wine, I'll snore like a pig. I'll get annoyed with tripping over your shoes all the time and the clothes that you leave strewn all over the bedroom. When we have our baby, we will be tired and we'll cry from exhaustion and we'll get it wrong and argue some more. You'll want to call the baby Rapunzel or Pocahontas and I'll argue with you because I like more traditional names like Mildred or Emma or Belinda or Rose. You'll badger me to be in the Summer Solstice play every year and I'll argue against it but then end up doing it anyway because I love you and I'll want to do anything to keep you happy even if that means waving my willy around in front of the villagers. You'll probably want to paint the castle bright pink and I'll grumble and moan about it as I buy the cans of paint and go up the ladder to paint it.'

Milly giggled. 'You make it sound so romantic.'

'But we will have hot sex every night.'

'Still not romantic.'

'And candle lit picnics on the beach under the stars.'

'Getting better.'

'But despite all our problems, I know we are supposed to be together, I know you are my soul mate.'

Milly opened her mouth to protest, but Cameron closed it gently with his fingers over her lips.

'Not because of some silly family curse that's been hanging over the castle for the last thousand years, not because you broke the stone heart or have the dragon tattoo or because of the cameo. I know we are soul mates because I can feel it in here, because I was drawn to you from the first moment that I saw you, not because you are beautiful, but because …' he struggled to find the words and Milly decided to help him out.

'Because it felt like we had known each our whole life. We weren't getting to know each other, we were becoming reacquainted.'

'Yes. Your tattoo about true love's kiss. That's how I feel about you. Before, I was sleeping but now with you I'm awake.'

Milly choked back the tears. 'I feel like that too.'

'Then come back with me to the castle and we can start our not so perfect life together.'

Milly stared at him and he leaned in to kiss her but she leapt back at the sound of a roar of a sports car. She watched Olivia drive out the village, her hair plastered to her head, and what looked like baked bean stains on her blouse. She didn't even seem to see them.

Milly looked back at Cameron. What was she doing, could she forgive him so quickly? She glanced over his shoulder at Igor, loading Cameron's car onto his tow truck.

'Your car's getting towed.'

'I don't care.'

Milly sighed, leaning her head against his chest. 'I'm so tired. I've lost my job, I'm humiliated in the national press and I've cried more tears than I even knew I had in the last twenty-four hours.'

'I'm tired too baby, but don't make the same mistake that I did and make a decision on our future based on exhaustion and emotions. Come back to the castle, have a sleep, I'll make you dinner and if you still want to leave, I'll drive you home myself.'

She reached up and kissed him, just briefly on the lips. 'I've already made my decision.'

Tears filled his eyes.

'I don't want that perfect future with you. I want the real one, the one that you just described.'

'With the farts and the arguing?'

Milly giggled. 'Yes, I want my future to be with you, in all its glorious and gory details. I love you, all of you and your stupidity hasn't changed that.'

He bent his head to kiss her, she wrapped her arms round his neck and kissed him back.

Eventually they pulled apart. 'So what happens now, shall I carry you off into the sunset, or is that too clichéd?'

'No, but as the sun won't set for hours yet, how about we settle for you carrying me over the threshold instead?'

Cameron scooped her up and carried her towards the castle. 'Let's go home, Mrs Heartstone.'

Milly rested her head on his shoulder and smiled. This was where she belonged.

EPILOGUE

One Year Later

'Hurry, they're all waiting for us,' Milly said, shoving her feet into a pair of silver sparkly heels.

'They can't start without us, 'Cameron said, fiddling with his tie.

'The first wedding in the castle, I am so frigging excited.'

'Yes, and Jamie says we have five more booked for this year and seventeen for next year. He thinks we'll get full really quickly once word spreads.'

'And no one is half-naked,' Milly said, straightening his tie.

'Yeah, the villagers aren't happy about that but it makes sense to do it properly. No one is going to want to get married here if it might not even be legal.'

'Sshhh don't let the villagers hear you say that, you know how protective they are of their little ceremony. I'm surprised that they have changed their Summer Solstice celebrations to come to this. The first time in nearly a thousand years that they haven't acted out the play, or so Gladys tells me.'

'They wanted to be here to support us. They know how important it is to us. Besides, opening the castle to visitors and offering weddings here is going to be a massive part of our business.'

'It looks beautiful out there, like a proper fairy tale wedding.'

Cameron smiled down at her. 'I wanted it to be perfect. I'd better go, I'm sure they all know what we've been doing.'

Milly blushed.

He turned to leave but Milly caught his arm. 'I have something I need to tell you.'

He smiled, hugely. 'I already know.'

She gaped at him. 'How? Because Lavender predicted it?'

'Because I found the pregnancy test in the bathroom … but the morning sickness was sort of a big clue, too.'

'You are going to be a marvellous dad.'

'I couldn't be happier,' Cameron kissed her. 'I love you Mrs Heartstone.'

'I love you too.'

Cameron looked at his watch, 'We'd really better go, I'll see you out there.'

He ducked out the door.

Milly looked around the honeymoon suite and smiled. It was the last room in the castle to be finished and Cameron had kept it a complete secret from her throughout all the renovations over the last year, only surprising her with it the night before. It was a perfect combination of the traditional and the modern. White curtains billowed around the four poster bed, caught in a gentle breeze from the large open windows. There was a tangle of pink fairy lights wrapped around the wooden branches of the headboard and above the white marble fireplace. One of her favourite parts was the gold silk chaise longue placed in front of the windows with views over the sea. Even now, as the sun had just disappeared beneath the waves, the moon tipped sea could still be seen. The en-suite bathroom was heavenly, with a step down jacuzzi surrounded by Greek style marble columns. She and Cameron had spent several hours last night enjoying that.

The other three rooms at the top of the towers had each been converted into themed family suites. The *Lion King* suite was probably her favourite, with bold, African style coloured walls, animal print bedspreads and cushions in the main bedroom, wooden furniture and a stone rustic looking bathroom, whilst the twin bedded room for the children had more of a cartoony feel with large brightly coloured lamps made to look like flower heads, rainforest style curtains and prints and murals from the film itself.

There was an Under The Sea Suite, themed around *Finding Nemo* and *The Little Mermaid* which saw lots of blue tones, and a Pirate themed room with beds made to look like pirate ships, treasure map blankets and treasure chest style tables and drawers.

Jamie had asked for a lot of their input when redesigning the inside of the castle. He wanted it to be something they were proud of and loved, especially as it had now become their home. So the themed rooms had been Milly's project while Jamie had helped oversee the other renovations. The other four rooms in the towers had each been split into two smaller, separate rooms, again combining the contemporary with the traditional. Brightly coloured bed covers and curtains had been added, but they had kept the traditional stone walls and four poster beds. Cold stone floors had given way to the luxury of carpets, open fireplaces had been replaced with gas log fires which were much safer, and the windows were made much bigger, affording stunning views over the fields, village or the sea for all the rooms and lending them much more light.

The secret passageways from each tower had been converted into proper fire escapes. Ensuring that the castle was safe had been the most expensive aspect of the renovations. The secret passageways and dungeons especially had to be reinforced and rebuilt in parts. And there were now fire exits in almost all parts of the building, ruining the traditional castle feel slightly but Jamie had ensured that it looked as natural as possible, especially from the outside.

The banquet hall had been pretty much left exactly as it was, which Milly felt was important considering all its history. Jamie had installed radiators though to make it a lot warmer, especially in the cold winter months, although they were hidden behind more traditional wooden panels so they weren't obtrusive. The guests would eat their breakfast and dinner in there, or, as today, the room would be used for weddings and parties.

Most of the parts of the castle that the customers would see had remained the same, apart from a lot of repairs. It was the behind the scenes stuff that had greatly been updated. The old courtyard had gone and the old kitchen had been vastly extended and modernised with proper fridges and cookers. A team of highly skilled chefs had recently joined the ranks of the ever growing staff. Jamie had been happy to hire most of the villagers for the smaller jobs, like gardening, cleaning and maintenance, whilst bringing in his own team of managers to oversee the day to day running of the place.

They had two more weeks before the castle was going to be officially opened for business and each of the bedrooms were already booked almost every night for the first two months.

Everyone had worked hard to make it perfect and Milly knew Jamie had enjoyed the project, both working alongside her and the challenge of keeping with the traditions of the castle while making it modern and exciting enough to get people interested enough to come.

Suddenly remembering the time, Milly quickly put on a pair of simple pearl earrings and the blue cameo which she had converted into a choker. She checked her appearance in the mirror one more time, trying to straighten her hair which Cameron had messed up a few moments before. But as she turned to go she caught Sophia smiling at her with approval in her reflection. She whirled round to look at her but she was gone. Neither she nor Cameron had seen Sophia since the treasure had been lost in the sea, as if somehow her spirit had been released with the treasure, so it was a surprise to see her now. Or maybe not, considering what day it was.

The moon glinted off her engagement ring for a moment. The tiny pale pink diamond was the only thing left of the treasure when they had returned to the cave. Milly wasn't sure if it was real or not, but the significance of it was so much more important when Cameron had converted it into a ring and officially asked her to marry him with it.

'I'm going to take really good care of him,' Milly promised the empty room, hoping that Sophia could hear her. A gentle breeze scented with flowers rushed past her towards the staircase and Milly followed it out.

She descended the staircase, feeling grand in her medieval style silvery dress, but as she stepped into the banquet hall, she was surprised to find it empty. Candles flickered over the dark surfaces and the delicate scent of the hundreds of white roses filled the room. The log fire was dying, the last embers glowing in the fireplace.

Where was everyone? A discreet cough from the side of the room drew her attention and she looked over at Jamie, looking stunning in a suit.

'You look beautiful, little sister,' he said as he passed her a bouquet of pink flowers interspersed with tiny crystals.

'Where's everyone?'

'Your wedding isn't taking place here, silly.'

'It's not?'

'Cameron wanted it to be perfect for you.'

Jamie offered her his arm and she took it in confusion. 'Thank you for giving me away today.'

'I wouldn't miss it for the world. Well, I did miss the first wedding but I can let you off for that as you didn't know you were getting married.'

'And I don't think it was a real wedding but don't tell anyone I said that,' Milly whispered.

Jamie escorted her past the staircase, down the corridor and over the drawbridge and Milly gasped when she saw what was waiting for her. A glittering silver round pumpkin carriage sat outside, and a white horse stood proudly at the front with a plume of pink feathers bursting from his head. The carriage sparkled in the moonlight, making it look magical and enchanted, as if it might change back into a pumpkin at any moment.

'Are you kidding me?' Milly squealed.

Jamie shook his head. 'Cameron has covered all the bases.'

He helped her aboard and then sat next to her. The horse and carriage swung into motion and they trundled slowly down the driveway towards the village.

'Where are we going?'

Jamie smiled. 'You'll see.'

Milly peered out the windows for some clue to what was going on. Were they going to get married on the village green again?

'Hey, don't spoil the surprise. Tell me about your new job.'

He was trying to distract her but she let him.

'I love it, I know it's only been a few weeks but I love being able to share my passion for history with people. I love teaching them about dendrochronology and historic architecture. I see these people come into the classroom with some vague interest in the topic and they leave all excited and passionate about it all. It's a wonderful feeling knowing that I've had that effect on them.'

'I can imagine what your lectures are like, you have such an engaging way about you. I wish my history teacher at school had as much passion as you.'

Milly smiled. 'And the best part is that the university where I'm lecturing is really close, so I don't have too far to travel every day.'

She suddenly leaned forward as out on the dark sea, a glint of gold caught her attention before the sea vanished behind the trees.

The village sat in complete darkness, even the lights at Igor's pub that never seemed to go out weren't on this time. So she was surprised when the carriage stopped in front of the pub doors.

Jamie stepped down from the carriage and helped her down. She followed him up the tiny path and into the pub. It was completely empty and only a few candle filled lanterns lit the way towards the cellar door. Jamie pushed the door open and helped her down the stairs. He went straight to the hole in the wall and she scooped up her silvery dress so it wouldn't get too dirty in the cave, but the floor had been lined with a red carpet. The walls glowed with more lanterns. Cameron really had pulled out all the stops.

They reached the end of the cave and thudded out onto the little wooden jetty. Waiting at the end was a small wooden boat that looked like a gondola with its curved prow head rising high out of the water. Jamie helped her into the boat and she sat down next to him. It rocked gently in the water as they settled themselves. To her surprise, instead of being punted out to sea as the gondola shape of the boat suggested, the driver switched on a small engine at the back and the boat purred quietly as the man drove them slowly out into the waves. As they rounded the rocks that jutted out into the water and neared their secret cove, Milly gasped. There were at least thirty other boats on the water, each with several occupants. What made her smile most was the sea of gold Chinese lanterns they were all holding.

It was just as she had described to Cameron the year before.

The boat drifted out deeper, where she could see Cameron standing on a much bigger wooden boat.

As she passed the other boats she could see some of her friends and all the villagers that she had come to know over the last few months. They started chanting 'Oogie' as she passed but she knew it wasn't a summons to eat her but to keep her safe on her journey at sea.

She couldn't stop smiling as her little boat pulled up alongside Cameron's. He bent over and helped her step aboard his boat.

'You are so silly, you didn't have to do all of this.'

'I love you, of course I did.'

Milly smiled at all the people in the boats that bobbed nearby. Belinda was grinning hugely on the nearest boat, standing with Lavender, Constance and Gladys. Even Gregory was with them, wearing a pink bow tie. He barked when he saw Milly and tried to jump over onto their boat but Gladys managed to hold him back.

The vicar that had married them the year before in that bizarre ceremony on the village green was standing in the boat with them, but thankfully this time the whole ceremony was in English.

Milly's heart was thundering against her chest for the whole time but finally the vicar pronounced them officially man and wife, and Cameron swept her into his arms and kissed her. Milly giggled against his lips and their guests cheered and clapped, releasing their golden lanterns into the night sky. Milly looked up at the wonderful light show as they floated out over the sea, it was beautiful and she couldn't quite believe that Cameron had done all this for her.

She undid her star bracelet and let it slip into the sea. Every wish, everything her heart desired had come true that day. She wouldn't be needing it again.

Gregory barked, obviously keen to put his seal of approval on the event and leapt across onto their boat, which toppled and quickly pitched both her and Cameron into the cool water.

They surfaced, spluttering and coughing and gasping at the cold and Cameron wrapped his hands round her waist, pulling her against him.

Gregory seemed to be grinning at them from the boat.

'Bloody stupid dog,' Cameron growled. 'I'm so sorry. I wanted it all to be perfect for you and … why are you laughing?'

Milly wrapped her arms and legs round him and kissed him hard, silencing any more of his protests. Eventually she pulled back.

'It is perfect. I just married my soul mate, it doesn't get any more perfect than that.'

He smiled, his face lit up by a hundred golden glowing lanterns floating above them and kissed her.

'And they all lived happily ever after,' she whispered against his lips.

The End

LETTER FROM HOLLY

Thank you so much for reading *Fairytale Beginnings*, I had so much fun creating this story and I hope you enjoyed reading it as much as I enjoyed writing it.

One of the best parts of writing comes from seeing the reaction from readers. Did it make you smile or laugh, did it make you cry, hopefully happy tears? Did you fall in love with Cameron and Milly? Did you like the completely bonkers villagers of Clover's Rest? If you enjoyed the story, I would absolutely love it if you could leave a short review. Getting feedback from readers is amazing and it also helps to persuade other readers to pick up one of my books for the first time.

To keep up-to-date with the latest news on my new releases, you can sign up to receive an email whenever I have a new book out here:

www.bookouture.com/holly-martin

I promise to only contact you when I have a new book out and I'll never share your email with anyone else.

I have two books out this Christmas set in the town of White Cliff Bay so here's to more giggles and laughs and lots more gorgeously sweet love stories, coming soon.

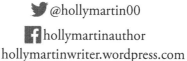

@hollymartin00

hollymartinauthor

hollymartinwriter.wordpress.com

ACKNOWLEDGEMENTS

To my family, my mom, my biggest fan, who reads every word I have written a hundred times over and loves it every single time, my dad, my brother Lee and my sister-in-law Julie, for your support, love, encouragement and endless excitement for my stories.

For my twinnie, the gorgeous Aven Ellis for just being my wonderful friend, for your endless support, for cheering me on and for keeping me entertained with wonderful stories and pictures of hot men. Although we have never met, you are my best friend and I love you dearly.

Huge thank you to my wonderful, incredible friends Kirsty Maclennan, Megan Milliken and Victoria Stone for the endless promotion, tweets, the excitement, the gushing and the love. You are amazing.

To my friends Gareth and Mandie, for your endless support, patience and enthusiasm. My lovely friends Jac, Verity and Jodie who listen to me talk about my books endlessly and get excited about it every single time.

For Sharon Sant for just being there always and your wonderful friendship.

To my wonderful agent Madeleine Milburn for just been amazing and fighting my corner and for your unending patience with my constant questions.

To my editor Claire for all your support throughout this book, and the other wonderful people at Bookouture; Oliver Rhodes, Kim Nash, the editing team and the wonderful design team who created this absolutely gorgeous cover.

To Julie Pope, Melanie Backe-Hansen, Alison Lodge, Sue and Philip Eades and the National Trust for your help with the research involved in this book.

To the best writing group in the world, you wonderful talented supportive bunch of authors, I feel very blessed to know you all, you guys are the very best.

To the wonderful Bookouture authors for all your encouragement and support.

And some other gorgeous people who have encouraged, supported, promoted, got excited or just listened; Rebecca Pugh, Lisa Dickenson, Sharon Wilden, Kelly Rufus, Simona Elena, Erin McEwan, Katey Beeden, Maryline, Jo Hughes, Dawn Crooks, Laura Delve, Jill Stratton, Emma Poulloura, Aga Klar, Catriona Merryweather, Lynsey James, Lindsay Hill, Ana, Alba Forcadell, Cesca Major, Rachael Lucas, Kat Black, Helen Redfern, Katy Gough, Emily Kerr Jaimie Admans Kate Gordon, Pernille Hughes, Louise Wykes, Pat Elliott, Shaun, Mark Rumsey, James Brown, Arron Davenport.

To all those involved in the blog tour. To anyone who has read my book and taken the time to tell me you've enjoyed it or wrote a review, thank you so much.

Thank you, I love you all.

Printed in Great Britain
by Amazon